LOVING LAVENDER FINCH

A NOVEL

KELLY BARGABOS

BOULAY PRESS
www.kellybargabos.com

First paperback edition June 2025

Printed in the United States of America

Library of Congress Cataloging-in-Publication
Data Control Number: 2025907131

ISBN 978-0-9994234-8-6 (paperback)
ISBN 978-0-9994234-9-3 (eBook)
ISBN 979-8-9986329-0-7 (audiobook)

Edited by Linda Lowen, Debbie Horan
and Melanie Zimmerman

Book Designed by GKS Creative

For my grandmother.

ONE

LAVENDER FINCH WAS BARELY AWAKE when she climbed the empty lifeguard chair to watch the sun take its place over the water. She ignored the signs that said, *Stay Off, Official Use Only* and *Violators Will Be Prosecuted.* The lifeguards weren't on duty yet and the beach was empty except for the giant-visor lady carrying the metal detector and the surf fishing guy wearing a Vietnam hat and black vest, his pole held by a PVC pipe while he sat in a low chair and smoked cigarettes. Lavender loved every moment at the beach but witnessing the beginning of a new day was her favorite. Almost felt sacred. Worthy of sacrificing sleep. She closed her eyes and pulled in the pungent air until she was full. *The calm before the storm.*

By the time Lavender got back to the beach house, Aunt Beck would be standing at the pantry cabinet with her hands on her hips and the doors swung wide. Disappointed with all the food left uneaten, she would assign the open bags of cereal and chips to be cleaned up by the end of the day. *We don't waste food,* she'd say. Uncle Rick and Uncle Ry would be making bets they'd both lose about finishing off that last twelve pack while the somber and sad undercurrent of *I can't believe it's over already* soaked into all of them. The next morning while it was still dark, Lavender's dad would pack the car and they would head north through Wilmington then Philadelphia then Scranton and finally, New York State and their hometown of Siena.

The Finch family had been renting a beach house at the Delaware shore for one week every summer ever since the oldest cousins were born. Her dad's parents died in a car accident when he was twenty-five and he and his four siblings were determined to keep their family close. As the only child of Ross and Sara Finch, Lavender couldn't relate to their sibling bond, but she'd had a front-row seat to the drama and tension she sometimes witnessed with her aunts and uncles, like when they fought over money or who got the ocean-front suite or who ate all the cereal that belonged to another family, and sometimes the drama was more serious like divorce, or one of the kids failing out first semester, or someone losing a job. The beach houses they rented got bigger each year and the annual group photo told the tale of a growing family, new babies, grumpy teens, old faces gone and replaced with new ones, but the original five siblings, Rick, Roxanne, Riley, Rebecca and her dad, Ross, never missed a year, and no matter what happened between them, love always won. Her dad liked to say, *they were a tribe that ran deep.*

Lavender and her cousin Jackie, thirteen months apart, were the youngest of eight cousins, which meant they were the lowest priority when it came to bedroom assignments and slept wherever they were told. Some years they shared a couch in the game room, some years they shared a queen-sized bed in the pool house, and others they camped out in sleeping bags on the floor. But they never minded. They were just glad to be there with each other and to be part of that tribe.

The quiet of the early beach was interrupted by a squeal. Giant-visor lady bent over and dug below the sand with her miniature shovel. She held her treasure close, right in front of her eyes, before unzipping her pink fanny pack and placing the item safely inside.

She looked up at Lavender with a satisfied smile and waved, as if she'd found exactly what she'd been looking for. Lavender smiled and waved back. *That will probably be me someday.*

Lavender shifted in the lifeguard chair to find a cooler section for the underside of her bare legs. The surfers she had been watching all week were way out from shore, bobbing on their surfboards in the water waiting for their next wave. A new set was coming in. She could tell by the swell that the first wave was going to be a big one. Not that Lavender had ever surfed but she'd been watching and studying them ever since that day in the Dewey Beach parking lot when she was six. She and Jackie were waiting while their parents loaded up the wagons with chairs, umbrellas, boogie boards, blankets and the cooler that held a bread bag full of tuna sandwiches. A faded yellow pick-up truck with a few teenagers in the cab and a few more in the back parked right next to them. They jumped out, grabbed the surfboards from the bed of the truck and headed over the dunes. Mesmerized by their tanned bodies and mysterious smiles, so sure of themselves, Lavender and Jackie spent the rest of that beach vacation, and all the ones after that, watching the surfers and trying to mimic their moves on their boogie boards. They'd ride the waves close to shore, squealing and laughing every time they caught a good ride and slid up on the beach, then waited for a thumbs-up or round of applause from the adults watching before they jumped up to chase another wave. Lavender hoped that someday she'd be brave enough to learn how to surf, but until then, she was happy to watch.

Her favorite surfer with the purple board made a move to take the next one in line. He turned quickly and laid down, moving his arms, slowly at first. He kept his head turned to his back. The wave was growing...he paddled faster...*Left. Right. Left. Right.* It would

crest soon. A few of the other surfers dropped back and let that one pass. He stayed with it. *Faster. Faster.* He waited until he was exactly in the middle of the rise, just before it crested. *Now.* He popped up fast and strong, his knees bent, his arms out. He knew he had it. Smiling, he leaned into the push and the pull of the wave's path while staying on top, riding the edge while it raced towards shore.

Lavender loved the ocean as much as she was afraid of it. She'd had scary moments where she caught the wave at the wrong time and got lost in its momentum, unable to control her own body until the wave had slammed her into the sandy bottom and then moved back out to sea. She'd had plenty of fat lips and scraped knees from getting caught in the *washing machine.* The ocean was undeniably strong and kept moving, no matter what. Lavender learned early on that a wave would never dodge her if she wasn't ready for it. It wouldn't change course to keep from crashing on top of her head or slow its roll towards shore if she wasn't paddling fast enough. She knew it had the power to take her out, and yet, she couldn't resist going back for more.

Purple surfboard crouched close to his board, lowering his center of gravity to stay on through this last push. *Almost there.* A quick fish-tail kick and he was done. *You made it.* Not that he was looking for it, but Lavender gave him a thumbs up anyway. He scooped his board up under his left arm and stood on the beach, waiting for his friends to come in. The sun was up, shining in full force without any clouds to break up the heat and the families began to appear to secure their spot on the sand.

Lavender was running out of time in the lifeguard chair. She was also running out of summer. Their beach vacation was always the last full week before Labor Day, the official end of the season. In just a few days she'd be a senior, then a graduate, then a college

student, and then what? All summer, people she didn't even know had asked her what her plans were, and what she wanted to do with the rest of her life. She was baffled that people expected her to have an answer. She was seventeen for god's sake. She had nothing stirring in her soul. Yet.

TWO

LAVENDER HELD THE BOARD on either side and turned her head to look at the next set of waves on the horizon. She started paddling. The tips of her fingers plunged down and she caught the weight of the water in the palm of her hand to pull her body forward. Her biceps, strong from scooping ice cream all summer at Ren's, were humming in tune with her forearms and hands. Lavender put her head down and focused. *Left. Right. Left. Right.* She looked behind her. Something was wrong. The wave was moving but she wasn't. If she didn't get herself in the right position, the wave would pick her up and instead of riding on top of its crest, she'd become part of it, rolling down, under and around as the wave pulled back out to sea. She'd be lost forever.

The waves pressed forward with or without her. She stopped paddling, closed her eyes, laid her body flat against the board. The hard surface against her stomach and chest slowed the pounding of her heart and the undercurrent in her belly. *Breathe in two, three, four. Breathe out two, three, four.* Still, the roar of the water pushing towards shore wasn't loud enough to drown out all the other noise in her head. *Are you excited to graduate? What are your plans after high school? What's your major? Will you go to law school? Med school? Become a teacher? Accountant? Engineer? So. Many. Questions.* The giant wave was headed right at her, but she didn't dare look it in the eye. Instead, she lay still on the surfboard and braced for impact.

Lavender's body jerked so hard she reached out with both arms to grab her bed and steady herself. She was not floating in the ocean. *Thank god.* She rolled over, hugging Mister Bean to her belly. She always woke up right before the wave got her.

Her phone chimed with a new message. Jackie sent her the pic from last Saturday night. The two of them lit up by the glow of a bonfire at the Lane, both holding a bottle of Bud Light and each other. Lavender smiled.

Hey cuz. The party's over. Lol. You
ready for school?

Ugggggh. Nope. Still in bed.

Get up lazy bones. Gotta look fresh
for your first day!

Wish i could fast-forward and just
get to bsu with you.

Well… wanna come see me next
friday? Killer party scheduled.

Yesss! Sounds awesome.

Sweet. We'll talk later. Let me know
how your first day goes.

Her first college party. Dorm room sleepover. Screw that wave, she was fine.

"Gimme an L...gimme an A..." Her mother's best cheerleader impersonation penetrated the closed bedroom door.

"Mom." Lavender put her pillow over her head.

"Gimme a V...gimme an E..."

"Seriously." Sara Finch had started every first day of school with this cheer. Until Lavender was twelve, she answered the call and responded with each letter. Since then, her mom played both parts with enough excitement for the two of them. No matter how much Lavender ignored her, she finished the entire eight-letter word. Once the cheer was complete, her mother opened her bedroom door.

"Good morning. Time to rise and shine to make your mind." Another longstanding tradition.

"Ugh. That doesn't even make sense." Lavender flung back her comforter and rolled out of bed. "I'm already up."

The floor was cool on her feet. She shuffled to the bathroom across the hall, turned on the shower and noticed it was due for a cleaning. That was on her. Being an only child had its burdens, but it also had its advantages and not having to share a bathroom was one of them. Which also meant that it was her *character-building* responsibility to clean it.

"Don't forget those hot spots..." her mother said as she retreated downstairs.

"Oh my god mother. It is too early for this," Lavender said as she swung the bathroom door closed. When she was little, her mom taught her that if she did nothing else in the bath or shower, she must wash her hot spots, meaning her armpits, her butt and everything else *down there*. Cute when she was seven, but at seventeen not so much.

She inhaled the coconut scent from her shampoo and was transported back to Dewey Beach smothered in suntan lotion. Someday she hoped to go to her favorite place on earth more often than once a year on Finch family vacations. Lavender didn't waste time in the shower. *Wash. Condition. Hot spots. Done.* Her best friend Jana took long showers. It was a constant source of tension in their house—her father yelling about the water bill, her brother knocking on the door and her mother wondering what exactly Jana did for thirty minutes. Not her.

Lavender stepped out and wrapped a towel around her hair and another around her body before crossing the hall back to her bedroom. Perfume gave her a headache, so she did the mom thing and rubbed her legs and arms with Fresh Coconut & Cotton body lotion before pulling on her jeans and top. The rest of her beauty routine was as fast as her shower. *Styling creme. Moisturizer. Mascara. Blow-dry only if it was below thirty degrees.* Despite Jana's horror, she didn't use concealer, foundation, blush, or the eyeliner that her friend said would make her dark blue eyes pop. Her low maintenance style suited her.

Lavender checked herself out in the full-length mirror on the back of her bedroom door. *Daughter. Cousin. Ice Cream scooper. Best Friend. What else?* She shrugged at her reflection and moved on to a more satisfying task, like making her bed. She arranged the pillows she had collected over the summer, all different shapes, sizes, and shades of red, on top of her new white comforter. She may not have figured out her future career choice yet, or who she really was, but at least her bed was made. She set Mister Bean at the center of all the pillows. The white polar bear that she and her dad made at Build-a-Bear for her fifth birthday had a cracked eye and his pink felt nose was faded and worn down to the hard plastic. When Bean was new, he would say, *I love you Lavender*, every time she squeezed his left paw. When she asked her dad how her new bear could love her when he wasn't real, her dad responded, *Oh that's easy. They're just words Rosebud. He's just repeating what he is supposed to say.* Her dad's answer was just words, but ones she never forgot.

THREE

"LAVENDER ROSE FINCH. A senior in high school." Sara Finch was still in her sweaty treadmill clothes, and after the wake-up cheer, she was back to the reality of her daughter's last first day of school. She'd been weepy on and off all week. "Where did the time go?"

Lavender shrugged and carved out a large scoop of extra-crunchy peanut butter and ate it from the spoon while she waited for her toast. It was a hypothetical question. With her only child getting closer and closer to adulthood, Sara would need a new hobby. Once her toast popped up and Lavender smoothed more peanut butter on it, she sat on a stool at the counter and looked out the kitchen window.

Sara poured Lavender a cup of orange juice and then herself a cup of coffee and leaned against the counter. "What a beautiful day. So nice outside," Sara said. "Are you excited? This is it...your last year!"

"It's just school."

"Speaking of school, any thoughts on the five campuses you want to visit this fall?"

"Five! What are you talking about?"

"Oh, I saw on the parents' Facebook group that you should apply to five colleges. Three that you really want to go to and would be happy to attend, one that is a real stretch, you know, like Harvard, and then a safe school, like a community college."

"I'm going to BSU, remember? Early decision," she said. In the vast sea of unknowns, there was one thing she knew for sure. One decision that had been made for years and years, and that was that she would be attending Beauville State University after she graduated. It had been her plan since her mother took her to a Bulldogs football game when she was ten years old.

"I know you've planned on that for a long time. I just wanted to give you options. What if…"

"What if what?" She cut her mom off before she could list all the possible things that could go wrong. For Lavender, there was no other option. That homecoming weekend at the football game, they sat with a big group of strangers that Lavender had never met before, yet they all knew her name. "Oh, this is Lavender!" "Sara, OMG, she looks just like you." "She's your mini-me." The strangers all hugged each other like they were brothers and sisters who hadn't seen each other in a while. Like they were a tribe that ran deep. They belly laughed before sentences were finished, danced in their seats to the music blaring in the stadium and somehow all knew exactly when to shout at the same time at whatever was happening on the field. She had never seen her mom have so much fun. Lavender wanted what she saw that day. She wanted to belong to people like that. To be known. She wanted it to be that easy.

"What if you don't get accepted?" Her mom was the queen of *what if. What if you get frostbite because you won't keep your mittens on? What if you trip and fall while you're running and bleed out because you don't have your phone? What if another driver slams their brakes and you don't see it in time?*

"I'm in the top ten percent of my class. I'll get in. It's a state school." Lavender tried hard to keep her voice even and hide the annoyance that was simmering hotter with each question.

"Ok. What if they don't have a strong department in your major?" the *what-if queen* asked.

"I don't have a major yet."

"I just think you'll regret it if you don't at least look at other places," her mom said.

"You loved it there. Why are you suddenly so against it?"

"I did love it there. But I want you..."

Lavender held up her hand to stop her mother from finishing her sentence. "Please stop. I'm not going to waste everyone's time and spend my weekends visiting places I have no interest in. I'm going to BSU. Isn't it my decision?"

"Okay, okay, okay...you're right. I'll stop. BSU it is." Her mother held both hands up. A sign of surrender.

"Thank you. But speaking of visiting colleges...Jackie invited me to spend the night with her...next Friday."

"On campus?"

"Yes."

"Hmph. What are the plans? No parties, right?" Her mom took a sip of coffee while her face looked like she was trying to solve for the square root of something. More *what ifs*.

"I don't know...we're just hanging out. No big deal."

"Isn't that homecoming weekend? Maybe Aunt Beck and I could come too. Stay in a hotel."

"MOM. Don't you trust me?"

"Of course. It's other people I don't trust," her mom said.

Lavender dug deep to find a softer tone of voice. "I need to get a taste of campus life if I'm going to be there next year, right?"

"Alright." Her mom's face relaxed. "I suppose it's okay. I know Jackie will look out for you."

"That's right." Lavender finished her toast and put her dishes in the sink. She moved to the living room, looking for her backpack.

"Do you have your schedule?" her mom asked, following close behind.

"Yes."

"Your lunch money?"

"Uh huh."

"What's your first class today?"

"Global Lit."

"What is that?"

She knew Sara wasn't really all that concerned with her schedule, but the nervous chatter was a way of trying to play it cool. "Uh…it's new this year, they're combining two subjects. Global and Lit."

"Hmm. Interesting. Geography and what?"

"I think it's what you used to call Social Studies and English."

"Oh, got it. Text me at lunch and let me know how your first day is going."

"Mom. It's not my first day of kindergarten," she said.

"Sorry Lav. I wish it was your first day of kindergarten." And then the slow roll of tears started. So much for playing it cool. "Can I have a hug?"

She hugged her mom and lingered a few seconds longer than usual. Her mom drove her crazy, like all good moms do, but Lavender knew it was a hard day for her. But the dorm room sleepover and first college party was on. Next fall she'd be on campus full time. Lavender just had to get through this year. *How hard could it be?*

"I gotta go Mom. I'm gonna be late." She unwound herself from her mother's arms and picked up her backpack. "See you tonight."

"I love you," her mother said as Lavender headed out the back door. She let her mom's words hang in the air as she kept walking to her car. Loving Lavender Finch was easy. Or so it seemed. At least for the people around her who threw the phrase at her like it was a simple game of catch. It wasn't right. For Lavender, it was more like monkey in the middle with the ball always just out of reach. She never quite believed them. Just like Mister Bean, a button was pushed and an *I love you* blurted out. Like it was expected. Programmed. A habit in this tribe so committed to love no matter what. *You're my daughter...my niece...my best friend...my closest cousin...so of course... push the button...I love you.* Love wasn't that easy. Or at least it shouldn't be.

FOUR

LAVENDER LIKED TO THINK the Chevy Malibu was a gift even though her grandmother had no choice but to give up the car, and most of the time, wasn't sure who Lavender was anymore. It was also the one thing her grandmother had taken good care of. No rust, no dents and only 75,000 miles. It was new the summer Lavender was born. White was not her favorite color on a car, but she loved the black interior. Most of all she was happy that she didn't have to ride the bus or need her mom to drop her off and pick her up. She was on her own.

Lavender shivered as she started the car and cranked the heat to take the chill off the windshield. The car was so old there was no Bluetooth connection for her phone. Old school radio was it. She and her dad had tried to get rid of the faint smell of cigarettes by shampooing the carpets and hanging the citrus air freshener he bought her. Then it smelled like smokey orange zest, but that was okay. It smelled like grandma. The dream catcher that hung from the rearview mirror had been there forever. In third grade, her grandma had picked her up from school because her mother was at work and couldn't take her to a doctor's appointment. Louise had burst into her third-grade class without knocking and walked right up to the teacher's desk. Her clip-on sunglasses were flipped up on her regular glass frames and the class watched silently as her grandmother talked extra loud to the teacher. Lavender's face burned hot and she wished for the superpower to disappear on demand and become invisible.

On the way home from the doctor's appointment, Lavender pointed to the odd-looking basket with leather tails hanging off it. "What's that?"

"It's a dream catcher," her grandma said. "Do you know what that is?" Lavender shook her head.

"It catches all the bad dreams you have when you're sleeping so they can't bother you or scare you once the sun comes up. Do you ever have bad dreams?" Lavender nodded.

Her grandma smiled at her. "Well then, I'll have to get you one of these for your bedroom."

Lavender thought for sure there'd be one under the tree that Christmas, or maybe wrapped up for her next birthday, but it never showed up. That is, until the Malibu. She finally got the dream catcher her grandma promised all those years ago. Maybe she should buy herself another one and hang it in her bedroom. It might stop the giant wave from breathing down her neck reminding her of her inescapable and uncertain future.

Lavender parked in the last row of the school parking lot. She was afraid other drivers would take the turn too wide into their own parking spot and hit her car, or they would park too close and fling their doors wide open when they got out, making a mark on her white car. She didn't mind the longer walk to keep her car dent free.

Over the summer, Siena High had installed a ten-foot metallic star with an arched tail, simulating the stream left by a shooting star. The new sculpture on the front lawn of the school was the gift from last year's graduating class. *Siena Shooting Stars.* No pressure at all.

FIVE

"LAVENDERRRRRRRRRR!" Jana skipped across the wide-open foyer to meet her with both hands up for a double high-five. "Are you ready to do this?"

As always, Jana with her perfectly flat-ironed hair, looked amazing in a pair of black jeans, an oversized white button-down that was just the right too-big-size to not look sloppy, and short, gold boots. Jana's entire high school goal was to be voted BEST DRESSED. In tenth grade, she explained to Lavender how she lined her clothes up in her closet and cycled through them in order, selecting the next top, the next pair of pants or the next dress, without checking in with herself to see what she was in the mood for that day. That way she wouldn't wear the same outfit again too soon. Not Lavender. Her daily wardrobe was directly connected to the day of the week, the time of the month, and her overall feeling about herself, and her stomach. She liked to keep it easy and comfortable above all else. Maybe if she took more care with how she looked she would get asked out on a real date. She wasn't interested in a hook-up at a bonfire, or in a school bathroom. She wanted to meet someone interesting who wanted to get to know her. The real her. Otherwise, what was the point?

"Hey, what's up?" Lavender hit her waiting high-five hands. "You're in my Global class, right?"

"Yeah. Ms. Clarke. I heard she's extra."

As they walked to their first class, the halls sounded like Aldersgate Pond when the migrating geese landed there for a break, their non-stop honking echoing off the open water as Lavender jogged the wooded trail. She often stopped just to listen to their noise, wondering what they were saying to each other. There was no use trying to have a conversation in the midst of all that squawking. They timed their walk to Global Lit perfectly and sat in their seats just as the final bell rang. She looked around the room. She knew every single person in that class. Clearly nobody new had moved to Siena over the summer. Was that possible?

It was obvious Ms. Clarke loved her job. She was genuinely excited to be talking to the class about the world events that happened over the summer.

"Class, I have wonderful news. A big part of your grade this year is going to come from a project I'm calling, *It's a Small World.* You know, like the song."

She's not going to sing for real, is she? No. Don't do it...

"It's a small world after all, it's a small world after all, it's a..."

She did. Ms. Clarke's big idea was to prove that instead of technology making people more isolated, she believed it connected people and made the world smaller than ever before. People, especially teenagers, just needed to take advantage of it. Not exactly a new idea, but she was excited about it.

Ms. Clarke combined her desire to connect teenagers across the globe with her passion for those that serve in the military and passed around a list of names, high school seniors who were stationed at different military bases around the world. Lavender scanned the list of names. Her eyes settled on Martin Luther Adams. Martin Luther. Interesting name that stood out from all the Tylers and McKennas and Codys of their generation. Maybe they would have something in common. Did he hate his name as much as she hated hers? Maybe hate was too strong a word. She didn't really *hate* her name, but it annoyed her. Really. What was her mother thinking? She had always wanted a different name. Unique was okay, but Lavender would have preferred one that was typically a boy's name, like Ronny, short for Veronica. Or Bobby, short for Roberta. Or Charlie, short for Charlene. She had grown used to *Lavender* and the comments and questions that went along with it. *Oh, what an interesting name you have. Were your parents hippies? How do you spell that? Is that your nickname or your real name? That's my favorite color or scent or whatever.*

So maybe she'd have something in common with Martin Luther Adams. The assignment was to email each other on a weekly basis. They were required to discuss a different topic related to technology each week. They would email each other through the school email server so Ms. Clarke could log in and monitor the assignment, and also make sure there were no nudies, sexting or any other inappropriate behavior happening in cyberspace between the new pen pals.

Of course, there was still more to the project. Ms. Clarke also wanted the class to fully experience the small world where they lived. Forty hours of community service had to be completed by the end of the school year in order to graduate. Ms. Clarke passed around another list.

"Let's pick one together," Jana said as she read the list. "Ooh, we can work at the Salvation Army daycare. We could play with kids."

"I don't think so." Lavender spent enough time babysitting Mrs. Gordon's kids.

"Oh come on. We'll have fun doing it together. Otherwise, it will be so lame," Jana said, making a pouty face. "What about the animal shelter? Yes! Puppies and kittens."

"Uh…you remember I'm not a big fan of furry things, right?" Lavender looked over Jana's shoulder at the list. Nothing really clicked. Daycare. Food pantry. Meals on Wheels. Park cleanup. She raised her hand.

"Lavender? Did you have a question about the assignment?" Ms. Clarke asked.

"Yeah, do we have to pick something on the list?"

"I guess that depends. What were you thinking?"

Lavender paused. She didn't have an answer right away. She just knew that she didn't want to work at the places on that list. She looked out the window and spotted her car in the parking lot. *Grandma.*

"How about a nursing home?"

"Umm sure. That's a great idea. Get me the name and contact information and we can set it up."

"Ewww. Why would you want to be around old people? Those places are always too hot and smell like pee." Jana plugged her nose and looked at her like she had lost her mind.

Lavender ignored the question. She had visited her grandmother once or twice since she'd moved in at the Betsy Ross home three months ago. She didn't mind the smell so much. You got used to it after a few minutes. If all she had to do was email some random guy a few times and spend an hour at the nursing home visiting her grandmother once a week, she'd sail through this senior year. Easy assignment, easy grade.

Jana leaned back and whispered, "Did you hear we have an assembly for 8th period today? Seniors only?"

"Yes, sounds exciting," Lavender said as she rolled her eyes.

She wondered how her grandmother would like the weekly visits, while Ms. Clarke was lost in her reverie of serving global and local communities. The bell rang and she and Jana and the rest of the class left the room while Ms. Clarke was still talking. "One more thing…we'll be reading *The Great Gatsby* too and having our own little book club!"

"See ya 8th period," Jana said.

"Yup," Lavender responded with a thumbs up and headed to her next class.

Lavender walked into the auditorium and scanned the room to find a seat. It had been a long day, and she really wasn't in the mood to talk to any more people about their summer vacations or summer jobs or summer hookups. She took a seat by herself and took out her phone. She had forgotten to text her mom all day.

Hey lav, haven't heard from you.

Hope your day is going great.

Remember how much i love you!!!

There it was again…the *I love you* toss.

"What a day!" Jana appeared out of nowhere at her right side, taking the empty seat. Lavender sighed and put her phone away.

"Right? Glad it's almost over."

"You wanna come over tonight and do homework?" Jana asked.

"Yeah, sounds good."

The bell rang and right on time, Hillary Charles was on the stage with a mic in her hand. "Attention. Attention. 1.2.3. Testing. 1.2.3. Can you hear me now?" Hillary giggled into the microphone.

"I'm so not in the mood for her right now," Lavender said and sank into her seat.

"Helloooo Siena Shooting Stars!" Jana and Lavender looked at each other and groaned. "My name is Hillary Charles and for those of you who don't know, I was voted class president at the end of last year. So, here I am. You guys, this is the most important year of our lives." Hillary's words were stunted and sing-songy at the same time, probably because her face was locked in a judgmental and condescending look that made her lips tight. As Hillary rattled off the due dates for college applications, final exams, graduation day, Lavender found herself tuning out. All the information they needed would be on the website and she could get the information when she was ready for it. She looked at the row in front of them, and to her left and right. Everyone, including Jana, was either taking notes on their phone or recording Hillary. What the hell? When did everyone get so serious about that stuff?

"Two more important announcements before we're done," Hillary went on. "Voting for Senior Superlatives will take place in March and the winners will be announced at the end of April. Second, senior night is June 14th, the Friday night before graduation. Everyone, and I mean everyone, will be announcing their plans for next year—the college they've chosen, and it's totally fine if you're one of those people who just don't think college is for you, the branch of military or the full-time job you'll be working at is fine."

"One of those people...hah!" Lavender snorted, "Who does she think she is?"

The bell rang, drowning out Hillary's voice for a few seconds. The audience stopped listening at that point and started to move out of the room. "See you later. Text me when you're on your way over," Jana said as they got lost in the moving crowd. Hillary's loud, shrill voice cut through the din of the parting mob. "Don't forget—we also need to think about the class gift we want to leave as our legacy. Let's make it happen, Siena!"

So much for easy. Hillary had turned senior year into decisions, obligations, and responsibilities. Lavender couldn't get out of that auditorium fast enough.

SIX

LAVENDER NEVER FELT MORE ALIVE than when she was running, especially in late September. Fall had always been her favorite season. Breathing in the perfume of the changing leaves, watching the trees turn from green to red or orange or gold, inhaling the smell of burning wood, the wind in her face that was chilly enough to make her nose run and her cheeks red, but not so cold she had to wear a hat or gloves yet. It was hard to explain, but all of it made her insides hum. Her brain stood still, her heartbeat made sense, and her stomach felt at ease. She didn't listen to music or carry her phone, which made the *what-if queen* bonkers, but she preferred to hear the cars coming up behind her, or the dogs barking at her, and she also preferred the silence.

Saturday mornings were her favorite. No time schedule. No rush to get to school. Just her and the familiar scenes of her town. Lavender ran the full length of her street, Sycamore, lined with Cape Cod style houses on small lots, with a fancier and bigger four-bedroom home with a two-car garage thrown in every other block or so. The west end of Sycamore ended at a T stop. A right turn took her down the main drag, past the five or six strip malls, alternating on either side of the road, that held the pizza and sub shops, the dry cleaners, Wegmans, Walgreens and perhaps a yoga studio or an Orange Theory. That route wasn't bad in the early morning, but later on a Saturday, the divided boulevard was crowded with people rushing to get their weekend errands done. Not her favorite.

She turned left, which followed the river to the old downtown six-block radius of 1930s buildings and storefronts that struggled to keep their charm, and businesses, going. Flags hung on the streetlights, each one with a local resident who had served in one of the wars. Ren's Sweet Emporium was on the corner of the last street before the railroad tracks and was also where she turned around and headed back home.

She did her best thinking when she was running. Her mind, focused on nothing more than putting one foot in front of the other, somehow allowed her to process the events in her life in ways she couldn't do if she was sitting still. She didn't understand it, but she came to accept it about herself. She ran for her. Not to be competitive, or to race, or to lose weight. She ran to stay sane.

The first day of school had come and gone. The first week was over. Senior year had begun. All the anticipation and questions and expectations were finally in motion. Moving forward. Still so many questions to be answered but Lavender preferred to focus on the things that were easy to wrap her head around. *Martin. Grandma. Gatsby. Done.* Then off to BSU. It was enough for now. She'd figure the rest out later.

Her stride lengthened as she rounded the corner, back on Sycamore, and saw the long and gradual hill in front of her. She lived at the top of it, so she had no choice but to run up it. She didn't mind. She liked ending her run with her lungs burning and her quads quivering from the final push up the hill.

After a post-run shower and breakfast, Lavender headed to the Betsy Ross nursing home for the first Saturday of her community service. Three months ago, she had watched her father pick Grandma up out of the backseat of their car and carry her into the place. Louise did not go quietly. "You liar. You said we were going to dinner," Grandma yelled. "Put me down, you shithead."

Sara followed behind, crying, and carrying the suitcase she had packed. "Don't leave me in this hellhole," Grandma Louise begged. The doctor had said it was time. Too many years of starving her brain on a steady diet of cigarettes and cheap beer had left her with dementia at sixty-nine years old. It seemed like a sad ending to a sad life.

Lavender wasn't sure her grandma would be glad to see her that day, or for the next forty hours of community service. Louise had never been the kind of Grandma that read stories or bought her dolls or pretty outfits. Lavender had never spent the night at her house. She doubted that Louise even knew when her birthday was. She'd always been a little jealous of her friends with grandmothers who took them shopping or to the movies or wanted to hang out with them in general. Her time spent with her grandmother had consisted of weekly check-ins with her mother to make sure Louise was alive and eating some sort of food and tagging along when her mother had to fetch her out of the North Siena Hotel or Sammy's on East Lake Street. Lavender had no grandparents on her father's side, and she'd always heard that Louise's husband had left when Sara was three, never to be heard from again. Grandma Louise was it. And even though it was her own life choices that had led her to where she was then, Lavender couldn't help but feel sorry for her. Was she lonely? Did she miss her own bed? When did things go so wrong for her that getting drunk was the only thing that could soothe her mind? What was she like when she was seventeen? Did she ever love again after her husband left? Or did he break her heart so badly she never recovered?

Lavender swung the Malibu into the last row of the parking lot. She looked at the one-story building in front of her. The Betsy Ross Home was a dull shade of white on the outside with some random pansies planted around the flagpole in the center of the front entrance. She had never visited Grandma without her mother. Lavender took a deep breath and got out of her car.

Inside the front glass doors, immediately on the right, was a counter with a reception desk behind it. There was a girl sitting at the desk with a small silver hoop in her nostril and a blue-stoned stud in her brow. A sleeve of tattoos extended out beyond the arms of the white jacket she wore. She was playing a game on her computer and did not look up when Lavender walked in and stood at the desk. Lavender cleared her throat. The girl slowly acknowledged her presence with a silent look.

"Hi. I'm here to see Louise DuBose?" she said.

"Sign in on this sheet. And make sure you sign out when you leave." The girl stood and pushed the clipboard in front of Lavender so she could fill in her name and the time of her arrival.

"Can you tell me where she is?" Lavender asked.

Tattoo girl looked at the clock on the wall. "10 o'clock. She's probably in the TV room. Just keep walking straight and you'll run right into it." She pointed down a long hallway.

The hall, and the entire place for that matter, was bathed in beige floor tiles and walls, with cheap art prints and bright lights and very few windows. She walked straight ahead. A woman with wild white hair and a purple housedress was walking towards her. She looked at Lavender like she knew her. Her hands clutched her enormous breasts as she lumbered down the hall. "Will you take me home?" the woman said in a high-pitched voice aimed in Lavender's direction. Did that woman mistake her for someone else? The woman in purple passed by and kept moving towards the front door, repeating her question out loud. "Will you take me home?"

Lavender kept walking towards the center of the building. The air smelled funky, like dirty diapers mixed with the faint aroma of beef gravy. Five hallways extended out in different directions from the TV room. A flag hung at each entrance with the name of the hall: Washington, Delaware, Pennsylvania, Potomac, and Maryland. She saw her grandma sitting in a blue rocking chair with big thick cushions. She looked up when Lavender walked in the room.

"Hi Grandma," she said, hoping that the use of *Grandma* would help her recognize her. Her grandmother stood up and looked her right in the eyes. Lavender smiled.

"I had a dream last night you were coming," Grandma said.

"You did? That's cool." She hugged the little lady in front of her. At five foot five she towered over her four-foot-eleven grandma. She looked better than the last time Lavender had seen her. She'd put on a few pounds and her hair had been washed and curled. She looked cute, almost grandmotherly.

"Do I know you?" Grandma asked.

"It's me, Lavender. Sara's daughter."

Louise studied her face and sat back down in the chair.

"Well sit down. You can't stand all day. You'll make me nervous."

She sat on the brown couch next to the blue chair. There were three other women in the TV room. Lavender wasn't sure what to do so she sat quietly and looked at Louise.

"So why did you come see me? Grandma asked. "Are you going to take me out of this hell hole?"

"Um, no. I think I'd get in trouble if I did that." She shifted in her seat. "It's for school. We need to complete forty hours of community service before we graduate. I asked my teacher if I could visit you as part of my assignment. Is that okay?"

"Suit yourself," Grandma said.

"Rita! Channel 12. It's 10:30," one of the women said.

"I wanna watch something else." Rita shouted loud enough for the whole building to hear.

"*Mary's* on Channel 12. You can watch something else later."

"I don't want to watch *Mary!*" Rita said through clenched teeth.

"Oh for Chrissake Rita, put it on 12." Grandma stood up, her shoulders squared, her tiny hands in fists at her side. "We are watching *Mary Tyler Moore*, like we do every goddamn day at 10:30."

Lavender sat up straight. Should she do something? What, exactly, she didn't know. But she felt like she had to be ready to run. The other woman made a move to grab the remote from Rita's hand.

"Sharon, you bitch," Rita yelled.

"You can have it back after our show." Sharon told her.

Rita picked up the matching blue footstool in front of the rocker and flung it low across the TV room. Lavender picked her feet up off the floor to avoid getting hit. Sharon changed the channel to 12 as the show's theme song was just ending. Lavender sank back into the couch and looked at her grandma, who seemed to be satisfied with the TV back on the right channel.

A tall muscular man in white pants and white shirt came in the TV room.

"What's going on in here?" He picked up the footstool and put it back in front of Grandma's chair. Rita huffed and left the room. Sharon sat down. All eyes in the room were fixed on the TV. Lavender looked at the ladies and saw that no one was paying any attention to the man in white. He looked around the room, looked at her, shrugged his shoulders and left.

"I've never seen this show Grandma. Any good?" she asked.

"We don't talk during *Mary*. Ask me at a commercial," Grandma said.

Lavender, Grandma, Sharon, and another woman watched the show in silence, except for an occasional giggle and comments about Mary's outfit and hairdo.

"I had a dress just like that one," Sharon said.

"You say that about every dress she wears," Grandma said.

"Stop talking. I can't hear." The other woman grabbed the remote and turned the volume up so loud she was sure tattoo girl at the front desk could hear it. For the entire thirty minutes of that episode, her grandma was spellbound by that Mary and her friends. Lavender was too. The clothes. The apartment. The way they talked to each other. Every conversation was intense. They argued. Got mad. Cried. But their friendship and love always won. Mary and her circle of friends and co-workers were a tribe that ran deep...just like the Finch siblings.

SEVEN

LAVENDER OPENED HER DOOR and crossed the room in the dark to turn on the lamp by her bed. She didn't like the overhead light on at night. Too bright. Lavender's bedroom was her favorite place in the house. She was mesmerized by the way the lamplight spilled across the soft gray walls she had painted over the summer. The new look of her bedroom had been her birthday present from her mother. The paint, the all-white curtains and bedspread, and the pillows, all those yummy red pillows, which had become her favorite part of the makeover. Two long narrow ones, the color of fresh roses, were at the top of her bed, with two square, crimson pillows with tassels placed in front. Stacked in front of those were three round, apple-red pillows with buttons sewn in the middle, while two triangle-shaped ones, the lighter shade of tomato flesh, finished the look on the bed. Three giant puffy pillows that were more the color of rosy cheeks after a run in the cold air were stuffed in the corner of the room. Those were great when she got the urge to lie on the floor and read.

It was Sunday night and she had to email that Martin guy for her Global Lit project. Lavender sat on the bed in her usual homework position. She rearranged the pillows behind her just right with one of the square ones across her knees to hold her laptop. She rarely sat at her desk anymore; the bed was way more comfortable. She played music from her laptop while she typed.

Hi Martin. My name is Lavender. I'm a senior in Ms. Clarke's class at Siena Central High. I picked your name for this *It's A Small World* assignment. Hopefully your teacher filled you in on this project, so you don't think I'm some rando emailing you, lol. I think this week we're supposed to discuss the impact of technology on interpersonal communication. Exciting, right? Any idea where to start? I think it's cool your family is in the military. Where do you live?
Lavender

Lavender hit the send button and moved on to her assigned reading of *The Great Gatsby* for the Lit part of the class. Less than five minutes later she heard the deep woosh of an email sliding into her inbox. *That was fast.*

What project? I have no idea what you're talking about…jk. (Yes, I knew some rando would be emailing me, lol.)
Hi there, nice to meet you. Love your name. Is it a family name? We're stationed at Guantanamo Bay in Cuba at the moment. Where is Siena Central High?
Martin

Haha.
Siena is a small town in upstate New York. Not much happening here. You might as well know the full name: Lavender Rose Finch. I know…My mother is very sentimental. Lavender Midnight is the perfume she was wearing on the night I was conceived. (This may be too personal since we hardly know each other, but it's the truth…) I'm not exactly sure where the Rose came from. Maybe he brought her a

bouquet that same night? And Finch, well that's the family name. A plant, a flower and a bird. Ugh. What about you? Martin Luther? I think it's very cool you're named after him. I always wished I had a chance to march on Washington. Lavender

Lavender picked up her book again and began to read chapter one. There was a knock on her door.

"Come in." She turned the volume down on her music.

"Hey Rosebud. What're you doing?" Her father was the only one who called her Rosebud, and he usually only did it when it was just the two of them, no one else around.

"Not much. Homework." She looked up and smiled.

"That's good. I'm going to bed soon. Early day tomorrow."

Every day was an early day for him. He was a contractor and had to be on jobsites by six a.m. She used to love to go to work with him. He would let her sit on his lap while he ran the backhoe and bulldozer. She loved the smell of dry dirt and diesel fuel, watching the sun come up on chilly summer mornings with the dew still on the ground. She'd have to make an effort to go with him again before she left for college. He'd love it.

"Okay Dad. Goodnight."

"Goodnight sweetie, love you." Her father smiled and closed the door softly, his words hanging in the air. She turned the music back up and tried once again to start reading but was distracted by her email inbox.

You're right, your mother <u>is</u> sentimental. Knowing the story makes it even more interesting though. I love your name. Mine is not what you think. My Dad's a Chaplain in the

Marine Corps. I'm named for the original Martin Luther. He was an outlaw monk in the 1500s. I can tell you all about him sometime, lol, if you're interested. I suppose we should tackle our serious subject for the assignment?
Martin

Lavender and Martin traded emails for the next hour or so. They did finally discuss Ms. Clarke's question about technology and communication. They both agreed that the ease of communication that technology provided—email, texting, Zoom, Facetime—did connect the world in ways that made it seem effortless to talk to someone in Cuba, or China, or South Africa. But they also talked about the dangerous side of technology—the girl from Lavender's homeroom that sent a picture of her boobs to a boy in their class, who then posted it on Instagram for the whole school to see. Martin told her the story of a kid on base who attempted suicide after he was tortured by his classmates in memes and videos. And then there was the lack of privacy. Every day in the news another company announced that they had been hacked. Her friends had started to conveniently *forget* their phones at home when they went out because their parents were tracking them and knew their physical location at every moment. It was too much. Lavender didn't like the feeling of being watched or her every move recorded. She didn't like knowing that true privacy didn't exist anymore. She used her phone only when necessary and carried it more for her mother's peace of mind than anything else.

Martin was just as passionate about the topic. They both told each other stories in their email exchange how spooky it was when ads or reels popped up about things they'd been thinking or talking about, confirming that the device was always eavesdropping. Or was all the content sneakily programming their minds, telling them what to think?

Lavender longed for a time she had only heard about. Like when her mother was a teenager, she would go out on a Saturday night and come home at a predetermined time. That was it. She didn't text her mother when she arrived at her friend's house. No tracking device was used to find out if she was really at the mall or the movies. Lavender wondered what it would be like to have more space for silence and room to breathe, alone with your thoughts without the constant interruption of texts and notifications and popups. Mary Richards, from her grandma's favorite TV show, didn't have a cell phone or computer and seemed to be legitimately fine without them. Life seemed more simple, more romantic, before all the technology took over.

She closed her laptop. It was late. She and Martin had completed that week's assignment successfully. Ms. Clarke would be satisfied with their discussion. *Yes, Ms. Clarke, technology created a small world, but also a world where privacy doesn't really exist, and this tether that connects people, also stifles independence, autonomy, and freedom.*

More importantly, she really liked Martin. He was easy to talk to and seemed interested in getting to know her. The real her. The way she wanted all those who threw the *love* word around to know her. To love someone, you had to know them. Their hopes. Their dreams. How could anyone know her enough to love her when she didn't even know herself enough? Most of the time, she didn't even know what she felt, what her dreams were or if she was even lovable. If she wasn't convinced of those things, how could they all be so certain? How could she possibly think that loving her was as easy as they made it sound? Just like Mister Bean, they were just words.

She couldn't tell anyone she felt this way. They'd think she was depressed, or that there was some dark hidden reason for her feelings. It wasn't anything like that. She had solid parents. Not perfect, but solid. They did all the right things. She was healthy, no terminal diseases with a sad ending in sight, no real trouble in her life, but if she was being honest, most of the time she felt like something was missing inside. Like nobody had really scratched the surface of her soul, including Lavender herself.

EIGHT

LAVENDER AND JACKIE pulled up in front of a three-story Victorian with a wide wrap-around porch and big windows. It was obvious that it had been a grand house once, but the chipped paint and overgrown grass left it looking sad and empty. "Are you sure this is it?"

"Yup. I'm sure," Jackie said.

Jackie's roommate had texted her the address. The roommate's boyfriend had a friend who lived in the house. The street was already full of cars. They crept around the neighborhood at five miles per hour for twenty minutes making sure they weren't missing an open spot or a car that was pulling out of one. Lavender wasn't much help. All she could think about was walking into a party where she didn't know a single person except Jackie. Did she choose the right jeans and top? What would she say when she met somebody new? They finally scored a parking spot two blocks away. Jackie had always been the older, cooler, sister Lavender never had. Jackie was the one who taught her how to ride a bike, dive into the deep end of a pool, surf a wave on a boogie board, and drive a car, so it made sense that Jackie would be the one to take her to her first college party.

Lavender was ready to have some fun and meet new people. She was so tired of the same group of kids she'd known since kindergarten. By the time they found a parking spot and walked up the front steps, the big old house was busting with music, people smoking on the porch, and every light turned on. The front door was wide open, so Jackie and Lavender looked at each other, shrugged, and walked in. Jackie had prepped her earlier.

"Just look like you belong, and you know what's up."

"Act like you've been to a real party before."

"Don't act like a high-schooler, and for god's sake, don't embarrass me!"

Inside the crowded house, people were standing in small groups, shouting to be heard over the music. Guys were in the kitchen mixing drinks and making a game of hitting each other in the crotch. "Why do they do that?" Jackie said, which was exactly what Lavender was thinking.

"I don't know. You would think they'd grow out of it at some point," Lavender said.

Girls were standing around checking each other out. Everybody had a plastic cup with a name on it. A beer pong table was set up in the dining room. Every corner of the big old house had something happening. The room pulsed with the energy of it all. Lavender pulsed too. Jackie spotted someone she knew and grabbed her hand. They wormed their way through the crowd.

"Hey," Jackie said, "This is my cousin Lavender."

"Hi." She smiled and nodded.

"This is Morgan, she's friends with my roomie," Jackie said.

"This party is going to be killer. You guys need a drink," Morgan said.

"Show us the way," Jackie said.

Morgan pointed to the keg in the corner. "There's the beer. And there is rum and vodka in the kitchen. Help yourself."

Jackie and Lavender moved to the corner and grabbed a couple of red cups. There was a black marker hanging off the keg by a shoelace. Jackie reached for it and wrote her name on her cup and then Lavender's and then filled them both with cold, foamy beer.

"Cheers Cuz. Here's to your first of many college parties."

Lavender knocked cups with Jackie and took her first sip. "Mmmmm, that tastes so good," she said. The first swallow was always the best—the foamy taste on her tongue, the burn of the bubbles in her throat, and the warm ember it left in her belly. Most of the girls she knew hated the taste of beer. Lavender loved the bitter flavor that was oddly sweet as well. And she loved the way it made her feel, ever since that first night she had tried it. Last summer, Jackie had scored some from her neighbor's extra refrigerator they kept in their garage. It was full of beer so they would never notice a few missing. They each drank two, maybe three, through straws to speed up the process and finish before Aunt Beck came home. Afterwards, they walked to the mall. Lavender's head buzzed with a strange but fascinating sensation. She felt lighter, like she had a secret no one knew. When she ran into Jana and the other kids from school, she was funny and easy with her words. That was the night she discovered that after a few beers, she just felt right in her own skin. Like she belonged there.

They moved around the house, beers in hand, saying hi to different people that Jackie knew from campus. "Flowers" came on and all the girls followed the unspoken mandate to head to the center of the living room, defiantly singing the words in unison, raising their cups, and their voices, for the chorus. When the song finished, Lavender and Jackie drained their first beer and moved back to the keg corner. Two guys came up at the same time to refill.

"Hey." The shorter one nodded to Lavender, while the other one chatted up Jackie. They seemed to know each other.

"Hi," she said.

"What's up?"

"Just hanging out, enjoying the beer and music," she tried to sound relaxed and cool, even though she felt tongue-tied and stupid. It wasn't every day she talked to a boy she didn't know, especially a college boy.

"I'm Travis."

"Lavender."

"Cool. Have I seen you around campus?"

Before Lavender could answer, his friend interrupted. "Hey, Jackie and I are gonna play darts, wanna join?"

Travis looked at her, as if he wanted to know what she thought. It was then she noticed brown eyes framed with the longest lashes she'd ever seen on a guy, and an easy smile that made her stomach flip a few times. She shrugged her shoulders in a *why not?* kind of way. Travis grabbed her hand as they followed Jackie and his friend down a set of stairs. She had hoped to meet a guy tonight but didn't think it would be so easy or fast.

Darts were set up in the finished basement of that huge house. The music was not quite as loud down there, but loud enough. Couples were dancing. There was a pool table in the middle with four guys looking very serious as they held their pool cues and surveyed the solid and striped balls strewn around the table. A huge television on the wall was playing *Ridiculousness* videos and there were two dartboards next to each other on the far wall.

Lavender was getting that familiar feeling that she loved when she drank a little beer. Her blood warmed up. She was feeling looser, uninhibited, lighter, like everything she said was interesting. She could do anything. Say anything. Be anything.

"Okay, it's me and Lavender against you two," Travis said.

"Let's flip a coin to see who goes first," his friend said.

The boys moved up in front of the board and pulled out a quarter. While they negotiated that critical step, Lavender pulled Jackie close and giggled. "OMG, can you believe this? He is cute! And seems really nice."

Jackie laughed. "He is cute. I've never met him before, but Jake is cool too. He's in my Economics class. We've been flirting for weeks."

The two girls knocked their cups together again, "Cheers" they said in unison and then took big gulps of their beer. Once the coin toss was settled the teams took their sides and the game began.

"I guess I should confess I've never played before," Lavender said.

"That's okay, I'll teach you," Travis said.

Travis took Lavender's arm and moved her into position, with her right foot lined up against the big piece of duct tape on the floor, her left leg trailing behind. He took her right hand and showed her how to hold the dart between her thumb and forefinger. Travis was standing behind her, with his left hand on her waist and his right hand on hers, moving her arm forward and back, showing her how to aim at the board. She could feel his entire body up against hers. It was warm. She felt the waist of his jeans and his groin against her rear. She was trying to focus on what he was telling her about darts, but between the beer and his body, her brain and crotch were buzzing. Maybe she would get a college boy kiss tonight. Maybe he would get her number and they could go out to dinner or a movie. Or both. A real date. He could meet her parents. They could be a couple around the BSU campus next year when she was there full time.

"That's it. You got it," Travis said.

Lavender held her arm straight, closed her left eye and squinted her right, looking over the top of the dart. She threw her first one and landed in the outside ring, right next to the number four. She was relieved that it landed on the board at least. "That's not very good is it?" Lavender asked.

"Not bad for a first throw," Travis said and kissed her check.

"Beginner's luck," Jackie said. "Two more practice shots and then let's play."

The four of them played at least four rounds of darts. Lavender was having a good time. Travis and Jake were easy to hang out with. She thought college boys would be more challenging, like she would have to be on top of her conversation and worried about acting adult. But it was easy. They seemed like they just wanted to have fun too.

"What do you think, Lavender?" Travis whispered in her ear. "Are you having fun?"

"Of course, this is great. I don't know how I've made it this long in life without playing darts," she said with her best smile.

"Beer run." Jake said and gave Travis the head nod to the side. While they were gone, Jackie and Lavender had a chance to check in.

"What's up with you and Jake?" she said.

"So far, so good. Who knows what will happen, but we're getting along pretty good. How about you and Travis? You seem to be cozy," Jackie said.

"I know. We just hit it off. Like, we're a natural fit," she said, still surprised at how easy it was to meet a nice college guy.

"I don't know anything about him. If I get a chance, I'll ask Jake what the scoop is on his friend," Jackie said.

The boys came back with four cups of fresh beer and the dart games continued. Lavender lost track of how many drinks she'd had, she knew she should slow down, get some water, but she didn't want Travis to think she was inexperienced or immature. She kept pace with him. It was just beer. She'd be okay.

In the middle of a game, Travis grabbed her hand, "Let's dance." They made their way to the center of the game room. Travis drew her close and wrapped his arms around her waist. She put her arms around his neck. He was just a couple of inches taller. They fit together perfectly. Lavender relaxed against his chest, surprised at how comfortable she felt. She thought she'd be more nervous. The beer helped. She noticed the buzz in her head getting a little louder and she was almost feeling too loose. She liked the feeling but didn't want to lose control of her body. What if she fell over? She'd be humiliated. She lost track of how many songs they danced to when Travis left her to go get another round of beers. Lavender looked around the room. *Where was Jackie?* She couldn't see her. Someone had turned the lights down. The crowd had definitely thinned out. She didn't see Jake either and guessed they probably went somewhere together. It was at that point she realized that her and Jackie had not made a plan to reunite if they got separated. They hadn't planned on separating.

Travis was back with two more beers. He grabbed her hand and pulled her into another room. They could still hear the music. "Let's dance in here, by ourselves. We can have some privacy," he said.

She nodded and resumed her position, entwined with him. "Do you know where Jackie and Jake went?" she said.

"I saw them upstairs. Don't worry, they're still here," Travis said. Travis nuzzled her neck. It felt good. But she wanted to slow things down. She backed up a little. "Come here," Travis said. He held her face with his right hand, pulled her in and kissed her. Gentle at first. His lips were warm and full. Her first college kiss.

She could count on one hand the number of boys she'd kissed, including the first one in sixth grade at the roller-skating party. None of them were memorable. Lavender's head reeled. Her ears felt plugged. She couldn't tell if someone turned the music down even lower, or if the room was soundproof. Travis kissed her so strong she took a few steps back. With his hand on the back of her neck, she felt his tongue enter her mouth. She pulled back and took a sip of her beer. "Let me get a drink," she said.

"Of course, let's sit and relax. We can talk." Travis pulled her towards the navy futon in the center of the room. Lavender stumbled and fell on to it, hoping he didn't notice her clumsiness. Travis closed the door before he sat down. It was dark, there were no lights in the room. They could still hear the faint bass of the music and footsteps and voices overhead. "How's your beer?"

"It's good. Really good. I probably shouldn't have any more though," Lavender said.

"Come 'ere." Travis took the cup out of her hand and set it on the floor. He pulled her close and kissed her, his tongue pressing into her mouth. His breath tasted like the last few sips of a warm, stale beer. Lavender could barely get a breath in. She was spinning. Travis stopped kissing her for a moment and gave her a chance to breathe.

"I should go find Jackie," she said.

"She's fine. Let's hang out. I want to get to know you."

"You can come with me. Maybe the four of us can go get food or something."

"That sounds cool. We'll go in a little bit," Travis said.

He kissed her again. His hands on her shoulders, then his lips were on her neck. She knew she was in over her head. *How many beers did I have? Four? Five?* Travis lay back and pulled her with him. They were face to face, his lips never leaving hers. His hands traveled to her breasts. That was a first. His hands were moving fast, too fast. He worked his way down to her waistband. His hand moved up inside her blouse.

"Travis…wait."

"It's okay. I really like you."

"I know. I like you too but…"

"Shh. Trust me."

"No, really, I need to find Jackie."

The kisses, his hands, the beer, the music all seemed to jumble together. Lavender felt like she was underwater. Drowning. Like she was trying to speak but the words wouldn't come out. She wanted to be cool. She wanted to be mature. She wanted to date a college guy. But she wasn't ready for that. She wasn't ready to have his hands on her breasts just hours after meeting him. *Where are we anyway? What room is this?* Lavender looked around the room again but all she could see was the futon. She knew she didn't want her first time to be there, in that dark room, after drinking too many beers. She wanted it to be special. Romantic. It wasn't what she had imagined at all.

Travis' hands were never still. They were on her breasts again. Her bra was unhooked. He must have unbuttoned her jeans too because his hand was in her pants and he was touching her. His fingers between her. *Oh my god, he was going to go inside.* She used her hands to push him away. But he ignored her and moved his hands right back. His finger went inside of her.

"Travis. No. Not now." *How can I get him to stop?*

"It's okay baby. Relax."

Baby. When did I become his baby?

"Do you want to blow me instead?"

What the fuck? Lavender was glad it was dark so he couldn't see the look on her face. She sat up, still looking for a way out. Travis had unbuttoned his own jeans and pulled himself out. He put his hand on the back of her head and pushed her down. "Suck it." Travis' voice had a different tone. *Where was the cute boy with the brown eyes, the long eyelashes, the smile?*

"I don't do that." She knew she sounded lame. Stupid. Childish. *I'm going to throw up.*

"You're not a tease, are you?"

He pulled her back down and kissed her, hard. He moved on top of her. She could feel him, bare against her stomach. He pulled her pants down. *No.* Lavender couldn't tell if she had made a sound. *Did I say no out loud?* She wanted to scream. If she screamed, Jackie would hear her. *No, no, no.* He was moving fast. His fingers, then she felt it. It was bigger than his fingers. It hurt. *What is happening?* He was on top, pumping hard and fast, not speaking. Lavender was paralyzed. She couldn't move. She tried to sit up but didn't have the strength. She wriggled and moved her head back and forth, side to side. *Is he holding me down? Why can't I move?* Lavender closed her eyes tight. Travis held her arms firm on either side. *No. No. No. Jackie.* Travis didn't say a word. He just kept moving. As if she wasn't even there. She didn't care anymore if he thought she was immature or not. Lavender began to cry. That was the last thing she remembered.

"There you are!" Jackie was standing over her with a worried look and phone in hand. "Why didn't you answer my texts?"

Lavender's head was pounding. She was covered with a blanket. *Where did that come from?* She sat up and rubbed her eyes.

"I left my phone in the car."

"Ugh. Why do you do that?" Jackie said.

"What time is it?"

"Six."

"Where is everybody?"

"Most went home. Some are passed out upstairs," Jackie said.

"Where's Jake?"

"Didn't Travis tell you? They had an early practice."

Lavender's jeans were pulled up, but she could tell they were still unbuttoned. She struggled to remember how she ended up there on that futon covered with a blanket.

"Oh yeah, he did mention that." She lied.

"So, how'd it go last night? What did you guys do?" Jackie asked.

She pulled the blanket up around her neck. *What did happen last night?* She was embarrassed and didn't want to admit to Jackie that she didn't completely remember.

"We just hung out and talked. I must have passed out."

"Yeah? Are you guys going to see each other again? Did you give him your number?

"Yup." She lied again.

"You don't look so good. Does my little cuz have her first hangover?"

"Maybe. I feel like shit."

It was true. Whatever was in her stomach wanted to come up and leave her body, and her head hurt so bad she felt it in her eyes. There was another soreness that she had never felt before. Like she'd been kicked in the crotch. Travis flashed through her mind. He was on top of her. Inside of her. She was saying no. *Why didn't he stop when I said no?* She pushed down tears. Her throat tightened. She remembered enough. *How could I let that happen?*

"Come on, let's get outta here. You need a grease plate from Rocky's," Jackie said.

Relieved to be interrupted from her memory of last night, Lavender moaned and pushed the blanket off her, hoping Jackie didn't see her button her jeans.

"I need to be home by nine to get to the nursing home. And, by the way, I'm never drinking again," she said.

Jackie laughed. "Yeah, right. Remember, you'll be a college girl next year. Parties every weekend."

Not if I can help it. Lavender wanted to get as far away as possible. Far away from that house, from the BSU campus, from Travis. She never wanted to see any of it, ever again.

NINE

LAVENDER PULLED HER CAR UP the steep driveway to Mrs. Gordon's house. Saturday night and she was babysitting for her old fifth-grade teacher. The truth was, she really didn't mind. Ever since the party with Jackie she was not interested in hanging out with anyone on Saturday night, or any other night really. She parked to the right of the driveway so she wouldn't block the Gordon's Lexus, walked to the front door and rang the doorbell. She could hear the commotion on the other side as Mrs. Gordon opened the door.

"Lavender! Kids, Lavender is here! Jim and I are so happy you could make it tonight. We just looooove when you babysit for us. Come in."

Lavender stepped in the foyer and Mrs. Gordon grabbed her in a big bear hug. She set her backpack on the floor next to the basket that held all the shoes. She raised her right leg over the basket and let her sneaker drop in and then raised her left leg and did the same thing again. Mrs. Gordon walked to the kitchen with her following.

"I was just telling my friend, Kristen Yaeger, about how much I looooove you. She might call you. I told her how responsible and mature you are...don't always have your phone in your face like everyone else your age...you can genuinely carry a conversation. Most kids today have lost the ability to talk to people. Don't know what's gonna happen to this world. Stevie, Sadie, come say goodbye to Mommy."

Mrs. Gordon was her own special whirlwind, but Lavender liked her. The most annoying thing she did was constantly tell Lavender how great she was. Getting her and her husband out of the house was always a little stressful but usually happened fast.

Stevie and Sadie came bouncing in the kitchen and latched on to their mother's legs. Mrs. Gordon shuffled over to the refrigerator with a 3-year-old on one leg and a 5-year-old on the other and opened the door.

"OK...so...there are hot dogs in here, and juice boxes, just one before bed though with dinner or their snack, and there is some leftover mac and cheese in here from last night." Lavender checked out the contents of the fridge while Mrs. Gordon was talking and saw what she was looking for on the bottom shelf in the left corner. She had to count fast, but it looked like there was seven bottles of beer. Good.

"And if they want a snack, they can have this popcorn." Mrs. Gordon pulled out a package of microwave popcorn from the cupboard and set it on the counter.

"Okay. Got it." Lavender said.

"Sadie, Stevie, go watch your video, Mommy needs to finish getting ready." Mrs. Gordon pried them off her legs and went upstairs to finish getting ready. Lavender picked up Stevie, grabbed Sadie's hand and led them to the living room.

"What are you watching? Can I watch it with you?" She settled on the couch with Sadie on her lap and Stevie sitting on top of her feet and an old Disney movie playing on the TV.

Mr. and Mrs. Gordon came back downstairs and stood silently by the front door. They liked to sneak out of the house to avoid any dramatic goodbyes. Mrs. Gordon took a pink sticky note and stuck it to the mirror in the foyer. She waved at Lavender, pointed at the note and moved her mouth, exaggerating each word as she explained it had the address of the party and both of their cell phone numbers on it. She waved goodbye and Lavender thought she mouthed that she would be home by midnight. Lavender gave her the thumbs up and a smile as they walked out the door. Sadie and Stevie were mesmerized by the singing animals and never turned their head.

At six o'clock, Lavender headed to the kitchen to cook the hot dogs and heat up the mac and cheese. "Stevie, Sadie, dinner's ready. Come eat dinner with me." They didn't make a move or a sound. "Come on guys. If you eat dinner with me, I'll play hide and seek with you after dinner."

"Hide and seek?" Stevie squealed and came running, repeating "Hide and seek, hide and seek, hide and seek..." about twenty times. Sadie followed her brother and they all ate hot dogs and macaroni at the kitchen counter.

After dinner, they played hide and seek until seven o'clock. She took the kids upstairs for baths, powdered them and put them in their pajamas, helped them brush their teeth and then negotiated how many books they could pick. After a twenty-minute discussion and twenty books thrown around on the floor, they picked three books each and settled on Sadie's bed to read.

Lavender alternated reading one of Sadie's books and then one of Stevie's, going back and forth in princess voices, and puppy voices, and whatever voice a moon makes, until all six books had been read. By that time it was close to 8:30 and time for bed. They said good night to Sadie, tucked her in and she carried Stevie to his bed and said good night to him.

They were good, as far as little kids go. And she rarely heard from them again once they were down. But her favorite part about babysitting was after the kids went to bed. Then she had the house to herself.

She cleaned up the kitchen first, loading the dishes in the dishwasher and putting the food away. Then she cleaned up the living room and turned on Netflix. She looked at her phone. Nine o'clock. They wouldn't be home for a few hours. She had plenty of time. She went back to the kitchen and headed straight for the fridge. Yup, there were seven bottles of beer. Cool. She had convinced herself that one or two missing would be less noticeable with an odd number of bottles. And there had to be more than three to begin with. Three or less and she didn't dare risk it.

Lavender looked around first to make sure one of the kids hadn't come down the stairs, and then she grabbed one. She took the mermaid bottle opener off the side of the fridge and popped the top off. She carried the beer back to the living room and sat on the sofa with her feet curled under her. With the kids upstairs in their beds, sound asleep, she could sip her beer and relax.

She finished that first beer and then grabbed the second one. She was halfway through a movie on Netflix and one more beer would get her to the end. She didn't dare have more than two beers. At least not there. She didn't want to push her luck and have Mr. or Mrs. Gordon get suspicious. Plus, she wasn't trying to get drunk while she babysat. She just wanted the gentle buzz from the beer to smooth out the ragged edges in her mind. She wanted to pretend, even if for just a night, that the party and Travis had never happened. Beer helped her do that.

Lavender drained the second bottle just as the movie credits started to roll and carried both bottles out to the kitchen. She made sure the mermaid was back in exactly the same place it was on the right side of the fridge, next to the sticky notes and

Sadie and Stevie's pictures. She rinsed out her bottles, dried the outside with a paper towel and then stuffed a little paper towel in each bottle so they wouldn't leak. She made sure to grab the two bottle tops, the used paper towels, in case they made the garbage smell like beer, and the empty bottles and carried them out to the foyer. She put all of it in her backpack and zipped it up. She'd drive by the AM/PM on her way home and put her garbage in the can on the side of the store. She went back to the kitchen to take a final look and make sure she had cleaned up any sign of what she had done. She checked the fridge again and made sure the five remaining bottles were orderly enough but not so neat it looked like she had messed with them. She played with the bottles until they looked natural there on the bottom shelf. She opened the cupboard beneath the sink and found the spray bottle of kitchen cleaner. She squirted the sink a few times and let the hot water run just to get rid of any lingering smell.

She took a trip upstairs to peak in on the kids and found them both sleeping sweetly in their own beds. All was good. Lavender went back downstairs to the couch to enjoy the rest of her evening. She picked up her phone to make sure there were no texts from Mrs. Gordon and to check the time. 10:30. Lavender scoured Netflix for something without any make out scenes that would trigger her back to the party and Travis. She couldn't let her mind go there. She lay down on the couch with Mrs. Gordon's fuzzy white blanket over her, thinking somehow that blanket could hide her from the memory of what happened. She was sure that Mrs. Gordon would not be so quick to throw the loooooove word around if she knew what kind of girl Lavender really was.

TEN

NOVEMBER 1ST WAS LOOMING. The deadline for submitting her BSU application for early decision was in a few days. And Hillary Charles never let her forget it. She asked her every single time she saw her if she had done it yet. Lavender sat down at her desk and opened her laptop. Half the high school would be applying there. Beauville State University was only an hour away from Siena, and because it was in-state, tuition was much lower than other schools. Her mom graduated from there, her cousin Jackie was a freshman, and everyone expected Lavender to be next.

But she hadn't thought about going to college in weeks. Ever since the party. She did everything she could to avoid thinking about it. Thoughts of BSU brought back pieces of memory that she was trying very hard to forget. She didn't want to go anywhere near that campus, and she was sure that boys like Travis were at every college in the country. If she let it happen once, it could happen again. The thought that somebody else could do that to her was unbearable.

But there was no way to get out of going to college. She'd be forced to explain why she had changed her mind after all those years of talking about going to BSU. And what else was there? If she didn't go to college, what would she do? She couldn't imagine a life after high school in Siena. Would she scoop ice cream full time? Or babysit? Neither of those sounded like a solid life plan.

She was determined to never tell anyone her secret. She was so ashamed of herself and couldn't stand to think of the shame her mother would feel, or her friend Jana. She hadn't even told Jackie. She found the college website and created her user account. Just seeing the BSU logo and picture of the campus on her laptop screen made her hands and insides tremble. With shaking fingers, she filled in the typical information on the form: name, address, email and birthdate. Someone knocked at her bedroom door.

"Come in."

"Hey Rosebud. What're up to tonight? Lots of homework?" her dad asked.

She looked up, smiled at her dad and swallowed her dread. She felt a moment of horror at the thought of her dad finding out what had happened. It would break his heart, and his image of his little Rosebud. "Nope. I'm looking at the college application."

"Oh, wow. Time for that already, huh?"

"Yup. That's what I hear. Early decision is due in a few days."

"Oh. BSU?" Her dad hadn't gone to college, so he wasn't as familiar with the process and the expectations. It was all very mysterious to him. She heard her mom's footsteps in the hall coming their way. *Oh boy, here we go.*

"What's up Lav?" Her mom poked her head in the bedroom and smiled, "What are you two talking about?"

"She's filling out her college application," her dad said, throwing his shoulders back and stretching his neck with pride.

"Oh right. That time already? How exciting." Her mom and dad looked at each other and smiled.

"I should get back to it, probably going to take a while."

"That's our hint Sara, let's leave her be," her dad said.

"Alright. Let me know if you need my help," her mom said as her dad took her hand and led her out of the room.

"Goodnight. We love you," her dad said as he winked at her and closed the door.

"Goodnight," she said.

She navigated back to the website and clicked on the link to the application. Lavender began filling out the profile information, her parents' names, her school details. There was a section on community service. At least she had something to write there so she filled in the name of the Betsy Ross Nursing Home and described her last two months visiting with her grandma and the other residents. She filled in her work history at Ren's Sweet Emporium and her babysitting for Mrs. Gordon.

The last part of the application was the personal essay. She had to pick one of the questions and then answer in eight hundred words or less. #1: What is your dream job and why? *No freaking idea. Next?* #2: What is the most dangerous thing you've done? How did you justify the risks with the reward? *I'm sure they would frown upon drinking beer while babysitting...* #3: Describe a challenge you've had to overcome and how it affected your life. *WTF*

Lavender stared at the screen. She couldn't move but tried to keep breathing. She closed her eyes. She heard the faint sound of muffled background music; she tasted stale, warm beer; she smelled the musty futon; she felt him on top of her. She slammed her laptop closed. Who was she kidding? There was no way she could fill out that application to BSU, or any other college. Nope. She needed another plan.

ELEVEN

LAVENDER PULLED INTO the Betsy Ross Home and found one of the last available spots to park. Must be a lot of visitors today. She wondered what the occasion was as she walked through the glass doors. The same girl with the tattoos and nose ring was at the desk with the phone to her ear, a red face and a loud voice. "I'm sorry, Mrs. Gates. I really am. But I cannot go get your mother and bring her to this phone. You'll have to pay for phone service in her room if you want to talk to her." Tattoo girl looked at Lavender and rolled her eyes. "Those are the rules. Yes. You can call on Monday and talk to the Director." She hung up the phone and brought the clipboard over to the counter. "Sorry about that. It's been a crazy day today."

"No problem," Lavender said. She wrote her name down and checked the time. "Do you know where Louise is? Oh, never mind. I know. It's 10:15. TV room, right?"

"That's right. Have a good visit." Tattoo girl sat back down at her desk.

Lavender headed straight towards the center of that beige world and tried to focus on something other than the smell. The temperature was way too high and didn't help the air quality. The woman with the wild white hair and purple housedress was walking at the center of the building, looking for a hallway to travel. She selected the one that led to the dining room, clutching her bosom and asking the question, "Will you take me home?" Lavender hoped she wouldn't run into her.

The room was empty except for her grandmother sitting in the same blue rocking chair, watching the television with her hands folded in her lap, her short legs up on the footstool with the blue Keds bouncing.

"Hi Grandma."

Louise looked up at Lavender and eyed her for a minute before she stood up.

"Hi."

She put her arms around Louise and gave her a hug. "Do you remember me Grandma? I'm Lavender."

"Did you come to take me out of this hell hole?"

"No. I'm here to visit you. I'm Sara's daughter." She set her bag down on the couch and took her jacket off. Grandma sat back down in her chair. "I made you cookies. My mom says these are your favorite." She reached into her bag and pulled out a clear, plastic container. "Oatmeal raisin."

"Oh. I love those. Can't get good food like that in this place."

Lavender opened the container and offered a cookie to her grandma. Louise took two and smiled. She put the lid back on and sat down.

"Aren't you going to have one?" Grandma asked.

"No. I'll have one at home. These are all for you." She handed her grandma the container. Grandma stood up and walked towards the hall named Potomac. "Where you going Grandma?"

"Let's go put these in my room. If I keep 'em in here those awful women will steal them." Her grandmother walked fast to the end of the hall. She turned in the last room on the left and opened the door.

"Is this your room?"

"Yup. Terrible isn't it?" Grandma said.

"Oh, it's not so bad…"

Just inside the door was the bathroom. Lavender peeked in and saw the white sink, toilet and tub. There was a string next to the toilet. The red knob at the bottom had *Help* etched in white letters. At the edge of the sink was a ceramic holder with one toothbrush and a tube of toothpaste standing inside.

There was a single bed and a small table next to the window. There was a fake leather chair on the right and a nightstand on the left. Lavender sat on the bed and looked out the window at the parking lot. The same afghan that had been on the back of her grandma's couch ever since she could remember was folded across the bottom of the bed. Her grandmother had made this brown, orange, yellow zigzag-patterned afghan many years ago when she used to crochet. She was glad to see that something had come with her from the trailer Louise had lived in all those years. Her grandma pulled a key ring out of the pocket of her navy sweatshirt and unlocked the door on her nightstand.

"You have to lock up everything around here," Grandma said. She opened the door and put the plastic container of cookies inside. Lavender spotted a small stack of picture frames inside the door of the nightstand. There was the senior picture of her mother on top, and she thought she saw her parents' wedding picture and another one she couldn't quite make out who the people were. "This place is full of thieves," Grandma said.

"Really?" Lavender wondered if that was really true or if dementia made you paranoid. She'd have to look that up later.

"Yup. Can't leave anything valuable out." Louise opened the nightstand drawer above the door. It was full of those small white tubes of Avon lipstick samples. There had to be fifty of them in there. Louise rummaged through the pile of white tubes and checked the bottom of a couple of different ones before selecting a color and painting her lips. She pulled out a hand mirror and smacked her lips together a few times before putting the mirror down.

"You want some lipstick?" Grandma held out a tube to Lavender with wide eyes. She paused for a few seconds and studied her face. "You look like someone I used to know."

"No, that's okay. I don't wear lipstick." She didn't know how she should respond to her grandmother's comment. Was it worth it to keep telling her who she was? That she looked familiar because she looked just like her only daughter, Sara? Would it just make her grandmother feel sad if she was constantly reminded that she had a life before that hellhole? And a family she didn't remember?

"Suit yourself." Grandma shrugged and put the lipstick back. "I don't like to go out with naked lips." Grandma put the tube back in the drawer and locked the nightstand. She dropped the key back in her pocket. "Let's go. It's almost time." Her grandma closed the door of her room and they walked back to the TV room. Sharon and Rita were both there.

"Where've you been Louise?" Sharon asked. "I thought you were going to miss it."

"I had to do something with my friend." Louise looked at her and winked, like they had a secret. Louise sat back down in the chair and Lavender sat on the couch. Her grandma kept her eyes on Rita and Sharon and slowly put her hand in her pocket. She pulled out a cookie and took a big bite before putting it back in her pocket, nice and slow. She stared at the TV while she chewed.

"*Mary's* coming on," Grandma said, nodding in the direction of the TV.

"Oh right. *Mary Tyler Moore.*" The theme song was just starting. Lavender leaned over and whispered so the other ladies wouldn't hear. "How's the cookie?"

"Shhh. I don't want to miss the music. Talk during the commercials."

Lavender smiled and swung her feet up under her, settling in to watch *Mary* with the girls.

TWELVE

HILLARY CHARLES STOOD in front of Ms. Clarke's Global/Lit classroom, clipboard in hand. "Hi everyone. TGIF, am I right? Today is November 1ˢᵗ and for those of you applying for early decision, the deadline for applications. Raise your hand if you're done." Hillary raised her own hand and looked out at the class. Since nobody responded or followed her directions, Hillary turned to her clipboard and began to call out names.

"Kyle?" she asked.

"Yep. Finished at 4 a.m.," Kyle said.

"Brandon?"

"Nope. Air Force Academy for me."

"Jana?"

"Of course. BSU here I come. Woo!" Jana looked at Lavender and smiled.

"Lavender?" Hillary asked. *Shit.* She pretended not to hear her name. "Lavender, did you hear me?"

"Ditto," Lavender said and nodded left, towards Jana. *Was ditto better than an outright lie? Doesn't matter I suppose. A lie is a lie.*

Jana gave her a thumbs up and a squeal while Hillary finished her list and turned the class back over to Ms. Clarke. How was she going to get out of it? Why didn't she just say no? Or pretend to have missed early decision? How long could she pretend that she had submitted her application to BSU? When would she tell everyone that she wasn't going to college after all? She just couldn't. *How did my life get so screwed up? How did I get so screwed up?*

She shook off her spinning thoughts and focused on the class topic which was the upcoming November election and voter registration. Ms. Clarke was explaining the importance of the election process in a successful democracy, and when she talked about the blood that was shed to give us the right to vote and represent ourselves, her eyes filled with tears and her voice caught in her throat. She talked about the Suffrage movement and the long, tedious, battle that women had to wage to be considered equal citizens. Susan B. Anthony, Elizabeth Cady Stanton, Alice Paul. Ms. Clarke stopped pacing and stood on her chair as she launched into Martin Luther King's "I Have a Dream" speech, reciting his words from memory.

Lavender looked around her classroom. Jana, looking sharp in a navy skirt and pink sweater, was filing her nails. Kyle, John and Brandon were passing a phone back and forth under the desks, trying to keep it hidden from Ms. Clarke. Which wasn't hard to do. Ms. Clarke was usually so engrossed in whatever topic she was talking about that she didn't notice the colony under her nose, busily avoiding the passion oozing out of their teacher. Serena, Emily and Kelsey looked bored and rolled their eyes at each other every time the boys stifled a giggle. Her mind wandered to Martin Luther. What was he doing at that exact same moment? Was he sitting in class? Or was he eating lunch? What did he wear to school that day? Was he thinking about her? She was anxious to find out more details about his life.

Ms. Clarke handed a stack of voter registration forms to Serena and asked her to pass them out to the rest of the class. Serena sighed but stood and walked from desk to desk making sure everyone in the class got the form. Ms. Clarke explained that for those students who had not turned eighteen yet, their form would register them for the election following their next birthday. Was Martin registered to vote? Did they have elections and voting booths on the base at Guantanamo?

Even though the form asked for the most basic of information, Ms. Clarke reviewed each line, giving detailed instructions. Name. Address. Are you a citizen? Have you voted before? It was painful to fill out the form as a group. Lavender was amazed that her classmates were confused by some of the questions.

At the bottom of the form was the section on political party. A low buzz started to cross the room. Ms. Clarke stressed the importance of aligning your beliefs on major issues with the political party that you choose. Kyle, John and Brandon launched into a serious discussion about gun control, regurgitating statements they'd probably heard their parents make about abortion, healthcare, the president and protecting the border. Jana had finished her form ahead of the group, set her pen down and picked up the nail file again. Lavender's parents weren't overly political and didn't seem to be lovers, or haters, of any political party or politician. She was pretty sure they voted but she had no idea what they were registered as or who they voted for. She filtered the buzz of conversation and observed that most of her class was checking the Republican box.

She wasn't sure which political party her views were most aligned with. She should do more research. But she looked at Jana, confident enough in her answers to resume her manicure. Emily, Serena and Kelsey compared their answers and made sure they had all filled out the form exactly like each other. She watched Kyle, Brandon and John continue to debate each other. Her mind wandered to Martin again. Which box would he check? Democrat or Republican? How did he feel about the voting process? What was his opinion on gun control, same sex marriage, abortion, healthcare?

There was so much Lavender didn't know, but she was confident that her beliefs didn't align with the rest of her classmates. If they were Republican, she must be the opposite. She checked the box for the Democratic party, put her pen down and flipped her form over, satisfied she had made the right choice. She looked out the window while she waited for the rest of her classmates to catch up. Was the sun shining in Cuba like it was in Siena? Did Martin have a window in his classroom? Would Martin send her the letter he had promised her?

In their last email exchange, they had another long discussion about technology and privacy and had come up with the idea to go old school and write to each other with pen and paper, mailing envelopes through the postal service, with stamps and everything. Neither one of them had done that before. Last Saturday, on her way to the Betsy Ross Home, she had stopped at the office supply store and picked up two nice pens, a pad of paper, and a box of envelopes. When Lavender asked the woman behind the counter at the Post Office for stamps, a plastic sleeve with ten different designs to choose from was plopped down in front of her and the woman asked, "Which one?" Lavender was caught off guard by the question but eventually settled on Waterfalls, staying far away from any designs with hearts, roses or love vibes. Martin was writing the first letter. How long would it take for the envelope to get to Siena from Cuba? Lavender caught herself smiling. She covered her mouth with her hand and looked around the classroom to see if any of them had noticed. It was a whole new world for Lavender, and none of them were part of it.

THIRTEEN

LAVENDER HELD THE ENVELOPE in her hands and stared at the handwriting on the front. He had used a blue pen on a plain white envelope. That was Martin's handwriting. His own hands formed those letters. She hadn't seen his face yet, they had decided to wait on Facetime or video calls, but she saw his hands, holding the pen, and the shapes and space they formed across the page. His letters and words were even, not exactly neat, but not messy either. They were careful. Thoughtful. Perfect. She ran her hands over the words. Her name in his handwriting. *Ms. Lavender Finch.* She felt him.

"Is that a letter for you?" Her mother's voice jolted her out of her pleasant trance.

"Yeah. It is." Lavender hoped to move the conversation along quickly so she could get up to her room and read it.

"That's unusual. Who is writing to you?"

"This kid, Martin. It's a project for school. No big deal."

"Hmph. I'm surprised they have you using the actual Post Office. What happened to email and text?"

"Well, it started that way, but we wanted to try the old-school, you know? More privacy and stuff."

"Interesting. Where does Martin live?"

"Cuba." She thought maybe one-word answers would squelch the questions.

"Cuba? How did you get his name? How old is he? Lavender! What if he's a creep? What if he's catfishing you?"

"Oh my god, stop. He is a senior in high school. His family is stationed at the base there. His father is in the military. Okay?" *Take a breath, what-if Queen.*

"Oh, alright. If you're sure..."

"I'm sure." Lavender scooped up her backpack and grabbed a drink. "Heading upstairs for homework." She was playing it cool on the outside but was dying to open the letter.

Dear Lavender,

I hope this makes its way to you. I don't think I've ever sent a "real" letter before. I've only signed the birthday and Christmas cards that my mother mails to my grandparents and other family back in the states.

I know we've been talking some through email, but I haven't told you all about me yet. Hopefully this won't bore you.

We've been in Cuba for three years. It's fine. Honestly not much different than when we lived in San Diego. The neighborhood we live in is mostly military families. The sun shines most of the time and it gets seriously hot in the summer. I think I told you my dad is a Marine and is currently serving as a Chaplain. He loves what he does. My mom works remotely for a company in California. I think she processes insurance claims, or something like that. She's home all the time. As far as parents go, they're pretty good. Only mildly annoying, lol. My sisters, on the other hand...they're a lot. I have two younger sisters. One in sixth grade and one in ninth. They're not too bad now that they're older... but they can be extra. They're involved in their own stuff like dance and soccer and their friends, so they leave me alone. Thank god. I torture them just enough so they'll have big brother stories to tell when they're adults. Don't worry...mostly nonviolent...well except for the doll who lost all her hair to my scissors, and hiding under their beds to grab their ankles when they jump from the floor to the bed. That one is my favorite. The screams...lol...

I can't believe it's already November of our senior year! Are you going to college? Do you know which one yet? I'm still trying to figure that out. I know I'll go to college at some point, but I'm not sure I want to go straight there after high school. I feel like I've been living on a campus my whole life moving from one military base to the next. I want to be free and roam, ha ha. I'm thinking about the Peace Corps, or something like that. Maybe a Missions trip. I don't know. Haven't confessed that to my parents yet...not sure how that will go over. I think my dad knows I won't follow in his footsteps to join the military or become a minister, but we haven't had the conversation. I do want to help people, but in my own way. I love photography and want to incorporate that into my career somehow. Still figuring it all out....

I don't think I've ever told any one person all that stuff about myself. Another side effect of military life...you never really have a chance to find your soulmate/childhood best friend. How about you? Tell me everything.

Good idea on the letter writing. Putting my thoughts down on paper was cooler than I expected. There is something about it...who knew?

Write back soon! I'm waiting...

Your friend,

Martin

Lavender closed her eyes and sank back on the big red pillows on her bedroom floor. There was something about letter writing that *was* special. She wasn't sure if it was seeing his handwriting in real life or knowing that his hands had held that same paper that she was holding in her hands. *Martin Luther Adams.* She moved to her desk and took out her own set of pen and paper.

Dear Martin,

Yes! Your letter made it here today. This is a first for me too. First letter I've received and now the first one I'm writing and mailing. Who knew acting like a boomer could be so fun?

Your life sounds a lot more exotic and interesting than mine. Whenever I tell someone I live in New York they always imagine the big city. But Siena is a small town about four hours north-west, I think. We are almost right in the center of the state. There are about 30,000 people in Siena, NOT six million, lol. I've lived here my whole life. Just me and my mom and dad. My parents are usually cool...my dad especially. He's chill, my mom is the opposite of chill and nosy, and loves to worry about things that will never happen, but overall I can't complain...lol. My grandma is in a nursing home and I'm visiting her every week to earn the community service hours I need to graduate. Do they make you do that at your school? I'm enjoying it, even though she barely knows who I am. I have a few cousins, most are older so I don't spend a lot of time with them. Jackie is only thirteen months older than me so she's like my big sister. She's a Freshman at BSU.

That's so cool that you're a photographer! What do you like to take pics of? Do you have one of those cameras with the big lens? Or do you use your phone? I'd love to see some that you've taken. I'm imagining you in a darkroom with papers hanging like I've seen in the movies...do photographers still do that???

I have a ton of homework tonight...ugh. Physics test tomorrow.
Thanks for writing. This is fun. Let's keep it going.
Your friend,
Lavender

Lavender folded the paper and placed it in the envelope. After addressing and placing the stamp on it, she set the letter on top of her phone so she'd remember to take it in the morning and drop it off at the Post Office on her way to school.

Who would have thought she'd make a friend all the way in Cuba? He was so easy to talk to. And not like the boys she knew. He seemed more mature, interesting, and comfortable in his skin. She had avoided his question about college. How could she explain that she had planned to go to BSU her whole life but one night at a party had ruined everything? She had ruined everything. What would he think if he knew the real her? He'd probably be disgusted and never want to hear from her again. *Maybe I never have to tell him. Or maybe I can move to Cuba after high school, and he can be a photographer and I'll be a writer.* She shook herself out of her daydream and opened her laptop. A few hours of physics would be a welcome distraction.

With her brain wore out from hours of calculating kinetic energy and contemplating spontaneous combustion, Lavender climbed into bed dreading the next day. Thanksgiving had always been one of her favorite holidays. Her parents loved hosting and cooking and just hanging out all day with her dad's family. Everyone was usually relaxed and in a good mood. Her routine had always been to go for a run before the company arrived, then help her mom and dad in the kitchen and set the table. Lavender loved the tradition.

Jackie came every year. They usually spent a lot of time in Lavender's bedroom, catching up on school and friends and the latest news, watching videos, listening to music. She hadn't seen Jackie since the party. After almost two months Lavender felt like she could breathe again. She'd had her period, twice. *Thank god.* She hadn't caught any diseases that she could tell. Bedtime was the worst. When she closed her eyes and turned off all the noise from her TV, her laptop, her phone, her latest book, and was alone with the silence, that's when it started. She remembered how innocent that night began. She had just wanted to meet new people and have fun.

I'm Travis.

Lavender.

Cool. Have I seen you around campus?

His smile. His long eyelashes. She searched the memories for the warning signs she missed. He was so gentle and patient when he taught her how to play darts. But also stood too close for just meeting each other. She should have known then. Why did she let him think it was okay to press up against her like that? She must have given him some kind of signal. Permission.

Let's dance in here, by ourselves. We can have some privacy.

Lavender's chest tightened whenever she got to that point in her memories, but she kept going. She re-lived it, night after night, trying to figure out what she did wrong. She searched the scenes in her mind looking for clues, looking for answers, looking for another outcome, secretly hoping that maybe it didn't end the way she was sure that it did. Maybe if she looked hard enough, she'd figure it out. *Why couldn't I stop him?*

The room had a smell. Maybe it was the futon. She couldn't quite describe what it smelled like, but she remembered it. It filled her nose and mouth. He had a smell too.

Travis. No. Not now.

It's okay baby. Relax.

Do you want to blow me instead?

That was when it got hard for Lavender to keep going. She cried softly. *No, no, no...* She felt the full weight of him on top of her. She rolled over and grabbed Mister Bean. The scenes got blurry at that point. Muffled. It was harder to see. She was still missing pieces that she didn't remember. She was sick to her stomach. Just like she was when she woke up that morning after the party. Once she exhausted all efforts to make sense of that night, she fell asleep. Some nights were longer than others. All were hard.

When morning finally came, she picked up her shame right where she had left it the night before. The endless loop bounced off the corners of her mind. *How could you? Why did you? What is wrong with you?* She longed for the day when all of that would leave her brain for good.

FOURTEEN

LAVENDER TURNED THE CORNER at the bottom of the hill and settled into her stride that would take her to the top. The air was chilly when she started out but perfect at the end of her three miles. Her runs kept her sane. The fresh air, the sweat, the focus on something other than all the things stressing her out, like college applications, her grandmother, and her uncertain future, gave her a chance to breathe again and forget about the party and Travis and pretend that she was the same old Lavender that everyone loved.

She arrived in the driveway as Aunt Beck and Jackie were unloading themselves and their bags filled with the bottles of wine and loaves of bread they had been assigned to bring for dinner.

"Hey Cuz. What up?" Jackie said.

"Not much. You know. School, homework, same old, same old."

"I feel like you've been avoiding me."

"Why would I do that?" Lavender laughed and hugged her cousin and then Aunt Beck. *Nope. Just avoiding what happened the last time I saw you.* She hoped she didn't sound as fake to them as she did to herself.

"I don't know. We haven't hung out in forever. You don't answer my text messages. I feel like you're ghosting me," Jackie said.

"Nah. Just busy and distracted with school. Come on, let's go upstairs." *Just busy and distracted with trying to find anything else to do after graduation other than go to BSU.*

She and Jackie made their round of obligatory hugs and fielded the usual questions from aunts and uncles they hadn't seen since the last family party and wormed their way to Lavender's room.

"Your room looks great. When did you do this?"

"Over the summer. New paint, new comforter. You like it?"

"Yesssss, especially after living in a dorm. I do miss my own room." Jackie settled on the floor on one of the big red pillows from the corner.

Lavender stretched out on her stomach on the bed. "So what is up with you? How is college? Tell me everything." She forced her voice to sound genuine and curious and light. Jackie told her about her professors and her classes and the food and the parties. She just listened and tried to focus on Jackie's life.

"Hey, did you ever hear from Travis after that night?" Jackie asked.

Fuck. Why did she have to say his name? "Uh uh. Nope."

"Oh. I thought you really hit it off and would at least text each other."

"Um, yeah, I guess, but I just have been too busy." Lavender swallowed hard and jumped up off the bed. She took off her running clothes in exchange for leggings and a sweater.

"Too busy for a college boyfriend? Who are you?"

Who am I? If you only knew... "Lol, I know. Serious student all of the sudden."

"He asked about you," Jackie said.

What? Her mouth dried up, like she had just swallowed a bucket full of sand. She could barely respond, much less play it cool. "He did? When? What'd he say?" she asked, avoiding eye contact with Jackie.

"I saw him that next week after the party and he just asked if I'd heard from you."

"What did *you* say?" She moved around her room, like she was looking for something. If she kept moving, maybe Jackie wouldn't be able to hear the panic in her voice or see the shame on her face.

"I told him I hadn't heard from you since the day after the party. That was it."

The only thing left Lavender could think to do was to change the subject. "What about you and Jake? Whatever happened with you two?"

"We hooked up a few times. I see him around campus and at parties. He's cool but not my soulmate, you know? I don't want to get serious my freshman year. You'll see when you come next year."

"Yeah."

"You should be hearing soon about early decision, right?"

Yeah right. "December."

"We'll have to start planning. I'm pumped to show you the ropes. I've got it down now. I'm so excited for us to be on campus together. We are going to have so much fun!"

Her bedroom door opened slowly after a knock. "Hey Rosebud. Dinner's ready."

Dad to the rescue. "K Dad, we'll be right there."

Lavender and Jackie went downstairs and found their place in the living room. The dining room table was extended into the living room with a long folding one from the basement. After everyone found their seat, there was a break in their conversation and her dad stood holding his glass.

"Let's take a moment and say thank you for the food before us, the family that surrounds us, and the good health and wealth that follows us. Cheers everyone." She caught her mom's eye while her dad was toasting and nodded at her. Louise was her mother's only family. They must miss each other on holidays. Did they serve a big turkey dinner to all the people who lived at Betsy Ross? She would see her on Saturday, like always, but wished her grandma was there with them. The adults clinked their wine glasses while Lavender and Jackie clinked their water and said, "Cheers."

The turkey, mashed potatoes, stuffing, rolls, carrots, green beans were passed down and around while everyone talked and laughed. *I wonder if Martin is having dinner right now?* Maybe in his next letter he would tell her all about it. Lavender tried to avoid direct eye contact with anyone but that only worked for so long. Her aunts and uncles tried to be nonchalant, but they couldn't help themselves.

"So, how's school?"

"Senior year...are you excited to graduate?"

"Going to BSU right? That's what your mom told me."

"Oh, how nice. You and Jackie will be together."

"So proud of you."

Would they be so proud of their beautiful and bright niece if they knew the truth about her? Would they still love her like they profess every time they see her? Lavender kept moving, shoving food into her mouth so she couldn't possibly answer all their questions. *Was it really lying if you only nodded and smiled?*

FIFTEEN

LAVENDER SIGNED HER NAME on the visitor log, nodded to tattoo girl and headed to the TV room in the center of the building. She thought the Saturday after Thanksgiving would be a busy visiting day at the Betsy Ross Nursing Home, but it was quiet. Almost melancholy. *Mary Tyler Moore* had just started on the television and Rita and Sharon were in their usual spots. Louise wasn't in her usual chair. *Hmmm. That's odd.* Lavender walked back out to the front desk.

"Hey, sorry to bother you, ummm, my grandma isn't in the TV room, do you know where she is?"

Tattoo girl looked at the clock. "That is odd, isn't it? She wasn't feeling well yesterday and spent most of the day in her room. Did you look there?"

"Oh yeah? Okay. I'll check her room. Thanks." Lavender smiled and walked towards the center where all the hallways branched off. If she remembered correctly, Grandma was in Potomac but had forgotten exactly which room it was. She walked down the hall and glanced in each door. The lady in the purple housedress was roaming the halls, but even she was quiet that day. The door to the last room on the left was slightly open. The light was off. Lavender peeked in. *There she is.* Her grandma was on the bed struggling with her socks. Lavender couldn't tell if she was trying to get them on or off.

"Hi Grandma." Lavender waved and smiled. She knew Louise needed a moment to process who she was and that she was there to see her.

"Hi. Are you here to help me?"

"Sure, I can help. What's up?"

"I'm trying to get these damn socks off so I can put lotion on my feet. They're always so dry when it gets cold out."

"Of course. Here, why don't you sit back on the bed. I'll help. I heard you're not feeling well? What's wrong?"

"I think I have a cold. I'm tired. My chest hurts. I just don't have the energy for anything," Louise said.

"I'm sorry to hear that. Why don't you lay back and rest, okay? We don't have to talk."

Her grandma nodded and lay on the middle of the bed, her head rested on two pillows. Lavender sat on the edge of the bed and took her socks off. She picked up the lotion on the bedstand and pumped a few shots in her hand. Lavender blew on it and rubbed her hands together a few times to warm it up. Then she picked up her grandma's left foot and began to rub the lotion on it. Her feet were dry and cracked. She took her time spreading the lotion around and massaging her toes, the ball of her foot, the arch and then the heel. After a few minutes, she could feel her grandmother relax her feet and unclench her toes.

"That does feel good. What's your name again?" her grandma said.

"Lavender. I'm your granddaughter."

"Oh right. I knew that."

Lavender finished the left foot and put her sock back on. She added more lotion to her hands and warmed it up again before she started on the right. She looked at her grandma's face.

Louise had closed her eyes and her breathing slowed. She might have fallen asleep. She looked peaceful. Lavender massaged her foot and wondered if Louise remembered all the years of drinking too much and avoiding her family. *Did she regret any of it? What was she like when she was my age? Did she have a boyfriend?* Lavender realized how little she really knew about the woman who had given birth to Sara. She finished the right foot and placed her sock back on.

"Are you cold?" Lavender whispered. Louise nodded. Lavender reach down and covered her with the blanket that was folded at the foot of the bed. Lavender wanted to know everything about her grandma. What had happened to her...or inside of her...that caused her to drink so much? She knew from her mother's story that Louise wasn't always that way. When Lavender's mom was young and her father was still around, Louise took care of Sara and her son, Michael. She cooked dinner and played with them, read them stories, baked birthday cakes every year and made them special party hats. But it didn't stay that way. Uncle Michael became sick and died. Her grandfather left and never came back. That's when Louise started drinking. *Was it the heartbreak of losing her son? Or the way her husband abandoned her? Did he leave her for another woman? What was the thing that made her give up?*

Lavender moved to the chair at the side of the bed. Maybe her grandma had a book or magazine. She opened the nightstand. Louise must not be feeling well because the door to the nightstand was unlocked. She moved some picture frames and looked under her slippers. She didn't see any books or magazines. There was a small shoebox with a rubber band around it. She pulled it out, trying not to make too much noise or have all the contents of the nightstand topple out. She slid the rubber band off and peeked inside the lid. The box was filled with envelopes. Old stamps and postmarks were on the front. There was also a small leather book. A diary. Lavender's body froze. She had crossed the line and invaded her grandma's privacy.

"My letters. You found my box. I've been looking for those." Louise's eyes were opened but she stayed lying down.

"Sorry Grandma. I didn't mean to snoop. I was looking for a book or something to read. The box was at the bottom. In here." Lavender pointed to the nightstand. "Do you want me to put them back?"

"No. I want to read them." She closed her eyes again. Lavender held on to the box and didn't look further. She felt like she needed permission. She'd wait.

"Can you read to me?" her grandma whispered.

"Sure. You want me to read letters or from the diary?"

"Start with the diary."

She opened the red leather cover that had the word *Diary* in gold embossed letters. She flipped to the first page and began to read out loud. She kept her voice soft. Her grandma closed her eyes again.

July 12, 1973

Well diary, I am on my way. Can you believe it? A high school graduate and now on a plane to Ojai, California! I am ready to change the world! It was hard saying goodbye to mom and dad, and Elsie and Ruth. I will miss them. But I can't wait to meet people I've never met before and to work hard and make a difference. This world is so mixed up right now and sometimes I wonder if we'll all be okay, but then I remember what President Kennedy said. I'm ready to find out what I can do for my country.

Wait. Her grandma went to California? *1973. She must have been seventeen. Same age as me. Wild.* After a few moments of silence, Louise opened her eyes. "Is this your diary Grandma? Was that you?"

"Yes, that's me. So long ago. Another lifetime," Louise said.

"Why did you go to California after high school? Did you know someone out there?"

"VISTA. I went to California to help the migrant families."

"Wow. That is so cool." Lavender couldn't believe she hadn't heard that story before. She kept reading.

July 19, 1973

I've been here for exactly one week. Everyone is so nice. I met some people my own age that came here from Ohio and Pennsylvania and Vermont, and someone from Florida. The landscape is so different—more brown than green and the hills and mountains are...different. But breathtaking and beautiful. The air is hot, sometimes stifling, but then there is a breeze that makes it tolerable. It even smells different here. I love to go outside and inhale huge giant breaths of this western air. This part of California doesn't look at all like what I imagined...I guess that's what I get for trusting Hollywood and the television for my research, ha ha. I am glad to be here. We have been going through orientation classes, learning some Spanish and getting settled. Tomorrow I start working. I am ready to get busy.

Louise was asleep. Lavender closed the diary. She didn't feel right reading it without her grandma. She sat by the side of the bed and watched her breathe. There was so much that Lavender didn't know about that woman. She wanted to read more of the diary and the letters in the box. Lavender leaned in close and whispered in Louise's ear.

"Grandma. I have to go soon."

Louise moved her hand to the edge of the bed and opened it. Lavender placed her hand in her grandma's and held it for a moment. Her mouth went dry and her throat tightened, making it hard to swallow. Her grandmother's hand was small and cold. Her fingers were thin, capped with longish nails. Lavender traced the purple vein across the back of her hand. They felt strong. She thought of the young hand that had written in that diary, fifty years ago. Lavender wondered if her hands would look like that someday. Her grandma's eyes opened slowly.

"Thank you," she said to Lavender.

"You're welcome, gram. I hope you feel better."

"I just need to sleep. Take that with you."

"Take what?" Lavender was confused.

"Take my diary. You can read it. I want you to know me before. I want you to know I wasn't always like this."

Lavender couldn't speak if she wanted to. She fought back the hot tears pooling in her eyes and held her breath. She kept the diary and placed the box back in the nightstand. "I will grandma. I'll read it and bring it back soon. Okay?"

Her grandma nodded and closed her eyes again. Lavender stood and moved the chair back in place out of the way so Louise wouldn't trip over it, then leaned over, kissed her cheek and whispered. "Goodbye grandma. See you next week."

SIXTEEN

"LAVENDERRRRRRRRR!"

She barely had her Malibu in park before she heard Jana's squeals. Lavender looked up. *Oh shit.* Jana was a crazy person running at her with a wild look on her face. She looked happy though. *Wait. Is today the day?* Dread filled every available space in Lavender's body.

"Hey Jan. What's up?" Lavender laughed.

"Omg...I'm in. I'm in. I'm in. Did you get the email?"

Lavender grabbed her backpack, locked the car and walked with Jana. She didn't say a word. She didn't have to. She let Jana do all the talking. As soon as she swung the door open into the main foyer, the atmosphere was electric. Buzzing. The excitement was palpable. Almost frenzied.

"Did you get in?"

"Did you hear Megan got rejected?"

"I can't believe Nick was accepted! His grades are terrible."

Her classmates were hugging and crying. Some were already sporting a sweatshirt or hoodie from their new alma mater. Overwhelm shared space with the dread inside Lavender. She and Jana made their way to Ms. Clarke's classroom, high-fiving and stopping to hug people on the way. She knew she had a frozen, fake smile on her face and her eyes were glazed over, but no one noticed. As long as she wasn't crying or sad-faced, they assumed she had received good news too. Including Jana.

"Oh my god, Lavender. We. Got. In. Can you believe it? It's really happening. We are going to be in college at this time next year." Jana settled in her seat and finally paused and took a breath.

"Yeah. I know. I can't believe it either," was all Lavender could muster.

"Okay, everyone. Take your seats." Ms. Clarke was attempting to get the class in order. "I know it's a big day, but we have work to do."

Hillary Charles came flouncing in and took her seat in the front. She was holding her clipboard, her face lit up with know-it-all superiority, just waiting for the opportunity to talk. Her hand was raised straight up in the air, her butt pushed all the way back against the chair.

"Yes, Hillary?" Ms. Clarke said. Hillary wouldn't put her hand down until Ms. Clarke let her do her thing.

"Ohhhh, thank you Ms. Clarke." Hillary took Ms. Clarke's acknowledgement as permission to take over the floor and bounced up to the front of the room. Ms. Clarke took a deep sigh. "Best day ever, am I right? Well at least for those that are going to college and applied early decision." Then her voice changed to a lower register, like you might talk to a four-year-old. "I understand not everyone is taking the same path. Some will apply later to multiple schools, and some are not choosing college. And that is a-okay. No judgement here."

Lavender cringed and looked around the room. There was a mixture of faces—some that looked just liked Hillary's—smug and ecstatic; then there were those who were ignoring the whole scene by looking down at their desk or the floor or their phone; and then those who stared defiantly back at her, daring her to engage with them and ask what they were doing with their lives after graduation.

"If you applied early decision and received the acceptance email, raise your hand. I'm compiling a list for Principal Edwards." Hands went up around the room. Jana had her arm as high as it could possibly go without unhinging from the socket. Lavender pretended to be distracted by her notebook, hoping that whole conversation would be over soon. Hillary scanned the room making check marks on her clipboard and murmuring to herself.

"Jana, Mara, Kyle…Lavender?" *This was it. The moment everyone would find out that I haven't really applied to BSU because I'm a fucking idiot who got drunk at a party and let Travis ruin everything. Let Travis ruin me.*

Jana kicked her. "Helloooo Lavender, are you awake?"

Lavender forced her mouth into a semi-smile and raised her hand for a split second and then pretended to be smoothing her hair.

"Lavender. Great." Hillary placed a check next to her name and kept moving. *That's it. The lie is down on paper now.* Hillary, and soon Principal Edwards, would think that Lavender had applied and been accepted at BSU. She didn't know how the hell she would get out of that lie. Thank God, Ms. Clarke took the room back over and Hillary sat down.

"Class, we've got a lot to do today. I want to do a mid-year check in on your project, *It's a Small World.*"

Lavender sunk into her chair and let her mind sink as well. She had no idea what to do or how to get out of that mess. Whenever she reviewed her options, none of them seemed possible. If she confessed that she'd never completed her application or submitted it, she'd have to explain why. Which would lead to the party and what she had let happen. She just couldn't do that. It was too embarrassing. She was too ashamed. How could she look her mother and father in the eye and tell them they she had too many beers and found herself in a room alone with a rando guy named Travis who thought she was the kind of girl who wanted him to do that? She could barely process it herself. How could Jana? Or Jackie? Or her parents? Lavender had to do something. At least before June. Once graduation was over and she had no place to go, her friends and parents would catch on. Whenever she tried to think through the problem and solve it, she couldn't get past the hate for what she'd done. The party was bad enough but now she was a liar too. Jackie had texted her five times since Thanksgiving and had invited her to another party. Lavender ghosted her. Hadn't even responded to her cousin. She hadn't been hanging out with Jana either. How do you spend time with the people closest to you when they don't know the absolute worst things about you? When they don't know what's literally keeping you awake at night? When they don't know about the biggest lie you've ever told? When they don't know your secrets?

"Lavender. Earth to Lavender. Helloooo?" Ms. Clarke came and stood at her desk. She looked up. "Can you tell us about your pen pal and your community project?" Apparently, Ms. Clarke had been going around the room and asking for updates. It was her turn. Relieved to be rescued from her thoughts, Lavender came back to class.

"Sure. I connected with Martin Luther Adams. His father is a Marine Chaplain stationed at Guantanamo Bay in Cuba. We've been emailing about the assignments. It's going fine." She left out how they'd been writing old-school letters and mailing them to each other. She didn't let on how much she really liked him or that he was her only friend now that she had cut Jana and Jackie out of her life. She wanted to keep what they had to herself for a while longer. It was special and she didn't want anyone's comments or opinions to ruin it.

"That's wonderful. Wow. Cuba. So exotic. Can't wait to hear more. And your community project?"

"Oh right. Yes. I've been spending time at The Betsy Ross Nursing Home on Walnut Street. My grandmother lives there. She was sick recently and I was able to help take care of her." She knew it wasn't as exciting as some of the other stories of working at community daycare centers and feeding the homeless, but just like Martin, it was special to her, and she liked that she didn't have to share it with anyone.

Ms. Clarke moved on and listened to the reports from the rest of the class. Her teacher seemed proud and thrilled that the students were executing her vision. Lavender was sure that most of her classmates just wanted to get the assignment done so they could move on. The bell rang, and Lavender could finally move on to a different class, Physics.

The rest of the day dragged as she tried to focus on everything except college applications and her lie. In 9th period, her last class of the day, Principal Edwards made an announcement.

"Good afternoon students. Today is an exciting day for many of our seniors. Early decision letters from colleges around the country have been received. Following is a list of those who've been accepted and the college they will be attending. Congratulations to all. We share in your pride and accomplishment. Godspeed." Principal Edwards proceeded to read a list of at least fifty names. The dread was back as Lavender listened to Edwards make his way through the alphabet.

"Tim Fairchild, Utica College. Lindsey Felder, SUNY Brockport. Lavender Finch, BSU…"

There it was. The lie was in the airwaves. Officially public and announced for all the world to hear. There was no turning back. Lavender wanted to throw up. She couldn't wait to get home and go for a run. Maybe she'd write a letter to Martin tonight.

When Principal Edwards was finally done reading the list and the last bell rung, Lavender made a beeline for the door and her car. She avoided eye contact with anyone, including Jana, and made it to the parking lot. She slid in her seat and exhaled. Her hands gripped the steering wheel on either side while she rested her head on it. *What a shitty day. So glad that is over.* She started the Malibu and turned on the radio. Maybe some music would turn the channel in her mind while she drove home.

Lavender entered her neighborhood and noticed new signs in the middle of some of the front yards. *Oh my god. I forgot about the signs.* The signs announced that a graduating senior lived in that house and what school they'd be attending in the fall. Lavender turned on to her street and there it was, slapping her right in the face. *No way.* The dread was replaced with full on horror.

Congratulations! Lavender Rose Finch is BSU Bound in the Fall. Go Bulldogs.

The lie was now in her front yard, in bold colors of blue and gold, for all the world to see.

SEVENTEEN

SARA FLUNG THE BACK DOOR OPEN before Lavender had a chance to get out of her car. "Best news ever, right?" Her mom was smiling but also had tears in her eyes.

"Who told you? How did you know to get the sign?" Lavender was unsure why her mom would assume she'd been accepted when they hadn't talked about it.

"Oh, you know, the mom group chat. Everyone was talking about it today. Somebody congratulated me and let the cat out of the bag. Plus, I've had the sign for weeks." Her mom hugged her. "My little girl is now a college girl. I am so proud of you. So is your father. I called him at work and we are celebrating tonight!"

"No, that's okay, we don't have to. It's really no big deal."

"No big deal? You're going to college. And not just any college but the one you've been dreaming about since you were ten years old. We are celebrating. Don't be so humble."

Lavender would not win that battle.

"We'll go to Losurdo's for Italian. That's your favorite."

"Can we just stay home and order pizza? I have a lot of homework." She gave it one more shot.

"No way. That is not special enough. We're going out," her mom said.

"Alright. Well, let me go get my homework done then." Lavender had to get out of there. It was too much. The way her mother looked at her, so proud, so satisfied, so loving. But Sara Finch didn't know what her daughter was really like.

"Oh here. You got another letter today." Lavender's mom handed her an envelope. *Thank god! At least one good thing happened today.*

Lavender grabbed the letter and made another beeline, that time for her room. She'd have a few hours before her dad got home, and she'd have to go to dinner to *celebrate*. She dropped her bag and flopped on the bed. Lavender held the unopened envelope up and looked at the handwriting. She felt the paper between her hands. She tried to feel Martin. She almost drifted off to sleep, holding the letter on her chest, before jolting upright to open it.

Dear Lavender.

Hi. How are you? I hope you're good. I can't believe Christmas is coming so fast. Three more weeks. Even though we're here in Cuba, Christmas is usually a lot of fun. They decorate the same way you do in the states, with all the lights and Christmas trees, and Christmas music is playing everywhere. The only thing missing is the snow, and all the commercial capitalism trying to get us to buy too much, lol, and making it all about spending. Has it snowed there yet? What's on your Christmas list? I'm hoping for a new camera and photo printer. My phone takes amazing pictures, but I want to be able to take my photography to the next level. There's this class I want to take in the spring. It's a Masterclass online with one of my idols. I can't wait for it. What's new with you? How's your grandmother? Louise, right? I hope she's doing well.

School is boring and typical. I think I'm starting to get senior-itis. I just keep thinking about getting this over and done with and moving on to the rest of my life.

I started reading The Great Gatsby. You said you were reading it for Ms. Clarke's class, so I thought I'd read it with you. I'll try to catch up. You're probably way ahead of me now.

I won't say Merry Christmas yet because you'll hear from me before then. Hey, what do you think of exchanging phone numbers? Maybe it's time to do an actual call? Even Facetime? I know most people our age avoid a phone call at all cost, but since we're doing it old-school, why not talk on the phone too? We'll be just like the boomers.
Write soon.
Martin

Lavender read the letter three more times. The dread and horror she'd felt all day was replaced with a warmth in her belly and mind. A warmth for Martin, who she had never met and hadn't known for long. She had so many questions. Was he going to get her a Christmas present? Is that why he asked what was on her list? *Oh my god. What would I get him?* He's reading her assigned book. *Why would he do that? Doesn't he have enough homework?* Should they talk on the phone? What if they didn't look like they each had imagined? What if it ruined the friendship they had developed by writing letters? Would it make it less special? Lavender wished she had someone to talk to about all of it. Jana or Jackie. But since she'd been ignoring their texts and invitations to hang out, she didn't feel like she could talk to them about Martin. Plus, it would open the door to more communication, and she was doing her best to avoid that. She had never been one of those girls with a whole gang of girlfriends, but she'd always had Jackie and Jana. It was an odd feeling to have no one to talk to. Lavender could lie there all night trying to find the meaning in his words. Martin Luther Adams was the most interesting person she'd ever met. And the only friend she had left. She moved to her desk and began to write him back.

Hi Martin.

I was so happy to get your letter today. Rough day at school… long story. I can't believe Christmas is almost here either. It has been getting colder but no snow yet. I'm sure any day now. My mom plans on putting up our tree this weekend. To be honest, I haven't even thought of what I want for Christmas yet.

She wanted to write, *a plane ticket to Cuba would be nice*, but thought it was too soon for that.

My grandmother is doing better. When I saw her the week of Thanksgiving, she was sick and not at all herself. She's warming up to me. She let me rub her feet with lotion and then she let me read her diary! She even let me bring it home with me. It starts in 1973 when she was on her way to California to work for AmeriCorps. Isn't that cool? I guess it is like the domestic Peace Corps. Have you heard of it? It was called VISTA when she went. I had no idea she did that when she was my age. I have a lot to learn about her…but I'm really glad that I'm getting the chance to do that.

I'm behind on my reading for The Great Gatsby so you're probably already ahead of me. What do you think so far?

I have a hard time identifying with the characters and all the money they have, but I love imagining what life was like back then.

Your class sounds cool. I need a new hobby. I don't have a clue what I want to do with my life.

A phone call! You are a boomer, lol, but I'm in, if you are. Maybe we can call each other on Christmas? I'm sure your day will be busy with your parents and sisters, but maybe later that night? What do you think? 10 pm Christmas night? Thanks for writing Martin. You saved my day today.
Write soon.
Lavender

Lavender sealed up the letter and found her grandma's diary in her backpack. She set it on the stand next to her bed so she could read it tonight before she fell asleep. Maybe it would distract her from her usual flashbacks of Travis and the party. But first, dinner at Losurdo's celebrating Lavender's college acceptance. What a farce.

EIGHTEEN

MRS. GORDON'S STEEP DRIVEWAY was no fun in December, but Lavender shifted into a lower gear like her dad had taught her and kept the pressure on the gas pedal, slow and steady. Lavender's social life consisted of babysitting, the nursing home and watching Netflix with her parents. She never thought that was what her senior year would look like, but she was getting into the rhythm of it. That lifestyle certainly kept the drama in her life to a minimum.

She parked to the right of the driveway so they could get their car out and before she rang the doorbell, Mrs. Gordon flung the front door open.

"Congratulations! We heard the news and saw the sign in your yard. Wow. Good for you, kiddo. Not that I'm surprised." Lavender stepped in the foyer and Mrs. Gordon grabbed her in the usual bear hug. "Kids, Lavender is here!" She smiled and said nothing. She was used to the comments and congratulations at that point and had become a pro at not responding, amazed at how easy it was to just let people talk and make assumptions. How easy it was to keep secrets. "I don't know what we're going to do next year when you're gone. I can't imagine having a new babysitter here. Stevie and Sadie are going to miss you!"

Lavender set her backpack on the floor and followed Mrs. Gordon to the kitchen while she went through the usual rundown of whose Christmas party they were going to, when they'd be back and what to feed the kids for dinner. Stevie and Sadie hung on her leg while they walked and talked.

Lavender turned towards the living room, "Who wants to watch a movie? With popcorn?" The kids squealed and she and Mrs. Gordon exchanged a look. She settled on the couch with the kids and searched for a movie to watch while Mr. and Mrs. Gordon did their silent sneaking-out-of-the-house act.

After dinner and the bedtime routine of pajamas and books, Stevie and Sadie fell asleep fast. Lavender was ready to settle into her own routine at the Gordon's house. She grabbed her backpack from the foyer. She'd brought her *Gatsby* book to catch up on her reading and her grandmother's diary.

When she was cooking dinner, she noticed that the beer shelf was re-stocked. The last time she babysat, she couldn't drink any because there were only two bottles left in the fridge. She wasn't that reckless. Lavender did one more check to make sure the kids were sleeping and also made sure she didn't have a text from Mrs. Gordon saying they were on their way. *All clear.* She popped open the first bottle and took a sip. It was cold and fizzy. That first taste was always so satisfying. Since she wasn't hanging with Jackie or going to any parties at the Lane, the only beer she had those days was at the Gordon's house. Lavender knew it probably wasn't the best habit to be drinking beer while babysitting, but if the kids were sleeping, there was no harm. It's not like she was impaired. She limited herself to two, most of the time, never more than three. And well within the suggested timeframe so her blood levels were below legal limits before she drove home. She was being smart about it. *It was better than drinking on a random dirt road with a bonfire and fifty other teenagers, right?*

She sat on the couch with her bottle and her books and waited for the gentle buzz to kick in and settle in her bones. The last few weeks had been harder than she'd expected. With the early decision results and everyone congratulating her and talking nonstop about college, she needed an escape, like drinking beer alone at the Gordon's house. It might sound lame to other people, but it truly was relaxing and the only time she felt like she could be herself and think straight. Lavender also knew that people would not understand if they knew about her questionable habit. She sipped her beer, turned on some music and tried to think of how she could get out of the college lie that was growing bigger by the day. *Maybe I could announce that I want to follow in my dad's footsteps in the construction business. Or something else that BSU doesn't have a major in, like nursing... or welding...or waitressing.*

She opened *Gatsby* and read a few chapters. She wondered if she would have been a flapper if she was a young girl in the 1920s. Lavender was amazed at how hard they partied. People always made the old days sound so innocent and G-rated, but it really wasn't. They conveniently forgot about all the drunkenness, the drugs and sex that was happening. *I'm sure there were guys like Travis back then too.*

When Lavender finished her first beer, she'd had enough of F. Scott Fitzgerald's world. After she got back from the kitchen with her second beer, she reached for the diary. Just like she did with Martin's letters, she liked to just hold it and try to feel the younger version of her grandmother. She ran her fingertips over the words and letters in her handwriting. She wondered if she and Louise would have been friends.

August 15, 1973

I made it one month! I'm so proud of myself for having the courage to move away, to defy everyone's expectations, and follow my dreams. I'm still surprised some days that I really did it. I have my moments of missing home. Like my mother's pancakes, the roast she makes on Sundays and her oatmeal raisin cookies, ha ha. The food here is okay, but not like Mom's. We finished the training and now I get to work directly with the families. I'm spending most of my time with the school-aged kids, helping them with their homework and with their English. When I'm not doing that, I'm writing. What's happening here on the farms and with the workers needs to be told. I love to meet the people and hear their stories. I love getting to know them. Such a different world than where I'm from. I'm sure this year will go by fast so I'm enjoying every moment. Our director has instituted a curfew for the volunteers. He says it is too dangerous to be out in the farming communities with all the protests and anger towards the migrant workers. Some people are upset that government programs like VISTA are here helping them. I don't understand it all, but I'm learning.

Lavender pulled out her laptop. She was so curious about all of it. 1973. The VISTA program. Ojai, California. The farms and the workers. What was the story her grandmother wanted to write about? Lavender spent the next two hours reading about the volunteer program and the lettuce boycott, the grape strike and Cesar Chavez. Her grandmother was right in the middle of history. She wondered if Louise remembered any of it. The stories Lavender found on the internet were sobering, and surprising. Why didn't they learn about that in school? The violence was disturbing. Why was it such a polarizing idea to pay people enough money to support their families? Or to have decent working conditions? Some were killed in the protests. That was a whole new world to Lavender too. She was anxious for her Saturday visit to Betsy Ross so she could ask Grandma about it.

By September of 1973, her grandma's diary entries had a different tone. She'd met someone.

M. and I managed to sneak out for a walk tonight after dinner. I told my roommate I was doing some extra English tutoring for one of the fourth graders in my group. I felt a little bad telling a fib...but the truth is, I'd do anything to see M. again. We met at the entrance to the vineyard and walked for an hour. There was no one there at that time of day. The vines are tall enough now to hide us. He is 17 too and hopes to join the military so they will pay for college. He's lived here since he was five years old, and his English is perfect. He's even teaching me some Spanish. I never thought I'd meet a boy like him here, and never thought I'd feel this way about someone I just met. But it must have been fate. The moon was almost full tonight, the air was cool, and we could smell the musty grapes that had been in the hot sun all day. He was waiting for me at the west gate, took my hand, and led me through the neat rows of grapevines. As soon as our hands met it felt like we'd known each other forever, and our hands had finally found the one they were supposed to hold. Mine, small and soft, interlocked with his, rough from his work in the fields. We talked about so much but also walked in silence. We are meeting again in two nights. What does Shakespeare say? "To sleep, perchance to dream." I will dream about M. tonight.

Her grandma fell in love in California. After that night, the entries were all about M. Their first kiss, the way they danced in the moonlight to a transistor radio, the first time they said *I love you.* Her grandma wrote about all of it. *Will I ever find that hand I'm supposed to hold?*

October 18, 1973

I'm not sure what I expected my first time to feel like, but it was more than I had ever imagined it could be. I didn't know you could feel such connection and depth with another human. We had our blanket laid out under the stars with our radio playing…so romantic…and it just happened. We didn't plan it. We didn't talk about it first. He kissed me. Told me he loved me today and would love me forever and I just melted into his arms. It was the most beautiful thing I've ever done. Our bodies connected but more than that, our souls touched. We were gone longer than we should have been and I was nervous about missing curfew. My roommate was asleep when I got back, thank god, so I will just fib again and tell her I got back earlier than I did. I don't care if I get in trouble. It was worth it. This love with M. has changed me forever.

Lavender had a lump stuck in the middle of her throat and a deep pit of sadness where her stomach used to be. Not for her grandmother, but for herself. Her grandmother's first time was a beautiful scene with two people willing to risk getting in trouble because they were so in love and had to let their souls touch in the deepest way imaginable. Lavender would never have that moment. She wasn't in love for her first time. She barely knew the boy and he didn't care about her at all. Her scene was disgusting and vile and made her want to vomit. She slammed the diary closed and looked at her phone. She'd lost track of time. Mr. and Mrs. Gordon would be home any minute.

She carried her bottles out to the kitchen and did her rinse and dry routine before placing the bottles in her backpack and setting her bag back in the foyer. She popped some gum in her mouth and checked the bedrooms one more time. Everything and everyone were where they belonged. *Where do I belong?*

NINETEEN

LAVENDER NEVER THOUGHT of herself as someone who loved Christmas, but seeing the shrubs in front of Betsy Ross all lit up with colored string lights made her smile. "White Christmas" was playing over the loudspeaker when she walked in the front door. The beige interior was overcome with garland and a large poinsettia display. There was a Christmas tree in the TV room with silver tinsel and a star on top. It was almost festive. Just as Lavender reached her chair, Grandma Louise looked up and smiled when she saw her.

"Hey gram."

"Oh hi. It's you again. Are you here to see me?" Louise said.

"I sure am. I brought your Christmas presents."

"You got presents for me?"

"Of course," Lavender said.

"I don't have anything for you."

"That's okay. I don't need anything."

"Let's go in my room. I don't want these nosey people knowing what I got. They'll steal it." Lavender and her grandma walked down the Potomac Hall to her room. There was a small round table with a chair in front of the window.

"You wanna sit over there at the table?" Lavender asked.

"Sure."

Lavender grabbed the other chair by the bed and brought it over. "How've you been feeling grandma? You were sick a few weeks ago."

"I was? I feel fine now."

"Oh good. Well here. Open your presents." She gave her the first package wrapped in red and green striped paper.

"Cookies! Are these my favorite?" her grandma asked.

"Oatmeal raisin. My mom Sara made them for you."

"Sara." Her grandma had a look on her face, like she recognized the name.

"Open this one next." Her grandma opened a set of coloring books made for adults, and a box of crayons and markers. Lavender had seen them in the bookstore and thought it might be a good activity. It seemed like there was a lot of time to kill in a place like that. "I thought the drawings of flowers and gardens and land-scapes were beautiful," she told her grandma.

"I haven't colored since I was a girl." Her grandma flipped through the pages of the coloring books, studying the different scenes. She opened the box of crayons and markers, took out a few and read the name of the color. "Hmmm. I like this."

"Okay. Here's your last one. I hope you like it. I wasn't sure what to get you."

Her grandma opened the last box. It was a small round speaker that Lavender had found at Target. It was made to look like a retro transistor radio, but it had wi-fi and Bluetooth. She could connect and download music from her Spotify and Amazon account and her grandma could play it in her room.

"Is this a radio?"

"Sort of. I can load music to it, and you can play it here in your room. Listen." Lavender turned on the speaker and set the volume at a level where they could hear it but not bother the room next door.

"Oh, that's nice. Jazz?" her grandma looked up at her. "I like jazz. I used to listen to music all the time when I was young."

"Cool. I'm glad you like it. Being able to do stuff like this makes all our new-age technology worth it." She placed the speaker on the stand next to the bed and left the music playing. Her grandma was smiling while they sat and listened to the soothing murmur of trumpets and clarinets and saxophones. Lavender then shifted to the Christmas playlist she had made.

"Do you wanna color with me?" Her grandma was eyeing the books Lavender had just given her.

"Yes. I was hoping you'd ask," Lavender said.

They sat at the table by the window with the Christmas music playing and colored for the rest of the afternoon. Her grandma was so excited when she completed her first picture, she wanted to hang it on her wall. Lavender walked out to the front desk and asked Tattoo girl for some tape.

"How's she doing today? Louise?"

"She seems good. I bought her these adult coloring books and she wants to hang up the picture she colored on her wall." Tattoo girl found a roll of tape in a drawer and handed it to Lavender. "Thanks. I appreciate it."

"Your name is Lavender, right? I'm Evelyn."

"Yes. Nice to meet you."

"Have you always been close with your grandma?" Evelyn asked.

"Nah, not really. We didn't spend much quality time together when I was growing up. At this point, I don't think she really knows who I am most of the time." Lavender avoided Evelyn's eyes.

"Bummer. It happens. But I believe on some level, they always know their people. Even when it doesn't seem like it." The phone rang and Evelyn nodded at her and picked it up. "Hello, Betsy Ross, how can I help you?"

Lavender took the tape and headed back to her grandma's room. When she got to the center, where the five hallways met, she looked around to see if anyone was looking. The coast was clear. She took one of the poinsettias off the bottom of the display and carried it back to her grandma's room.

"Oh hi," her grandma said as if she was seeing Lavender for the first time that day. "Someone brought me coloring books and crayons."

"Nice. I brought tape so we can hang your pictures up." Her grandma had finished another one. Lavender set the poinsettia in the corner and hung both pictures on the wall before she sat back down in her chair at the table.

"Grandma. I've been reading the diary you gave me. The red one with the gold letters? Remember, you gave it to me when you were sick." Her grandma didn't respond. Just kept coloring. "You went to California after graduation?" Her grandma's hands stopped moving. Lavender could see she was thinking about the question.

"I did go to California. I haven't thought about that in years. I don't wanna think about it either."

"Really? It seemed like you loved it? No?"

"I said I don't want to talk about it. I left all that behind when he left. Let's have a cookie."

Who left? Who is 'he'? Lavender didn't want to be pushy and risk that her grandma would get upset. But she was confused. Louise seemed so happy based on what she'd read in the diary so far. *There must be more to the story.* Lavender hadn't told her mom about the diary yet, but maybe it was time to ask Sara some questions. "Yes, a cookie sounds good." Lavender lifted the plastic wrap off the plate and grabbed them each a cookie while "Have Yourself a Merry Little Christmas" played on the new speaker. It was getting dark even though it was only four o'clock and the Christmas lights glowed red and green and gold and blue on the snow.

Her grandma held out her hand across the table. Lavender placed her hand on Louise's and they sat like that for a while. She didn't know if it was the lights outside, or the music, or because it was Christmas, but for the first time, maybe ever in her life, Lavender felt close to her grandma. Like they knew each other. Like their hands were touching but so were their souls.

TWENTY

LAVENDER WOKE UP on Christmas Eve dreading the day and night in front of her. Every year, the Finch tribe gathered at her Aunt Beck's house for a night of endless eating, games, and a white elephant gift exchange. It was always a fun time, but that year, she was not looking forward to the questions about college and if she was excited to graduate and what her major was going to be and what she would do with the rest of her life. She was also not looking forward to seeing her cousin Jackie, which was a strange thing to be feeling. They were like sisters. But she had been avoiding Jackie and ignoring her invitations to hang out or go to parties for months. The texts had slowed down lately. She guessed that Jackie had given up at that point, but it was going to be awkward to see her in person. They'd never been awkward before. They'd always been able to talk about anything. Jackie was the one who explained the things no one said out loud, like how you manage to breathe and not drool while having your lips locked with someone else, and not only how to insert a tampon for the first time, step by step, but also what it felt like inside of you. Everything Lavender knew about her body, and boys, and beer, she learned from Jackie. *Why didn't she tell me about boys like Travis?*

She wished she could just stay in bed, but it was generally not in her nature to sleep all day. She checked the weather app on her phone to see if it was too cold to go for a run. Thirty degrees was her threshold. The temp was a crisp twenty-five. *Thank god. I can stay in bed a little longer.*

She hugged Mister Bean to her chest and rolled over. She'd still been having that surfing dream on and off, but lately she was enjoying it. Her vivid and life-like dreams had always been almost like watching a movie in her brain. Sometimes she could even get up in the middle of the night to go to the bathroom, come back to bed and re-enter her dream. Jana thought she was crazy, but it happened. Lately, when she went to bed at night, she willed herself to fall asleep and start dreaming as fast as possible so she could turn off the life-like memories of Travis and the party that haunted her while she was awake. When she was dream-surfing, she was the old Lavender. Lavender before. The Lavender that hadn't got drunk at the party and lost her virginity to a super creep named Travis. She missed that girl. The wall of water in her dream that she could feel coming up behind her didn't scare her as much as it used to. Maybe she could learn to surf and avoid the crashing wave altogether.

"Lav, you up?" Her mom knocked on her bedroom door and jolted her out of her sleepy spell. "It's after ten."

"I'm up." Lavender sounded grouchier than she meant to.

"Can I come in?"

"Yes." Again, she sounded more annoyed than her mom probably deserved.

"You got something in the mail." That news made Lavender sit up. Her mom opened the door with a box in her hands. "I think it's from your friend in Cuba."

"Oh nice. Thank you for bringing it up." Lavender gave her mom a smile to make up for her attitude.

"Are you going to open it?" her mom asked. Lavender knew her mother was hoping to be a part of the opening process and wanted to see what Martin had sent her.

"I will. Later."

"Ok. Merry Christmas Eve. Are you excited?"

"For?"

"Christmas silly."

"I guess. I mean, I'm not a little kid so it's not as exciting as it used to be, but sure."

"What's up with you lately? You haven't seemed like yourself. Is everything okay? At school?" Her mom sat on the side of the bed.

"I'm fine. Why?" The grouchy voice was back.

"I don't know, you just seem closed off and withdrawn. I haven't seen Jana around in months. You haven't texted Jackie back or hung out with her."

"How do you know that?" She already knew the answer. Her dad's family didn't practice the concept of privacy and traded headlines about their lives, like it was all fair game. Her and Jackie had coined the phenomenon the FFTNN when they were ten and eleven. The Finch Fast Traveling News Network.

"I talked to her mom. Aunt Beck said Jackie thinks you're mad at her but doesn't know why."

"That's ridiculous. I'm not mad at her. I've just been busy," Lavender said.

"Ok, if you say so. But it seems like you've cut off your friends and social life. The only places you go these days are to the nursing home and the Gordon's house to babysit." Lavender rolled to the opposite side of the bed and stood up, hoping that would change the subject. She pulled on her pajama pants that she'd left on the floor last night and put her hair up in a pony, letting her mother's words hang unanswered. Lavender wasn't going to engage. "What about this boy? Martin? What's his story?"

"He's nice. We're friends. Just a school project." Her voice was circling back to that annoyed tone. The one she used to let her mother know she didn't want to talk about whatever they were talking about.

"If he's sending you Christmas presents, seems like more than a school project, but if you say so…"

Lavender saw her grandmother's diary on her desk and changed the subject. "Hey. Did you know Grandma went to California after she graduated from high school?"

"I think I heard that once. A volunteer program…did she tell you that?"

"It was VISTA, the domestic version of the Peace Corps in the seventies. Now they call it AmeriCorps."

"Hmmmph." Her mom usually got quiet and stopped engaging when the subject of her mother came up. Now that Louise was in a safe place where she couldn't drink anymore and was eating three meals a day, Lavender's mom didn't talk about her much.

"It's pretty cool…there was a lot going on in 1973…the migrant farm workers were protesting and boycotting and people were fighting for better conditions…it was a major story back then. At least in California. And Grandma was there. I didn't know she ever did anything like that."

Her mom let out a big sigh. "She wasn't always like the person you knew growing up. She used to be different. She was smart and interested in everything. She loved to meet people and learn their stories. She loved to read. She took me and Michael to the library every week. She tutored adults and children while we hung out and read books." A heaviness seemed to rest on her mom.

"Why did she change?" Lavender asked.

"All I know is that my big brother died, my father left, and my mother was never the same again. I was so young. She didn't talk about it. It was hard."

In that moment, Lavender felt her mother's pain in a way that she never had before. It must have been hard to grow up with a mother who was distracted with drinking and not present in any meaningful way. Her mom had lost her brother and father. *That must have been devastating.* Maybe that's why she was a hovering, helicopter mom with a what-if obsession. To make sure Lavender had a different childhood than she did. It made sense and she understood her mother more than she ever had. "I'm sorry Mom. That must have sucked for you." Lavender hugged her mother.

"It's all ancient history. When I had you, my life was never the same." Sara let out another sigh and stood up. "Now, it's Christmas, let's talk about something happy."

They brainstormed about whether they should bring lasagna or macaroni and cheese, or maybe both, to Aunt Beck's Christmas potluck and made a plan to get to the grocery store before the crowds got too crazy. "I'll be downstairs and ready to go in 15," Lavender said.

Her mom paused before she left the room. "Sounds good. I love you."

Lavender thought about saying *I love you* back to her mom, but her habit of not responding was hard to break. She set the box from Martin on her desk and ran her hand over the letters on the top. He had placed stickers of snowflakes and Wise Men and Santa on all the sides of the box. She would wait until later that night to open whatever Martin had sent her. She wanted to be in the right mindset and take her time.

TWENTY-ONE

THE PARTY AT AUNT BECK'S went as expected. She could have written the script herself. The questions came, almost on cue, along with the well-intentioned comments, the excitement, the infatuation with Lavender and what a lovely young woman she'd grown into and how proud they all were of her. *Loving that Lavender Finch was easy…if they only knew how messed up I really am…*

The hardest part of the night was Jackie, also as expected. Their hug was stiff and forced before they retreated to Jackie's room out of habit. The conversation was stilted and shallow and Lavender knew it was her fault. Jackie was guarded and wasn't sharing the intimate details of her life anymore. It made sense. Since Lavender was distant and focused on keeping her secrets and lies to herself, Jackie returned that with her own distance and space. They were both faking it and Lavender was sure they both felt it.

But she ate all the delicious food, played the games, and at the end of the night, couldn't wait to get home and return to her room. Her sanctuary. She kept the overhead light off, turned on the bedside lamp, and sat on the floor with her big red pillows. She reached for her phone and turned on some Christmas jazz. She closed her eyes for a few minutes and thought about Martin. He was probably with his sisters and parents and other families stationed at the base in Cuba, playing games and eating food, just like she did, but he was most likely enjoying it, because he didn't have to pretend like she did. Lavender wished that she could be with him and his family for Christmas and leave Siena, school, BSU, and everyone that went along with it, behind. *Someday.*

It was time. She ripped the brown tape from the top and sides and carefully opened the box. There was a card. The cover of the card was a painting of a beautiful, blue, night sky, with a wistful pattern of bright yellow stars and the path they seemed to form. Inside, the card was filled with Martin's words.

Lavender,

Merry Christmas! I hope this package makes it to you in time. It was hard trying to figure out what to get you but also fun. Where are you at in The Great Gatsby? I need to know so I don't spoil the plot for you…I finished early. Sorry. I haven't had much to do over Christmas break so I've been reading a lot. Did I tell you that I don't have a lot of friends here? Hopefully this doesn't make me sound like a weirdo, but I'm just not into football or video games or partying. Unfortunately, that means I'm not the most popular guy at school. It's not that I'm an introvert or anything, I just feel like I don't have much in common with the other kids my age. Like I was born at the wrong time or something…it's hard to explain, ha ha…I start my photography class after New Year's. I'm pretty pumped about that. Also, I've been doing some reading about AmeriCorps. I looked up some stories from 1973 when your grandma was in Ojai. So interesting. I saw some amazing photography from that time by news journalists. AmeriCorps is still actively accepting volunteers for assignments. I'm thinking about going that route after graduation instead of the Peace Corps. I know my parents would be happy if I stayed in the US instead of going to a

*remote village in a faraway country. The card I sent you is
one of my favorite paintings. It's Vincent Van Gogh's Starry
Night. (Sorry if you already knew that and I sound like a
pompous ass, but wasn't sure if you were into art...) I have
that poster hanging in my room. I love star gazing and with
the warm weather here, I can get out most nights and just
lie on my back and stare. I've been thinking lately how cool
it is that you could be looking at the exact same stars as
me...1500 miles away...that thought makes me smile.*

*Don't forget. I'm calling you tomorrow night (Christmas
Day) at 10 p.m. I think we should stick to audio only and not
be on camera. It's not that I don't want to see you (honestly,
I'm dying to) but in keeping with our old-school theme...ya
know?*
Merry Christmas, again.
Martin

Lavender lay back and closed her eyes and recited his words in
her mind. *He's dying to see me? He thinks about me when he's looking
at the stars? He looked up stuff about my grandma?* The drama of
Lavender's Christmas Eve with her family was a distant memory
now. She only thought about Martin and it felt good in her body.
Her stomach was at ease. No racing thoughts in her mind. She felt
warm and safe with him. She remembered the presents and sat
up to look inside the box. There were four presents individually
wrapped in the most beautiful silver and gold paper with ribbon
and bows. Gift wrapping was not one of her skill sets. She had
only sent him three presents and they were not that well-wrapped.
Since he wasn't going to get a white Christmas in Cuba, one of
his gifts was a snow globe with a quaint little village inside. She

sent him a vintage photography book that she had found at her favorite bookstore, and her third present was a glass kaleidoscope just because it was beautiful and unique.

She opened the first from him. It was a red, knitted scarf with a small note inside. *To keep you warm on your runs.* She wrapped the scarf around her neck and opened the second. It was a globe. Instead of a snow globe, it was a beach scene with a surfer girl riding a wave and sand-colored glitter when you shook it. *Oh my god. I got him a snow globe, how weird is that! We got each other the same thing.* Lavender smiled and hugged the globe to her heart. The note with that one said, *This could be you some day! Your dream come true.*

The third present was a music box. A miniature of the *It's a Small World* ride at Disney World. The song played when she picked it up. *This one's for you, Ms. Clarke,* the note said.

She could not believe the gifts he'd come up with. He was so good at that stuff. She thought about not opening the last gift because she didn't want to ruin his good streak. How could he possibly top the first three? *Would he think my gifts were lame?* Lavender had put a lot of thought into his presents too, but she wasn't sure she had aced it like he did.

Martin's fourth present was shaped like a book. Lavender peeled off the pretty paper. It was a leather-bound diary, red with gold embossed letters and a strap that wrapped around it. *Just like my grandma's.* A small piece of paper fell out when she opened it with only four words on it. *The story of you.*

Lavender fell back clutching the red book to her chest, with the globe and the music box at her side. The scarf, in her favorite color, still around her neck. It was too much. She couldn't hold back what she was feeling. Once she let one tear fall, the others followed and soon she was sobbing. *How is this possible? We've never even met.* She wasn't sad. That wasn't it. She felt seen. Like for the first time in her life, someone genuinely knew her. Martin touched her in places that no one ever had before. He touched her soul.

TWENTY-TWO

AFTER ALL THE ACTIVITY of the night before, Christmas Day was always quiet and cozy at Lavender's house. They all slept in and after opening presents, her mom made pancakes or french toast with bacon and homefries and her dad cleaned the garage or worked on some project in the basement. There was usually a nap later in the afternoon. Since Lavender was five or six, her and her dad had a tradition of going to a movie, just the two of them, every Christmas Day night.

Lavender delayed getting up and read her *Gatsby* book in bed, trying to catch up with Martin. Every character in the story had secrets and things they were hiding—love affairs and shameful pasts and life-altering decisions that didn't necessarily lead to happiness or contentment. The plot was a downer and she felt sad every time she closed a chapter. She couldn't wait to be done with that book. *Maybe it hits too close to home.*

"Lavender! Breakfast is ready." Her mom yelled from the bottom of the stairs.

"Coming."

Relieved for a break in the story, she closed the book and headed downstairs.

"I'm starving," her dad said, with a big grin on his face. As a construction worker in the Northeast, wintertime in general and the holidays were his time to relax and enjoy some time at home. He was always in a good mood during that time of year.

"Me too. This looks great Mom."

"A lot of carbs, but hey, it's Christmas. I'll have to do some extra treadmill tomorrow," her mom said. Sara was always conscious of what she was eating and how much and what she would have to do to *work it off*. A true Gen-X woman.

"Hey Lav, what movie do you want to see later?"

She pulled out her phone and looked up the theater. "How about the new Tom Cruise movie? It starts at 5:45." A 5:45 movie should get her home in plenty of time before the call with Martin.

"Sounds good. I'll meet you in the living room at 5 ready to go."

They both liked to get there early enough to buy popcorn, Twizzlers and get a good seat. They also liked to watch all the previews.

"Ok. I'll buy the tickets now to save us a step," Lavender said.

"Great. I have a bottle of wine to open and my favorite Christmas movies ready to watch too …," her mom said. She loved the tradition as much as they did.

"So Rosebud, what's up? How you been doing?" She knew her dad was genuinely interested. He didn't usually pry or try to ask leading questions. He really wanted to know.

"Oh, you know, living the dream, lol…" She wanted to keep it lighthearted and off the subject of her.

"School good?"

"Yeah…you know…just trying to get through my big projects for graduation. *The Great Gatsby*, forty hours of community service and the *It's a Small World* pen pal."

"Wow, that sounds like a lot. You've been spending some time with Grandma right? How's that been?"

"It's been good. Interesting, actually. I'm learning some things that I never knew, but I still have so many questions. How much do you know about her?"

"Well…by the time I met your mom, Grandma was drinking pretty heavy then. In the bars every single day, all day…she was nice enough to me but…," his voice trailed off.

"Mom won't really talk about her," Lavender said.

"You know Rosebud, there's a lot of history there. She put your mom through a lot."

Her dad went on to tell her stories that she'd heard pieces of growing up. A bartender called him once to tell him that Louise was passed out in a ditch. Her dad picked her up and took her home. And the time when Lavender was four and her father's aunt was dying, so her parents begged Louise to stay sober while she babysat Lavender. She promised she would. But when her parents went to pick her up, no one was home. They found Louise and Lavender sitting at a bar with a beer and a coke in front of them. Then there were all the times Ross had to pick her up because she was too drunk to drive, and the time she was arrested and needed bail money. There were a lot of stories.

"Why do you think she drank so much? Doesn't sound like it was a very fun life for her either."

"I don't know…I think people who drink like that are probably hiding from some pain or secret or something they're afraid of… the booze is just a symptom of something bigger…but what do I know? I'm glad those days are over for all of us."

Lavender was relieved when they arrived at the cinema. She had brought the mood down with the questions about Grandma, so she made an effort to change the channel for both of them and bought her dad his popcorn, soda, and candy.

The movie was loud, fast-moving and more epic-chase-scene focused than on story or dialogue, but it was entertaining. Lavender's thoughts were preoccupied with Martin and their upcoming phone call. *Would it be awkward? What if I don't have anything to say? Or worse yet, I sound like an idiot? What if he is a weirdo?* Even with all her doubts, Lavender had a good feeling about Martin and was excited to hear his voice and talk to him.

She also thought about what her dad said. *Was I headed down the same path as my grandma? Is that why I like drinking beer so much? What if I become an alcoholic?* Her mind was spinning with worry about her own habits and secrets. She just couldn't imagine getting that far gone though, where she'd drink all day at the expense of everything and everyone else in her life. Then again, probably nobody plans to get to that point.

Lavender and her dad were both quiet on the way home. It was a long movie, so it was almost nine o'clock by the time she got back to her room and plugged her phone in. She wanted to make sure she was fully charged before ten. She sat at her desk and made a list of things she wanted to talk to Martin about. Just in case she got tongue-tied or her mind went blank. Her phone was always in silent mode, so she made sure the ringer was on and the volume turned up. At 9:55 she connected her earbuds and tested them to make sure they worked. She kept her eye on the phone even though the ringer was on. She couldn't remember what her ringtone was set to. She hadn't heard it in so long. Exactly at 10:00 o'clock the call came in.

"Hello?" She barely let it ring twice before she answered.

"Lavender. It's Martin. Hi."

"Hi." She laughed a little.

"This is wild, isn't it? Have you ever talked on the phone with someone you hadn't met in person yet?" His voice was amazing. Not high-pitched. Not too deep. Soothing. The kind of voice that could read anything and make it sound good.

"I don't think I ever have," she said.

"How was your Christmas? Did you get my presents?"

"Christmas was good. Your presents were amazing. I've been wearing the red scarf nonstop, everyone loves it. And the diary was perfect. All of them were so thoughtful. Thank you."

"Oh good. I'm glad. I sweated over those."

"Really?" She laughed out loud. "You made it seem easy."

"Yours were good too. Thank you for making sure I had snow on Christmas and that photography book was dope."

They spent the next hour on the phone, both excitedly jumping from one subject to the next. They talked about *Gatsby* and school and taking pictures and their families. There was no dead air. It was like they'd been having this conversation forever. The words just flowed.

"Do you think we can do this again? Talk on the phone?" Martin asked.

"Definitely."

"Sunday nights at 10?"

"Great idea. That works." *Wow, zero to sixty. We're going from never being on a phone call with a stranger to talking every week. That was fast. But I'm in.*

"Hey Lavender."

"What?"

"I love your voice. So glad I got to hear it. You sound like someone I've always known."

"Awww. I don't think anyone has ever said that to me before. I love your voice too."

They eventually hung up after a few attempts at goodbye. Lavender got ready for bed. The phone call had been the perfect ending to her Christmas day. She lay in bed but instead of rushing to sleep and willing herself to dream, she only thought of Martin and the conversation they just had. For the first time in months, she fell into sleep without thoughts of the party and Travis and her college application that was never submitted. She finally knew what she wanted to do after high school. She wanted to meet Martin in person. She wanted to go wherever he was.

TWENTY-THREE

LAVENDER AND JACKIE had spent New Year's Eve together every single year, their whole lives. Somebody in the FFTNN hosted a party. The adults drank more wine than usual and played music and card games and laughed like they were teenagers, while she and Jackie hung out in one of the bedrooms and listened to their own music, had pizza and ice cream and any other snack they could dream up. They'd watch movies until it was time for the ball to drop and pass out around 1 or 2 a.m. It was a blast and held her favorite memories with her cousin.

But that year, she just couldn't face any of it. The questions, the comments, the admiration, the easy love, and most of all, the awkwardness between her and Jackie. So, she agreed to babysit for the Gordon kids on New Year's Eve. It wasn't so bad. The kids got to stay up an hour later than usual but they were still too young to stay up until midnight so she would get her alone time. There was plenty of beer in the fridge and a new show she wanted to start bingeing on Netflix.

Lavender was on her second beer, she had turned on some music, feet curled up on the couch in the fancy living room, almost at the end of *The Great Gatsby*. She was determined to finish the book that night. Over the last few months, she'd grown used to spending time by herself. Even though she never had a big friend circle, Jackie and Jana had been part of her life as long as she could remember. She missed Jana's text banter throughout the week about who had hooked up with who and the latest argument with her brother. She even missed how Jana kept her up on all the celebrity gossip and latest fashion trends.

She smiled when she remembered how horrified Jana was when she found out Lavender didn't wear the appropriate underwear. They were getting ready to start their junior year and Jana was inspecting her new school clothes. Jana did not approve of most of them. Too boring and basic in her opinion. But when she saw the bag from Victoria's Secret she squealed. Jana pulled out a dark pink bra and gray panties. She looked at Lavender with her eyebrows scrunched and her mouth open, shaking her head. "Lav, why? This is what my mom buys." Jana moved over to the top drawer of her dresser and started grabbing the bras and panties and held up a fistful. "These are the mom-jeans of underwear," Jana said.

"What are you talking about? They're cute. And comfortable."

"Lavender Rose Finch. Every girl our age is wearing a thong. They're pretty and sexy and the boys love them. And they look better under your clothes. No panty lines."

"I tried. I hate the feeling of a continuous wedgie! Besides, I read somewhere that they're not healthy for you."

Jana gave up arguing with her and closed the top drawer while shaking her head and sighing. Lavender would be the only non-thong-wearing senior at Siena High. She was okay with that.

Her relationship with Jackie was different, more like sisters. They could finish each other's sentences and usually knew what the other was thinking. Neither one of them could remember a time they didn't know each other. The family vacations, the birthday parties, the holidays, the sleepovers. They knew everything about each other. At least they used to. *Maybe I should just tell her what happened with Travis. Maybe she could help me figure out what to do.*

She tried to imagine how the conversation might go with Jackie. *Remember that night at the party? Remember Travis? He wasn't such a nice college guy after all. And he wasn't interested in me. He just wanted to get in my pants, literally. He had sex with me on that smelly futon in the basement. It was awful and I didn't want him to do any of it, but I couldn't stop him. I hate myself for what happened, and I can't stop thinking about it.*

At that point, Jackie could look at her and be disgusted, or sympathetic, or judgmental or worst of all, dismissive of what a big deal that was to Lavender and how much it had changed her life. She couldn't take that chance. She was too ashamed. She also worried it might make Jackie feel bad. Like she hadn't protected her younger cousin. When she was five and fell off the edge of the pool at the beach house, it was Jackie who grabbed her hair and pulled her to the surface. When a random girl at the beach took her boogie board, Jackie found her and demanded it back. When she was twelve and a boy at the movies snapped her bra, Jackie whipped around and kneed him in his crotch. He and his friends were so shocked that they left the theater without a word. Lavender didn't blame her cousin for what happened at the party and didn't want Jackie to blame herself. It was easier for Lavender to keep it to herself and be alone. She could pretend none of it had ever happened and ignore the gnawing memories, most of the time.

She needed to get back to her book but went to the kitchen for a third beer first. She had time. The Gordons would be out later than usual on New Year's Eve. With her third beer in hand, she pushed Jana and Jackie out of her mind and opened her book. It took her twenty minutes to finally finish the story. She didn't care for *The Great Gatsby* and couldn't wrap her head around why it was considered such a classic and required reading at that. She knew there were at least two movies that had been made. An older one with an actor she couldn't remember, and a newer version with Leo DiCaprio as Gatsby. The writing was solid, and she supposed the literary merits were there, but the characters were sad people who should have made different choices, and the ending was tragic. After all the secrets and lies, the betrayal and violence, after all the parties and bad behavior, none of them ended up better off or with the one they supposedly loved. Definitely not a love story.

She picked up her phone to check the time. She had a text message from Mrs. Gordon.

On our way home early. Migraine
Ugh.

Holy fucking shit. What time did she send that? Ten minutes ago. Fuck. They'd be here any minute.

Lavender kicked into high gear. She ran to the kitchen with her three bottles. She rinsed them out, throwing water everywhere, and grabbed paper towels so fast and rough she knocked the towel dispenser on the floor. She left it there while she raced to get the bottles in her backpack. She just barely got them in, and the bag zipped up when the front door opened. Mrs. Gordon looked surprised to see her in the foyer. Lavender's heart was thumping so hard in her chest she talked louder than normal so Mrs. Gordon couldn't hear it.

"Hi Mrs. Gordon, how are you feeling?"

"Oh, terrible. I have the worst headache. Such a bummer on New Year's Eve especially. How were they?"

"They were perfect, as usual. No problems." Mrs. Gordon walked to the kitchen. Lavender followed her. They both saw the paper towels on the floor and the water everywhere at the same time. *Oh shit.*

"What happened here?" Mrs. Gordon bent down to pick them up and moved to the freezer to get an ice pack. "Did Stevie or Sadie make this mess?"

"No…it was me. I think it fell when I was cleaning up after dinner and one of the kids needed my help with the TV. I forgot to come back and clean it up. Sorry about that."

"No worries. Thanks for tonight. I need to go to bed. I'll call you soon." Mrs. Gordon handed her cash and went upstairs.

Lavender exhaled for the first time since she saw the text. That was a close call. Too close. *What am I doing? I have to stop this habit.*

She left the Gordon's house and got in her car to drive home. She paused for a moment, realizing that she hadn't allowed for enough time to pass. Her body couldn't have processed all that beer yet. *I'll be ok.* She hadn't finished the third one though, and her head wasn't buzzing. *I'll go super slow.* She popped some gum in her mouth. *It's only a mile or two. It's fine.*

Lavender drove twenty-five miles per hour, stopped at all yellow lights, used her blinker and made sure not to roll through any stop signs. She also held her breath, the entire way it seemed, until she pulled in her driveway, safe and sound. She exhaled and slumped down in her seat. She couldn't believe she did that. *What an idiot.* She sat still for what seemed like an hour. *I could have killed someone.* She couldn't move. *So stupid. I guess I can add drunk driver to the list of things people don't know about me.*

Lavender finally got out of the car and went inside the dark house. Her parents were at the New Year's Eve party at Aunt Beck's. *Thank god.* At least she didn't have to face them right now. She could get to her room and be asleep, or at least pretend to be, by the time they came home. No one would ever know. Except for Lavender, that is.

TWENTY-FOUR

LAVENDER HADN'T PLANNED on going to visit her grandma on New Year's Day, it wasn't her typical Saturday time slot, but after what had happened the night before and a restless sleep, all she wanted was to be with someone...someone who wouldn't ask questions. If she stayed in her room all day by herself, she would replay last night over and over in her head. *Why did I have that third beer? Why did I have any beer at all? What kind of idiot gets behind the wheel of a car? I should have come clean to Mrs. Gordon and faced the consequences. Why did I?...I should have...What's wrong with me?* Those thoughts would spiral into thoughts about the party and her college disaster. She couldn't text Jackie or Jana and she didn't want to face her mother or her father. With the holiday, both would be home with not much to do but focus on Lavender. She had to get out of the house.

Lavender walked through the double doors at Betsy Ross and immediately felt at home. Evelyn was on the phone as usual but winked and waved. She pointed at the phone and twirled her finger in circles. Lavender nodded, signed in and headed to the TV room. Her grandma was in her chair. *Thank god.*

"Hey, I know you," her grandma said with a shy grin.

Lavender burst into tears.

"What's wrong? Are you hurt?"

"No...nothing's wrong...I just...need...a hug..."

"I can do that." Grandma stood up from the blue chair. Sharon and the others were silently watching the drama unfold. With her short frame, grandma moved to Lavender and wrapped her arms around her and squeezed. "Come 'ere sweetie. It's okay."

When Lavender felt her grandmother's arms around her, she cried even harder. She couldn't remember a time they had hugged like that. It felt safe. It felt good. When she came up for air, her grandma said, "Sit down honey. Let's watch some TV. Mary's coming on."

Her grandma sat on the couch and patted the spot next to her. Lavender sat down but then pushed her legs and feet out the length of the couch and laid her head in Louise's lap.

"Psst. Sharon. Go get that afghan off my bed. The girl needs to rest."

Sharon obeyed the order without a word, hurried to Louise's room and brought back the crocheted brown, orange and yellow blanket that was usually on grandma's bed. Louise flung the afghan across Lavender's body and with her hand, moved the hair in Lavender's face behind her ear. Her grandma's hand rested on Lavender's back.

Sharon sat back down in her grandma's usual spot. The *Mary Tyler Moore* show theme song came on and they all sat in the TV room without saying a word. They sat through one episode and then another and then another. Entranced by the voices, the forced laughter, the old-fashioned conversation of the show, Lavender lost track of time. She sat up with a start and wasn't sure if she fell asleep or was just so relaxed she completely zoned out. The TV room was empty except for Lavender and her grandmother.

"Oh wow. What time is it?" Her grandma shrugged. Lavender looked at her phone. 2:34 p.m. She'd been there more than four hours. "I'm sorry grandma. Did you miss lunch?"

"Bah, who cares? Food is terrible anyway. Do you feel better?"

"I do. Thanks for letting me sit with you all this time." Her grandma was quiet. Louise looked tired. "I guess I should get going. Make sure you have an early dinner, okay?" Her grandma nodded, not taking her eyes off the TV. Lavender folded the afghan and left it on the couch. She bent down and gave her grandma a hug. "Happy New Year Grandma. I'll see you Saturday."

Lavender walked back down the hallway and signed out at the desk. Evelyn was gone and a woman she had never seen before was on duty. That was the longest Lavender had every stayed at Betsy Ross. It was exactly what she needed.

TWENTY-FIVE

LAVENDER PARKED in the back row of the school parking lot. It was the first day back after the holiday break and everyone was greeting each other like they'd been reunited after months apart, when in fact it had only been ten days. Jana was usually dropped off by her brother and would wait on the sidewalk until she saw Lavender's white car approaching the school. Then she'd run, her face grinning and bursting with news that could be anything from the life-changing bagel she had for breakfast, to a comment on her Insta account, or perhaps the latest fight between her and her brother. Jana was nowhere in sight. There's only so much ghosting a person can take before they stop texting. Before they stop trying. Lavender felt bad about hurting Jana's feelings. Jana didn't deserve it. Jana believed they were going to be at BSU together in the fall and wanted to plan how they were going to decorate their dorm rooms, compare their class schedule, run through the list of potential sororities they'd rush and of course, review their personal brand and style they'd be adopting as college freshmen. But how do you stay close to your best friend when there was so much you haven't shared with her? There was her grandmother's diary. And Martin. And Travis. The party. Things just kept adding up. With every conversation, the lie became bigger and bigger and Lavender didn't know how to stop it. She didn't see a way out or through. So she said nothing.

Lavender walked into the school by herself scanning the foyer, again, Jana was nowhere in sight. She headed straight to Ms. Clarke's class. She'd be early but at least she wouldn't be hanging out in the hall by herself looking like she had no friends. She thought about Martin and how his first day back to school was going. Was he as lonely as she was? Their Sunday night phone calls had been going well so far. In fact, they had gone from awkward to comfortable. She'd gone from nervous and intimidated to excited and sure of herself. Their talks were easy but deep at the same time. Martin had become her only friend and the only one she really talked to, besides her grandma. Martin didn't ask too many questions about BSU in the fall. Not yet anyway. She hadn't really lied to him so far. He didn't know that she'd been sure of her college choice since she was ten, and she hadn't told him that she filled out the application and submitted it for early acceptance, when she absolutely did no such thing. He also didn't see her day-to-day life, so he didn't know that she had shut out her best friend and her cousin and had become a loner. She had been honest with Martin so far, but she hadn't told him everything. With Martin, she could pretend that she never went to that stupid party last September, she could pretend she never met Travis. She could pretend none of it ever happened.

Hillary Charles was already in Ms. Clarke's classroom and eyed Lavender as she came in by herself and sat down. "Where's Jana?" Hillary said. "You two used to be joined at the hip." Lavender didn't respond. The bell rang and Jana came through the door. Lavender watched her ex-best friend closely waiting for eye contact so she could wave or something. Their eyes met briefly. Lavender smiled and waved and mouthed, *Hi*. Jana met her gaze but didn't wave or smile, just nodded.

Ms. Clarke looked excited to be back to work after the break. She stood at the front with her face grinning and bursting with news. "I know you're all excited to see each other again, but we have a lot to do today." A collective groan rippled throughout the class followed by sighs. But their teacher powered on. "We are officially in the second half of the school year and the countdown to graduation has begun. We need to make sure everyone is on track with their community service, the *It's a Small World* assignments and *The Great Gatsby*."

Hillary raised her hand. "Ms. Clarke, may I address the class please?" Ms. Clarke stretched out her hands and motioned for Hillary to take the floor. "Hi everyone. Speaking of countdown, over the break, I created a countdown timer with all of the important dates for us. Senior pictures, yearbook, Superlatives, Senior Ball, Class Night and of course, graduation…" Lavender sunk in her seat and sighed on the inside. *What the fuck? The sign in the front yard wasn't enough, now I have to face a countdown timer. Like it's a ticking bomb about to explode and blow up my life?*

Hillary asked everyone to take out their phones and save the countdown timer on their home screen. As the class was buzzing with excitement, Lavender took out her phone as instructed, so no one would suspect that she wasn't just as excited as her classmates about all of it. But instead of going to Hillary's website and marking the countdown timer, she tuned out and wrote an email to Martin.

Dear Martin,

I'm in Global/Lit and had some free time so I thought I'd get a jump start on our next topic for discussion, which is Artificial Intelligence, aka AI.

I. AM. TOTALLY. FREAKED. OUT! I read the article and

listened to the podcast that Ms. Clarke sent us. Holy shit. #1) AI is going to outsmart us and probably take over the world, and #2) AI will probably be the thing that causes human extinction. Why is no one else worried about this???? I mean I know it can also do our calculus homework and write our papers, but is that worth the risk? Did you hear the story of how that stadium in Australia used an AI engine called Sebastian to scan their internal systems during every concert to look for cyber threats but then one night Sebastian literally took over and hacked into the sound system and started speaking in Persian? Sebastian taught himself to speak Persian! This seems to be a case of where technology could be in danger of destroying us rather than helping us. Is it just me? I also get that it could be life-changing for senior citizens and people with disabilities. Why can't we harness it for good and not for evil? It seems like the same old story of ego and greed driving those in positions of power to be blind to the danger. I heard that the CEO whose company invented the AI technology always carries a backpack that has what he needs to shut down the AI monster at a moment's notice. If that rumor is true, we should all be afraid. We could all get caught up in *The Matrix*. I'm not sure that most people really understand what is happening. What say you????
Lavender

Lavender hit send on the email just as Ms. Clarke was trying to wrangle the class back from Hillary. Before she had a chance to put her phone back in her bag, she noticed a new text. It was from Jana.

Not sure what i did to make you hate
me, but i will leave you alone. C ya
around.

She sunk in her seat and put her phone away. What could she respond with?

I don't hate you; I hate myself.

I'm an idiot and I don't know how to tell you that.

I'm a liar and a slut and I drink too much beer.

I'm scared and lost and don't know what to do.

It's not you. It's me.

As Ms. Clarke continued her round robin to check the status on their senior projects, Lavender counted down the weeks in her head. Twenty-three. Twenty-three weeks until graduation. Twenty-three weeks sounded like a long time, but it would go by fast. 160 days. Tick. Tick. Tick. She needed a plan. A plan to get out of all the lies before they came crashing down on her and she couldn't save herself. Just like that damn wave always chasing her in her dreams.

TWENTY-SIX

SUNDAY NIGHTS HAD BECOME the best part of her week. No matter what had happened at school Monday through Friday, or how lonely Lavender felt without her two best friends in her life, her conversations with Martin filled the void. He had become her closest friend, even though he was so far away. The strangeness of it all was not lost on her. Sometimes she looked around her life and didn't recognize what it had become. Her only friends were a boy in Cuba she'd never met and a grandma who wasn't 100% sure of who Lavender was. And yet, they were the two people who knew her the best. The only two people that she let behind the wall she had carefully constructed around her heart and life. She felt something missing with Jackie and Jana gone, but Martin and Grandma Louise made up for it. Lavender hadn't seen that coming. Her parents were steady as usual, but they probably assumed she was distracted with senior-itis and getting all her requirements done for graduation. Sara Finch would talk to anyone who would listen about the empty nest she was dreading and the void that was coming in her life. But the fact was, Lavender had nowhere to go after graduation, which was in 126 days to be exact, but who's counting? There was a knock at her bedroom door.

"Yeah?"

"Just me Rosebud."

Her dad slowly opened the door, as if he was afraid to bother her or find her changing her clothes. He really was the sweetest.

How am I ever going to break his heart and tell him the truth? "Hi Dad. Getting ready to jump on a call. It's for school."

"Okay. Just wanted to say Goodnight. Love you. Sleep tight."

"You too." Her dad closed the door as gently as he had opened it.

It was almost ten, there wasn't much time before her phone would ring. Lavender had sent Martin a Valentine's Day Card with a box of M&Ms. They had discovered that they both had the same favorite candy and fantasized about one day going to the M&M store in Times Square together. She thought he might not be able to get all the new variations of the candy in Cuba, so at Walgreens, she filled her basket with a bag of every flavor they had available—mint, peanut butter, pretzel, milk, dark and white chocolate, peanut, caramel and even a root beer float flavor. They talked of how the little round pieces were so perfect because you could hold the candy in your mouth long enough so that the shell dissolved and then there'd be soft, chocolate goodness on your tongue. So silly and juvenile but also oddly weird that they both had the same favorite candy. *Was it a sign?*

Lavender had also included her senior photo and a few other pics—one of her as a five-year-old and a super awkward eleven-year-old. They were sticking with the old-school theme they had started with the letter writing and phone calls and decided to exchange actual printed pictures before they saw each other virtually. If she timed it right, he would receive her envelope with the pics and the M&Ms on Valentine's Day. What if he liked girls with flat hair and extra eyelashes who wore thongs on the regular? She didn't want him to be disappointed, but it also gave her a little flutter in her belly to take that chance. She couldn't wait to receive his picture. Strangely, she didn't have an image in her head of what he might look like. She didn't really care. She liked him.

Her phone rang. She let it go through two cycles before she answered. "Hey you."

"Hay is for horses...."

"Oh, so now you're the king of dad jokes too?" They both laughed.

"How was your week?" Martin asked.

"It was fine. Nothing too exciting. But it's better now."

"Same."

"I finished *Gatsby*, did I tell you that? Finally...oh my god..."

"Great. Let me know if you need help on your paper. Hey...I wanted to ask you if have plans Wednesday night?"

"Wednesday? I mean, I never have plans, so no..."

"Well then, Lavender Rose Finch, would you like to go on a Valentine's date with me?"

"A date? How would that work?" Lavender's stomach backflipped into her throat.

"Well, I thought we could go to the movies. We're in the same time zone, and we have a theater here on base. Maybe we could watch a movie at the same time but separate. Then talk about it after. I'm a strict no phone person inside the movie. Hate that."

"Sure! I'm up for it."

They spent the next fifteen minutes looking up movie times and discussing logistics of their meetup. They agreed that they would use their cell phones and texting that night so they could stay connected until the movie started. They weighed the pros and cons of the latest Star Wars episode, the newest Marvel hero story or *The Matrix*, which was just re-released for the 25th Anniversary of the movie. They decided on *The Matrix* because it fit perfectly with the discussions they'd been having about technology, and it also seemed interesting. Lavender was shocked at the turn of events but played it cool. She was glad he couldn't see her face. *My first real date. And on Valentine's Day!*

They talked for an hour before they both started to get sleepy. They had a new way of ending their phone conversation where they would play each other a song and when the last song was done, they ended the call. They took turns on who went first. So far, they had discovered that they both loved most genres of music from all the generations. Martin introduced her to Jack Johnson and Cat Stevens and Neil Young, and she introduced him to Billie Holiday and Stevie Nicks and Norah Jones. Lavender was driving home from school the week before with her mind cluttered and packed with thoughts of the impending doom of graduation and the aftermath. Her chest was on lockdown, unable to take a full breath. She had turned on her radio and some angry death metal song was blaring, which just amped up the mental load in her head. She tuned to the next station and heard a song that had been playing that night at the party and images of Travis and the futon flooded her mind and she felt like she might throw up. She changed the channel again and again...nothing helped. She flipped to AM radio and heard soft, slow sounds of horns and a voice that made her feel like she was in another world. Lavender was able to exhale, slow down and it made the drive home tolerable, almost enjoyable. She found out later that she had discovered the afternoon Jazz hour that was on WSIE every day from two to four. From then on, that's the channel she listened to on her way home from school most days. That music affected her like no other she had ever heard. Her shoulders lowered a few inches and her mind quieted.

Martin's song finished playing, and without a word, Lavender hit play on "I'll Be Seeing You" by Billie Holiday. She thought it was appropriate for their future meet up someday. They both listened to the piano and the horns and the slow-moving story sung with that voice…it felt like they were sitting in a club somewhere far away but together. *I'll be looking at the moon, but I'll be seeing you…*Billie's voice trailed off. There were no words they could say that would be a better good-bye and so they both hit end on their phone at the same time.

Lavender felt connected to Martin Luther Adams in a way that she had never felt before, for anyone. Lavender fell asleep thinking about Martin instead of Travis. She fell asleep smiling on the inside and the outside, instead of crying herself to sleep.

TWENTY-SEVEN

THE FIRST THING LAVENDER SAW when she opened her eyes was a single red rose that hadn't fully blossomed yet. It was on her bedstand with a note. She knew exactly what the note would say. *To my little Rosebud. Happy Valentine's Day. Love Dad.* He never forgot the day and it was the only time he came into her room without permission. She smiled as she imagined him carefully opening her bedroom door without making a sound and tiptoeing over to her bedstand, all done in the five-a.m. darkness before he left for work.

The next thing she did was look at her phone. No texts. Jackie and Jana usually sent her a *Happy Valentines* text with a meme or a gif, then they'd spend the rest of the day making fun of clingy couples and commiserate how the holiday was really a conspiracy to make single girls everywhere feel bad about not having a boyfriend. She usually dreaded the day, but that year would be a milestone. Not only her first adult date, but a virtual-long-distance date with someone she'd never met in person. She wished she could fast-forward through her classes and V-day bullshit at school and get to the good part. Movies with Martin.

Next to the rose on her bedstand was the card she received in the mail yesterday. Lavender and Martin made a deal to wait on opening the cards if they arrived earlier than the actual day. Lavender picked up the pink envelope and studied the writing.

She never tired of seeing her name written by his hand. When she pulled the card out of the envelope, a photo dropped on her bed. Lavender sat up and turned on her bedside lamp. It was his senior picture. *Yes. That's him. Martin Luther Adams.* She hadn't imagined what color hair or eyes he might have, or whether or not he had freckles or dimples, but she wasn't surprised at all when she saw him for the first time. His hair was dark brown and slightly curly, his eyes were blue, the same color blue as his button-down shirt. He wasn't smiling but he wasn't scowling either. He looked open and approachable and like he was ready to say something important. His arms were folded one on top of the other on the desk in front of him. He looked relaxed and confident. Comfortable in his own skin. *He looks familiar to me. Like I've seen him before.* Lavender snapped a pic of it with her phone so she could have it with her in case she wanted to look at him again. Then she placed Martin's photo in her bedstand drawer.

Inside the pink envelope was a dark charcoal-colored card with a red heart on the cover outlined in gold glitter. The *Happy Valentine's Day* was inscribed in gold letters on the inside along with a handwritten message from Martin.

Lavender,
I'm glad we met (thanks Ms. Clarke) and look forward to meeting you in person someday. Can't wait for our date tonight! Hope you have a great day and don't get too annoyed with all the typical V-day stuff at school. I'm dreading it too.
Love,
Martin
p.s. No laughing...I despise posing for school photographers!

Love. He used the Love word. Lavender stopped. *What does that mean? Like, love you like a friend, a sister or just because it's Valentine's Day?* She never believed anyone when they said that to her. Because they didn't know her. How could they love her? But with Martin it was different. It felt almost normal or obvious or just the way it should be. He did know her. Well, most of her anyway. Even though he didn't know all her secrets, he still knew her better than anyone else had in her whole life. And for the first time, she felt like maybe she could say it back someday...and mean it.

Lavender would have liked to just stay in bed all day and write in her diary, look at Martin's picture and wait for the movie that night. But the only way to get to her long-distance date was to get out of bed, shower, get dressed and move on with her day.

Lavender found a gift bag with a card on the counter that her mom must have left for her.

"Happy Valentine's Day Sweetheart! I got you something."

She was not surprised that Sara was lurking close by to witness the big reveal and Lavender's response to the gift.

"Thanks mom. You know you don't have to, right?"

"I know...but it is my last year having you home with me, so it is my prerogative."

Lavender picked up the gift bag with different colored sweetheart candies all over it, with the cute sayings like...*be mine, too hot to handle, love you 2*...Inside the bag was pink tissue paper wrapped around something soft. Lavender pulled out an oversized, bright-red, V-neck sweater.

"I know you don't normally wear anything this colorful, but you seemed to really like red this summer when you were buying all those pillows for your bedroom, so I thought, 'why not?'"

Lavender held the sweater up to her body and smiled. It was super soft. She liked it. She was even surprised herself. "It's beautiful Mom. I do like it. In fact, I think I'll wear it later tonight." She imagined her dark jeans and short brown boots to complete the outfit. *Perfect for my date with Martin.* Jana would be proud of her.

"Yeah? Oh my goodness, that's awesome. So happy you like it." Her mom was beaming. "Do you have plans tonight?"

"I'm going to the movies actually...with some friends." Not a complete lie. She was going to the movies. It was just with one friend, without the plural.

"Nice. I'm glad you're getting out. You've been kind of a loner this year..."

She knew her mom was fishing for a conversation and more details, but Lavender didn't take the bait and let the words hang in the air while she finished eating her peanut butter toast. She didn't want to get into it with her mom...her day was off to a good start. Better than any Valentine's Day she could have imagined. She didn't want anything to ruin it. "Happy Valentine's Day Mom. And thanks for the sweater...I really do love it."

"Have a great day. Love you," her mom said.

Lavender picked up her backpack and gym bag and headed out the door. She was hoping to get a run in after school.

Siena High School was buzzing. She could feel it from the parking lot. The foyer was swimming in pink, white and red streamers.

Cardboard hearts of different sizes were hanging from the ceiling. Students were selling four-inch heart pins at a table in the center of the foyer. At five dollars you could buy a red heart with TAKEN across the center, or a pink heart with AVAILABLE or the white one with NO COMMENT.

"Lavender!"

"Come buy a pin."

Lavender nodded at the table with a fake smile. "No thanks," she said.

"Oh come on. It's all in fun."

"All the money we raise goes to our class gift."

"I'm good." Lavender kept walking. She saw Jana in the hall standing with a group of other senior girls. They locked eyes for just a second before Jana turned to the one next to her and smiled. *She has a red pin on. Jana has a boyfriend. And I don't know about him.* Her shock quickly shifted to a sad realization that Jana had moved on with her life. Who could blame her? But still…she had never felt more alone in that school as she did right at that moment. Lavender took out her phone and looked at Martin's picture. She could have bought a red pin too. But that would have caused too many questions, and she didn't want to spend the day explaining about a boyfriend who lived thousands of miles from Siena, New York. Lavender wanted to keep him to herself.

The rest of the day was filled with red-pin girls smug and giddy with boyfriend status, and those flaunting the pink pin to make sure everyone knew they were open for business. The guys were trying to play it cool and ignore the whole thing, but some had red pins that their girlfriend had bought them, some thought they were funny and bought all three pins. *I wonder if Martin would buy a pin if he were here. Probably not.*

Lavender decided to get out of there and go for a run at lunch time and avoid the cafeteria scene altogether with heart-shaped frosted cookies and couples being extra clingy and affectionate. She was trying to preserve her good mood that started that morning. She wasn't into all the V-day nonsense at school, but she couldn't wait for her own date later that night. Running in February could be iffy. She loved being outside in the cold air but slipping and falling on ice was no fun. The sun was bright at lunchtime, so it made it feel ten degrees warmer than it really was. They had about a foot of snow from a storm last week that hadn't melted yet. It didn't get any better than running on a day like that in the dead of winter. Blue sky. Sunshine. Snowbanks lit up like they were plugged in. Lungs full of cold air. No matter what was going on in her head, running quieted her mind. It steadied the back and forth. It made her feel strong and gave her a break from all the noise inside her head. *Jana. Jackie. BSU. Martin. The party. New Year's Eve at the Gordon's.* The list was growing.

After the run, dressed and ready to finish the day out strong, she walked down the hall to seventh period. *Oh shit.* Hillary Charles saw her from the other end of the hall and lasered in on her. "Lavender. We have a crisis."

"We do?"

"Yes...I'm preparing for our Class Night and got a list of accepted students at BSU." Lavender's stomach clutched.

"So...."

"Your name wasn't on it."

"Hmmm." Lavender shrugged and looked Hillary in the eye. Hillary waited. "What do you want me to do about it?"

"This is serious. Aren't you worried? I mean, what if they lost your application? Or deleted you from their system by mistake? Or got you mixed up with another student? Aren't you freaked out?"

"I'm not worried. I'm sure it's fine."

"Do you have a contact there? Are you going to call? Email? Do you want me to see if I can get in touch with someone?"

"No. I'll handle it." Lavender started to walk away. Hillary grabbed her arm.

"Lavender. Is there something you're not telling me?" Hillary eyed her suspiciously. "You can tell me. I'll help."

"There's nothing. It's not a big deal. I said I'd take care of it." Lavender turned and walked away, hoping that Hillary couldn't see the panic in her walk. She focused on moving swiftly but not like she was running away, just trying to get to seventh period. She focused on breathing normally and coughed a few times to get rid of the lump that was trying to form a solid in her throat. One hundred and twenty-three days...tick...She needed a plan. Once in her seat, she took a deep breath, looked at Martin's pic on her phone before the bell rang and exhaled. But the secrets and lies were still there, even with the good things happening in her life. *I have to tell someone soon, or I will be the thing to explode.*

Because Lavender got her run in at lunchtime, she was able to make another stop before getting ready for the movie date with Martin. She bought a bouquet of flowers, a valentine's day card and a box of chocolate-covered cherries at the grocery store and headed to Betsy Ross.

"Hey. Happy Freaking Valentine's Day," Evelyn said and rolled her eyes.

"Tell me about it. School was so annoying," Lavender said. "How's it been here?"

"Mostly the usual. We put up a few decorations and they had heart cookies at lunch time. Oh, and we spent the entire hour of arts and craft today making cards."

"Nice. Sounds better than my day." Lavender finished signing in and waved before heading down the hall.

"Will you take me home?" The lady in the purple house dress greeted her.

"Maybe someday." Lavender smiled and kept walking. Her grandma wasn't in the TV room. She walked down Potomac and found the room. "There you are." Louise was sitting in her chair by the window. "Happy Valentine's Day Grandma." Her grandma looked up and smiled at Lavender.

"Hi. Are you here to see me?" Louise asked.

"Yes, of course I am. I brought you these."

"Flowers? For what?"

"It's Valentine's Day."

"Oh. How nice. You brought me flowers. I haven't had flowers in a very long time."

"I brought you these too. You like chocolate, right? And a card."

"Wow. You are very nice." Her grandma sat down at the table by the window and worked on getting the plastic cellophane wrapping off the flowers and the vase they came in. She also opened the candy.

"Here Grandma. Open the card." Her grandma took the card and opened it slowly then pushed it back over to Lavender.

"You read it to me. I don't have my glasses on."

"Sure." Lavender read the outside cover. "A Grandmother's love is sweet and hard to beat," she opened and finished the sentiment from the inside. "...and I wish you a day filled with the sweet love you deserve. Happy Valentine's Day. I'm so happy that I've gotten to know you this past year. Love, Lavender Rose Finch, (your granddaughter)."

Her grandma reached out and squeezed her hand and said through tears, "That's the nicest thing anyone has ever said to me." Lavender smiled. The day took a turn towards perfect again. Her heart was full. She decided to try something.

"Guess what Grandma?"

"What?"

"I'm going on a date tonight."

"With a boy?"

"Yes! Well sort of...he lives far away so we're doing a virtual date. We're both going to see the same movie at the same time, alone in our separate towns, but together..."

"Oh." Her grandma looked like she was trying hard to process what that meant. "I see. That's fun."

"I'm excited."

"Do you like this boy a lot?"

"I do. He's nice and smart and thoughtful...different from the other boys I know."

Her grandma looked lost in a dream. "I liked a boy like that once. He was special." Lavender moved in closer. She knew her grandma was talking about M. from the diary but didn't want to disrupt the memory.

"What was his name?"

Her grandma put her head down slightly and moved her hand to her mouth. After a minute like that she looked up. "M. It began with an M."

"So does mine. His name is Martin. Isn't that funny Grandma? We both liked boys with names that start with M." Lavender laughed softly. "Do you want your flowers on this table or by the bed?"

"Hmmm. How about by the bed? Then I can look at them when I wake up." Her grandma smiled.

"Sounds perfect." Lavender stood and moved the vase to the bedstand and placed the card next to it. "I'll leave the candy over here on the table, okay?"

Her grandma stood up too. "I'll have some after dinner."

"Great. I've gotta run grandma. Need to get ready for my date, but I'll be back Saturday as usual, okay?"

"Okay."

Lavender bent down and hugged her grandma. There was a familiar and warm sensation between them. She held on for longer than usual and whispered in her ear. "I love you grandma." She wasn't even sure her grandma heard her, but it didn't matter. For the first time in her life, she said those words out loud and really meant them. That pint-sized woman had stolen her heart. She might not know Lavender's name or exactly who she was, but they were connected at a level so much deeper than their names. She was sure of it.

After her visit at Betsy Ross, Lavender stopped at home to put on the red sweater her mom had given her that morning, her favorite dark jeans and short, brown boots. She smoothed her hair with some styling cream and a quick blow-dry. Mascara and lip gloss finished the look. Jana would have said, *OMG Lavender. You*

look so good. You should dress like this every day. Lavender smiled thinking of her saying those words and how proud she would have been. Even though her and Martin were not doing screen time, she wanted to look good on her date. While she was getting dressed, she got a text from Martin.

> Hey. R u almost ready? I'm heading
> out. Lmk when you get there.

The movie theater was crowded with mostly couples, a few families, but hardly any single people. Lavender didn't care. She was on a mission. She got her water, M&Ms and popcorn and found a seat in the center of the row, at the front of the second section. She liked to put her feet up on the railing. She settled in and took her phone out.

> Hey. I'm here. In my seat. R u?

She waited while the three little dots danced on her phone.

> Yes. In my seat too. Do you have
> your goods?

> Lol. Yes, popcorn, water, m&ms.

> I'm pumped for the movie.

> Me too.

> You look nice.

> Very funny.

> For real. What are you wearing?

My new red sweater, jeans and
boots. You?

Black t-shirt, jeans and sneakers.
Put on cologne too.

Oh man. I can smell it.

This is fun.

The previews are starting.

Ok. Here too.

I'm going dark.

Same.

Text me when you get out.

Ok. I will. Watch the movie.

You watch the movie.

Goodbye, lol.

Shutting down for real this time…

The previews started and Lavender sunk in her seat and opened her M&Ms. She'd never been to the movies by herself before, but she didn't hate it. She didn't have to listen to someone whispering next to her or worry about anything really. She was able to exist in her own little world and get lost in the big screen in front of her. She got lost in *The Matrix*. Almost three hours later the credits rolled and Lavender took out her phone. Nothing from Martin yet. She texted him.

Wow. That was incredible. No
words…i'm heading home.

By the time she got to her car, she had a text from him.

No kidding. Amazing. I'm still
processing.

When she pulled in her driveway, she had another text.

I know it's not sunday, but since it is
a date night, you wanna talk on the
phone?

Yessssss. Call me in ten.

It was almost eleven o'clock so both Lavender's parents were in bed when she got home. She ran upstairs, put her pajamas on and settled in bed just before her phone rang.

"Hi."

"Happy Valentine's Day," Martin said.

"Thank you. And thank you for the card. It was really sweet."

"You're welcome. Thank you for mine. You are beautiful, you know that?"

"Stop. I am not. I loved your pic. I saved a copy on my phone, lol."

"Haha, I did the same."

"So? What'd you think of *The Matrix*?" Lavender asked.

They spent the next half-hour debating whether or not the characters were stuck in a computer game, and how they only addressed Keanu Reeves as Neo so maybe he finally hacked the ultimate computer system and got inside people's minds. Or not. They decided they'd have to watch the next movies in the series to get more information before they could really come to any solid conclusions.

"What was your favorite part?" she asked Martin.

"The fight scenes."

"Oh, of course."

"You?"

"My favorite parts were the dialogue. Very subtle, you could almost miss the words if you weren't paying attention…"

"Which ones did you like?

"That we're just a *mental projection of our digital self* and *never send a human to do a machine's job*. I mean, this was twenty-five years ago, imagine if they made that movie today."

She left out the other quotes from the movie that had also jolted her in her seat. *The answers are coming.* She hoped that was a sign that she could figure out how to get out of her lie about college without having to tell everyone what happened with Travis. *The mind has trouble letting go.* No matter how much she tried to not think about it, or how much she focused on other things happening in her life, the blurry memories of that night haunted her, always lurking around the corner, jumping out when she least expected it. That line in the movie validated that at least it wasn't just Lavender's mind that worked like that…it was human nature. The one movie quote she was dying to share with Martin but wasn't ready to yet was… *No one can tell you you're in love. You just know it. Balls to bone.* Another sign from the universe.

"Hey, you know what? We should put all this *Matrix* stuff in an email chain for Ms. Clarke's assignment. It fits with the technology and AI topic. She'll love it and we can get credit for it," Martin said.

"Sweet! Great idea," Lavender said.

"What did you think of our date?"

"I liked it. Even though we're so far apart and it sounds weird, I felt like we were together."

"Me too. We'll have to do it again."

"Maybe we could do the same thing at home. Watch a movie together."

"Yes. Let's watch the next *Matrix*. Sunday night?"

"Perfect."

"It's a date. Maybe a little earlier since the movie is probably a few hours? Does eight work?" Martin asked.

"Let's do it. I'll research where we can stream it," Lavender said.

"Hey Lavender."

"Yes?"

"Thanks for being my valentine."

Lavender smiled. She had that same feeling she got with her grandma earlier that night. "It was my pleasure. Best Valentine's Day I've ever had." She could almost feel Martin smiling on the other end.

"Ready for a song?"

Lavender cued up the song she had planned for tonight, Ella Fitzgerald's "My Funny Valentine." Then Martin ended that night with "I'll Be Seeing You." As the haunting notes of the song trailed off and they both pressed the end button, Lavender felt seen. She felt loved.

It was the best day ever. She refused to let thoughts of Hillary Charles, BSU, Travis, or New Year's Eve push out the wonder of everything else that happened that day. Her date with Martin, her hug with her grandma, the song they just listened to, the card Martin signed with the word love…she wanted to fall asleep thinking that maybe love wasn't as far out of reach as she thought.

TWENTY-EIGHT

MARCH IN SIENA was a pivotal month. It meant that you had survived the harshest part of the winter season, in length, temperature and snowfall, and spring was once again on its way. It wasn't quite there yet but signs of hope began to emerge. In March, a Lake Effect event, so named by the weather team at Channel 3, could dump twenty inches of snow on the ground and then three days later, the snow was melting, the first robin was bouncing around the yard, and daffodils were trying to wiggle their way up and out of the ground. For Lavender, March also meant that shit was about to get real and she better figure out what the hell she was going to do about her college application that was never submitted, her acceptance to BSU that never happened, and what she was going to tell her mother, Martin and Hillary Charles about all of it. Oh yeah, and the most important thing…if she didn't go to college after high school, what exactly would she do with her life? That damn wave was breathing down her neck. 94 freaking days…

"Hey…you guys…up here." Hillary's shrill voice jolted Lavender back to the auditorium. She had been hanging out there for all of 8th period waiting for the end-of-day assembly to begin. Jana was sitting on the opposite side of the room with Megan and Mallory and Tamra. *What the fuck? Why is she hanging out with them? They are snobby and fake and she's better than those girls.* Jana caught her staring and Lavender waved hi. Jana didn't wave back. "Today, we are exactly three months from

Class Night on June 14th. And then graduation is two days later. OMG! Can you believe it? Does everyone have their countdown timers synced and bookmarked?"

She didn't need to look at a countdown timer. Her brain was already ticking away. 94 days. Got it.

"So, here's what you need to know. Number one…when you leave today, please take your ballot to vote your Senior Superlatives. We will announce the winners at the end of April. Every vote counts! Number two…if you haven't already, please make sure I have your post-graduation plans…college acceptance, the major you are enrolling in, if you're undecided just put that down, and again, if you're one of those people not going to college, that's fine…really…it's fine…just let me know what your amazing plans are so you can be included in the Class Night festivities. Number three…Get your Senior Ball tickets… the money we raise will go towards our class gift…"

There was that phrase again…*those people*…is she really that clueless? Lavender went to nudge the person next to her and roll her eyes before she remembered that Jana wasn't there. She had no one to nudge.

Lavender hadn't changed her mind about college. It had been six months since the party and Travis. But in those moments when she allowed her mind to acknowledge the memories, it felt like yesterday. She had no interest whatsoever in a campus where boys like Travis roamed, searching for girls like her, so they could take whatever they wanted without considering if they had permission to take it. *He stole from me. He stole my first time. He stole my senior year. He stole my college experience. My friends. All of it. I can't undo it. I can't pretend it didn't happen. And I can't tell anyone. I never should have let him. I should have been stronger. I should have screamed louder. I shouldn't have been so stupid to think that this boy actually liked me and wanted to know me.*

"And the categories are..." Hillary's voice moved the needle in her mind from the Travis track of traumatic memories to the more outrageous topic of Senior Superlatives. Lavender was flabbergasted that it was still a thing. Her generation prided themselves on being more inclusive and accepting of diversity and rejecting the societal norms that their parents grew up with. That is, until there was an opportunity to separate from the pack and be recognized as smarter, prettier, stronger, better...Some of the category names were updated to sound less discriminatory and more casual and fun, but the end result was the same. *I'm better than you.* She didn't plan on voting and certainly was not campaigning for any of the categories listed.

"...Relationship Goals, Most Athletic, I Want Your Hair, Who Wore It Best, Most Likely To Go Viral, Most Likely To Have The Most Followers, Lol formerly known as Class Clown, Most Likely To Get Canceled and finally, my favorite, hint hint Siena High, Most Likely To Be CEO." Hillary finally took a breath and asked for any questions.

The assembly ended after her classmates spent ten minutes asking Hillary about the voting process, and other questions like would there be a runner-up for the categories? Or was it first place and second place? Or were there actual prizes? When exactly would the results be posted? As Lavender left the auditorium and made a beeline for the parking lot, someone handed her a ballot.

"Lavender! Wait for me." *Damn it. I thought I was safe.* Hillary Charles was coming at her. She kept walking. "Lav! I know you see me. Wait up." Lavender stopped and turned towards Hillary without a smile.

"What's up?" Lavender said.

"Did you call the admissions office?"

"Umm, yeah, it's all worked out."

"So, you're good?"

"I'm good." She tried to answer her questions in a way that also avoided blatant lies.

"Does that mean you're on the acceptance list now?"

"I said, I'm good."

"Okay, if you say so...let me know if I can help you."

Lavender started walking again and Hillary stayed with her, talking. "Are you excited for the Ball?"

"I probably won't go." *Shit. I haven't even thought of that yet.*

"What???? You have to! It's our Senior Ball."

"So? It's just a dance." Hillary grimaced at that response.

"You know you don't need a date, right? Plenty of people go with friend groups." *Well, that rules me out. No friend group here at Siena.*

"I know. I'll think about it."

"Okay. Promise?"

"Yes, promise." At that point, Lavender would say anything to stop the conversation and get Hillary to move on to her next project. "See you later Hillary."

Lavender bolted through the front doors leaving Hillary standing in the foyer watching her head to her car. The days were getting longer now so she had time for a run before dark if she hurried. A run was exactly what she needed after that assembly and conversation. She did her best thinking while moving. She had to come up with a plan. And soon. Hillary was right about one thing. Time was running out.

TWENTY-NINE

"TELL ME, LAVENDER ROSE FINCH, if you could do anything after high school, and earning money wasn't important, or you didn't need approval from your parents, or you weren't thinking about a career that was sensible...and you weren't afraid...what would you do?"

Lavender paused for a long moment. She had a hard time even dreaming about a future or imagining what she really wanted to do. She couldn't get past the wall of shame, secrets, and lies in her life to see anything else.

"I honestly don't know...what about you? Tell me what Martin Luther Adams would do."

"I would go to Costa Rica, or maybe Colombia or Ecuador and take pictures, work on my photography, and immerse myself in a new culture. Oh yeah, and surf."

"Is that what you're planning? Have you decided yet?" Lavender asked.

"I will do all of that, someday. But first, I think I need a transition year in the States since I've been in Cuba for the last four years with my family and all the other military families. I need to get my bearings and figure things out."

Lavender was still spinning after the assembly on Friday and the countdown timer in her brain was ticking, ticking, ticking...91 days...she wanted to tell Martin everything, but that dread in her gut was back and her chest was seizing up.

"Sounds like you have it all figured out. Where in the States?"

"I'm thinking about submitting my application this week to AmeriCorps. They have assignments right now in California, Appalachia, Alaska, and a Native American reservation in South Dakota."

"California would be cool. That's where my grandmother went after high school."

"That's right. I remember you saying that was in her diary. Did you ever finish reading that?"

"Yeah. The entries stopped suddenly. It was weird. There were a lot of blank pages. I'm taking it back to her on Saturday."

"What about you? Are you excited for BSU? Do you know who your roommate is going to be yet?"

Lavender paused for another long moment. She could lie, tell him she was excited and couldn't wait to find out who she'd be sharing her dorm room with, or she could evade his question and change the subject. She had become really good at that. Or she could be somewhat honest without revealing everything. "Hmmmm, no, not really excited…if I'm being honest."

"No? What's up with that? I thought that was your first-choice school?"

"It was. But now that it's a reality, I don't know any more if it's actually what I want. Not sure I want to go to college at all." There it was. The first time she'd said it out loud to anyone. She held her breath.

"You don't have to, right? Would your parents force you to go?"

"I doubt it, that's not really their style, but I think they'd be very shocked and wouldn't understand my change of mind." She didn't mention that she'd also break their hearts.

"They might surprise you, ya know. Sometimes parents do. You should talk to them."

"I will at some point." Lavender left out that the reason she hadn't talked to them yet was because that would mean she'd have to tell them why. She'd have to explain what changed her mind and why she had lied about it all year. She'd have to tell them about the party and Travis. But Martin just accepted her change in plans as perfectly reasonable. He was one of the most non-judgmental people she'd ever known. Of course, he didn't know the full truth either.

"What would you do if you didn't go to BSU? Get a job in Siena?"

"I haven't thought that far ahead."

"You should come with me..."

Martin's words hung in the air for what seemed like hours but was only sixty seconds or so. "You mean to AmeriCorps?"

"Yeah, why not? You could apply too. It's not college, but it's also not staying in your hometown, living with your parents, and working some random job."

"Maybe...that's an interesting thought."

Martin's invitation had sparked a new idea for Lavender's future for the first time in months. She promised to spend some time that week researching the AmeriCorps website, looking at the application and considering the possibility. *Maybe I could do that instead of BSU.*

"That would be sweet. We could finally meet each other and also spend some real time together." Martin's excitement was little-boyish and cute and made her smile. "Hey, you know what else?" Martin said.

"What?"

"We need to go on another date."

"Yeah? What did you have in mind? More movies or something else?"

"Something else. I'm thinking about it."

"I'm game. I'll think of ideas too." She had something else on her mind she'd been wanting to ask Martin. "Hey. I've got a question for you. Are you going to your Senior Prom?" She held her breath for the answer. She'd been wanting to ask him for weeks. Did he have a girl at his school that he would take?

"Nah, I mean, why? What's the point? If I can't take you as my date, I don't want to go."

Phew. Lavender quietly exhaled all the air she'd had in her lungs. "Awww, that's sweet. I don't wanna go to mine either. I haven't broken the news to my mother yet."

"Oh yeah, mothers love that shit. I'm sure mine already assumes I'm not going."

"Mine will be bummed."

"You ready for a song and sleep?"

"Yes. Thanks for not judging me about college."

"You can tell me anything. I'll never judge you."

"Goodnight Martin."

"Goodnight Lavender."

It was Martin's turn to play the first song. Lavender scooched down into her bed and snuggled with Mister Bean and placed her phone on the stand next to her. She closed her eyes and listened to a Cuban artist sing a love song in Spanish.

After his song was over, Lavender pressed play on the song she'd had on repeat all week. Green Day's "Wake Me Up When September Ends." The haunting song was a cry to the universe. Travis and the party happened last September and Lavender wanted someone to wake her up when the nightmare was over. So far, she wasn't sure it would ever be over.

THIRTY

"HI GRANDMA." Lavender bent down and squeezed Louise's shoulders and gave her a peck on the cheek. All the ladies were in their usual spots on Saturday morning watching *Mary Tyler Moore*. Lavender knew she wouldn't get much of a response or conversation until the show was over. She set her backpack down on the floor and took her usual seat on the end of the couch, closest to her grandma's chair.

In that episode, Mary found out that a man she was dating had a wife. He was married. It was quite the scandal. Once the show was over and the mini crisis was resolved, the crowd in the TV room dispersed to the cafeteria for an early lunch. If only problems got resolved that efficiently in real life.

"Are you hungry? Do you want to get some food? I'll go with you," Lavender asked.

"I could eat, I suppose."

Lavender held out her hand to her grandma and helped her out of the chair. "Well let's go then." They both moved down the hall to the cafeteria. The smell of gravy and french fries enveloped them as soon as they turned the corner. "Smells good."

"The food is shit in this hellhole," her grandma said.

Lavender shrugged and sat at a small round table across from Louise. The workers served them both plates of hot Turkey sandwiches, smothered in gravy and fries on the side. There were also some green beans to round out the meal. She dug into the plate of food hoping her grandma would too. It seemed like her grandma was shorter and thinner every time she saw her. "Mmmm. Not bad," Lavender said as she proceeded to finish a big bite of the sandwich and nibbled on some fries dipped in the gravy. The two ate in silence and let the chatter of others fill the space between them. Louise ate half her sandwich but didn't really touch her fries.

"You don't like the french fries Grandma?"

"They give me a stomachache."

"What a bummer. I'd eat them every day if I could."

When they had both eaten half and pushed their plates in the center of the table, one of the staff came and removed the dishes.

"Hey Grandma. I brought your diary back." Lavender reached into her backpack and pulled out the small leather book.

"Where did you get that?"

"You gave it to me a few months ago, when we were hanging out in your room."

"I did?"

"Yes, of course. I wouldn't have taken it without your permission." Lavender smiled at her.

"Oh. We need to get that back to my room and put it away. I don't want anyone in here getting any ideas about stealing it."

"Yes, let's do that," Lavender said.

They walked back through the hallway to the center of the Betsy Ross home and then branched off down the Potomac hallway to her grandma's room. Lavender sat on the end of the bed. "Can I ask you some questions about your diary?"

Her grandma shrugged her shoulders and sat down on the bed next to her.

"Do you remember going to California after high school to work in the VISTA program?"

Her grandma thought for a minute. "Was it The Peace Corps?"

"Sort of."

"I wanted to join the Peace Corps but my parents didn't want me to leave the country, so I went to California with that other program...I can't remember the name of it."

"VISTA."

"That's right. I moved away all by myself. That was a big deal back then."

"Were your parents mad that you didn't go to college?"

"No. They weren't college people. They were surprised when I announced my plans but not mad. They expected me to get out on my own and make my way."

"That's awesome they were so chill about it. Parents today expect you to have your whole life figured out, what you'll major in, where you'll go to college, who you want to be...," Lavender's voice trailed off.

Her grandma picked up the diary and stared at the red cover with the gold embossed letters. She opened the book and studied her handwriting, running her finger over the pages. "Seems like a different life..."

"There was a boy you met. In here you called him M." Lavender waited for a response while Grandma Louise looked out the window.

"Miguel."

"That was his name? Miguel?"

Her grandma nodded. "He was a sweet, sweet boy."

"What happened to him?"

"They sent him away. We loved each other so much, and they wouldn't let us be together." Her grandma slammed the diary closed. "That was it." She reached over to the bedstand and rummaged behind a few boxes to hide the diary from view and closed the door.

"You never heard from him again?"

"No."

"And then you went home?"

Her grandma lay on the bed with her head on her pillow and closed her eyes. "They sent me away too."

Lavender reached for her grandma's hand and clasped it. "That's so sad. Why would they do that?"

"It was a different time. People weren't as open-minded then. He was a migrant worker from Mexico. I was a teenaged white girl from a small town. There was already so much happening with the protests and the workers fighting the owners for better pay and safer conditions. News reporters were all over the farm. They didn't want another scandal to add to all the drama."

Lavender saw the box inside the bedside stand. "But the letters?" Her grandma pulled the box onto the bed and fingered the old envelopes. Lavender saw her grandmother's writing on the front. They were unopened. "You wrote to him, didn't you?"

"I did. I tried to find him...tried different places I thought he might be...but..." Her grandma put the letters back in the box, into the bedstand and shut the door, hard. "I never heard from him again."

"Oh grandma. That is terrible." She had never gotten that much information out of her grandma before. Her head was spinning, but Lavender kept going. "What did you do after that?"

"I came home and met your grandfather and got married. End of story."

Lavender knew enough to know that wasn't quite the end. "My mom told me that she had an older brother."

Her grandma opened her eyes and looked directly into hers. "I had a son. Michael." Louise sat up and reached back into her bedstand and found another book. A small blue photo album. There were tiered stacks of plastic photo sleeves on each side with each sleeve holding two or three small photos. "Here he is."

She took the book from her grandma and looked at the photo. Louise as a young girl, not much older than Lavender, holding a baby wrapped in a blue striped blanket and a blue knit cap on his head. A handsome man stood next to her, his hand on her elbow. He looked serious.

"Is that Grandpa?"

"Yes. That was my husband. Roy." Her grandma sighed.

They sat on the bed together and looked at every single picture in that album. The little boy grew to be a toddler with dark hair and brown eyes. His dimples and wide grin made Lavender smile. "He looked like a sweet boy."

"He was." Grandma Louise picked up one of the pictures and held it for a few moments while she kept moving through the album.

"That must be my mother?" There was a new baby in Louise's arms with a pink knitted cap and the same man standing next to her, holding her elbow. Same unsmiling face.

"That's Sara. My daughter."

Lavender stared at the picture, looking for a hint of the mother she knew. She followed the trail of pictures with Michael bending over his baby sister, kissing her cheek, holding her bottle, holding her hand. The boy grew to about three or four, the girl learned to stand and then walk.The last picture in the album was the four of them. Her grandma in a light blue dress, her grandpa in a suit, with Sara and Michael standing in front of them, also in a dress and suit. There were baskets in front of them. "Easter Sunday?"

"It was Easter. Our last one."

The tears in her grandma's eyes spilled onto her cheeks. Lavender stood and grabbed a tissue for her, then held her hand and waited. She wanted to keep asking questions. She was so curious to find out the thing that ruined her and made her give up. The thing that made her want to spend her days drinking. "What happened after that?" Lavender asked in a soft voice.

"Your grandpa left. Michael died." Louise laid back down on the bed.

"I'm sorry Grandma. That must have been so sad. And hard for you." Lavender lay down on the bed next to her grandma with her head on her shoulder.

"Life is hard sometimes."

"Why did Grandpa leave? Did he find someone else he wanted to marry?" Lavender tried to ask it in the gentlest way she could.

"Oh, that was a disaster from the start."

"What do you mean? You didn't love him?"

"I was so sad, and desperate, when I came home from California. I needed to get married as fast as possible. He was just the first boy who asked me."

Why would she have to get married? Why would she settle for a man she didn't love? "I don't get it Grandma."

"I was pregnant," Louise whispered.

With Miguel's baby. Her uncle had a different father than her mother did. Lavender lay still but her mind was spinning with the news. That must be why they sent Miguel away and then Louise. That was the scandal they wanted to avoid. *A teenaged girl gets pregnant by migrant worker.* Not a headline that anyone wanted then. It was 1973. She knew enough to know that young girls getting pregnant without a husband wasn't as accepted back then. Her grandma must have been so scared. "Oh," was all Lavender could think to say.

They both lay on the bed and let that memory hang in the air for a bit. Lavender pulled out her phone and turned on the speaker she had given her grandma for Christmas. She played some slow and soft instrumental jazz mix. "Hey Grandma. Is it okay if I ask you more questions?"

"It's okay."

"Did Grandpa know you were pregnant from another boy?"

"No. I was afraid that if I told him, he wouldn't marry me. If I wasn't married soon, I would have to give our baby up for adoption, so I kept that to myself. I lied. I was so ashamed and alone. My mother wouldn't understand. My friends wouldn't either. I was worried what they would think of me. If I could do it over again, I would tell everybody."

"What would you tell them?"

"The truth. That I met a boy in California named Miguel and we fell in love. I would tell how sweet he was to me and how much I believed in him and how we dreamt of a life together. I would tell them that I wanted to marry him and have our baby."

"Do you think they would have accepted that?"

"Maybe. Maybe not. But at least I would have told my truth and not kept secrets and lies inside me. That's what made Grandpa leave."

"He found out?"

"When Michael was sick, we were both so scared that we would lose him. It consumed us. At one point, Michael needed blood. His type didn't match the combination of me and your grandpa."

"So, he figured it out?"

"He was a smart man. I told him everything." Lavender noticed her grandma's hands were shaking. "I told him the truth, and he left me, and he left Sara. I know he was angry and hurt. He had every right to be. But he told me he loved me. He told me he'd never leave me. He told me he'd do anything for me. We made vows. As soon as he found out the truth about me and Michael, he left all of us." Lavender pulled the blanket up from the bottom of the bed and covered her grandma up. "That broke me."

Her grandma's sadness and despair hung in the room over them.

"A few months later, Michael died. It was like being torn away from Miguel all over again, only this time, part of me tore too. I would never be in one piece again."

Lavender squeezed Louise's hand as they both lay there with the weight of their family history on top of them. It was enough. No more questions. She knew enough now to understand the story of her family. Her grandma's heartbreak and loss, her mother's childhood, even her own childhood and why she felt like she grew up without a grandmother at all. Lavender began to cry, not because of her grandmother's story, but her own story. Her own loss. By the time she was born, her grandma had been trying to fill her brokenness with booze for so many years that she couldn't see the new baby, the new little girl, that needed her. Lavender finally understood the woman that was her grandma, and the life she lived, but was it too late? Could they make up for all the years they lost? Lies, secrets and shame had ruined her grandma's life. *Would my lies and secrets and shame ruin me too?*

THIRTY-ONE

LAVENDER COULD HEAR THE WATER trickling free from the melting ice and snow as she ran through the streets of Siena on Sunday morning. The Spring thaw had started. There was still enough white on the ground to create a glare from the full sun that shone bright in her eyes. No matter how chilly it felt at the start, she'd have to take some layers off mid-way through her run.

She jumped puddles and avoided black ice while she replayed the conversation she had the day before with Grandma Louise. She had no one to unload all the information to since Jackie and Jana weren't around, and she wasn't ready to talk to her mom about all of it.

It felt like she had two fifty-pound weights on each shoulder. On one side was the realization that her grandma was once a young girl, open-hearted and eager to find her corner of the world. Just like she was before that college party in September. Her grandma found a cause worthy of her hard work and intelligence, she found a boy worthy of her love and passion, and then it all got ripped away. Louise's heart was broken when she and Miguel were forced apart. Before that wounded heart could heal, a man who promised her everything, broke it again. The final straw, losing her baby boy—the only thing she had left of the life she really wanted—created a wound so deep and cavernous Louise never recovered. As sad as the story was, everything Lavender knew about her grandma, her mom, herself, mingled together in a moment of clarity that made perfect sense. She and Louise were not so different and that is what weighed on Lavender. Her grandma lost her ability to love anyone or anything and couldn't allow anyone to get close enough to love her. It was too risky. *Maybe that's why I don't believe people when they tell me they love me or why I always feel like their love is always out of reach, like a game of monkey-in-the-middle. It was passed down from my grandma.*

There were other similarities too. Like the lies, the secrets, and the shame. With so much in common, Lavender couldn't help but wonder if she too would become an alcoholic. She counted the number of nights she drank beer over the last year and still felt it was below average compared to the other seniors in her class. The difference was, Lavender mostly drank alone. And enjoyed it. *Does that mean I have a problem?* She sneaked beer while she was babysitting. Mrs. Gordon would be so surprised, and pissed, if she ever found out her beloved Lavender did such a thing. Then there was the night she drove home after having too many beers with not enough time to process the alcohol through her system. *Am I just like my grandma? Will I spend my days chasing a buzz on a barstool instead of living a life I can be proud of?*

Bearing down on the other shoulder was the haunting memories of Travis and what happened to her at that party. She was getting better at not torturing herself by letting the scenes play on a constant loop in her mind, but it was always there. Heavy. Lurking. Piled on top of that were the lies she told every day by not coming clean on her BSU plans and the fact that she had not applied, had not been accepted and had no intention of going to any college campus, anywhere.

Her chest was almost always tight, holding the heart that was pounding in sync with the countdown timer ticking away the weeks and days, *eighty-four*, until she'd be forced to expose it all to everyone. She tried to play out different scenarios, but she couldn't get past the look of horror on everyone's face when they learned who Lavender really was. *Drunk slut at a party with a boy on a futon in the basement. Beer-drinking babysitter who drove her car and could have killed someone. Liar who pretended all year to be going to college next year.* She didn't see a way out.

Then there was Martin. He was the one bright spot in her life right now. She felt closer to him than she'd ever felt to anyone, even Jackie or Jana. He was so easy to talk to and comfortable to spend time with, even though it was only on the phone or through letters or virtual dates. He had submitted his application to the AmeriCorps program and was making plans to go to California after graduation. Lavender envied his clarity and confidence. He wasn't weighed down with secrets and shame and indecision. Maybe that's why she liked being with him so much. He was free and she wanted that too. He was also smart and funny and so different from other boys her age. So different from the Travis' of the world. *Martin would never do that to a girl.* Lavender had spent some time looking at the website and application for AmeriCorps. *Did he really want me to go with him? Or did he just say it because he thinks I'm going to college and wouldn't really say yes?*

She rounded the corner into her neighborhood, avoiding direct eye contact with the yard signs that were still there, shouting the college plans for the high school seniors who lived in the houses on her streets. She had to get out of there. No matter what happened after everyone learned the truth about her, Lavender couldn't stay in Siena at home with her parents. Living in a house filled with disappointment and a town empty of all the kids she'd gone to school with for the past thirteen years would be the worst-case scenario.

AmeriCorps was a viable option. Respected organization. Legitimate work for a cause. Real-world experience. Travel. Zero college parties. There really was no downside to the idea. Once her parents recovered from the shock of who their daughter really was, they would probably be on board with the plan. Lavender could pretend that she got the idea from her grandma and wanted to follow in her footsteps.

Lavender bounced up on the curb and sprinted the last 100 yards to her driveway. The future wasn't so scary anymore. She still had to figure out how she could divert everyone away from their expectations for her life without exposing herself and all her secrets, but that giant wave rushing to catch her, had less power than it did before. After her run, she would fill out the application. She would go to California. She would be with Martin. Maybe she would learn to surf.

THIRTY-TWO

"LAVENDER IS HERE," Mrs. Gordon yelled, opening the front door wide for her to enter. Lavender set her backpack down in the foyer and gave Mrs. Gordon the hug she was waiting for. "We're so glad you could make it on such short notice, and a school night!"

"No problem, Missus G. Happy to do it."

"Stevie. Sadie. Come say hi." They ran into the kitchen and hugged each one of her legs and then chased each other back out of the room. "Time for bed. Run upstairs and brush your teeth. We shouldn't be too long, two hours max. Do you have homework? Senior year is almost over, omg, do you have senior-itis?" Mrs. Gordon talked nonstop as she put her coat and lipstick on, grabbed her purse and Mr. Gordon from in front of the TV. She lowered her voice as they made their escape, "They are in their PJs and had dinner already. After they brush their teeth they can go directly to bed."

"Got it." Lavender gave her a thumbs up.

"Okay, see you soon." The Gordon's exited out the front and closed the door quietly behind them.

Lavender headed upstairs to finish the nighttime routine and get the kids to bed. Both Stevie and Sadie piled on Sadie's bed so she could read to them at the same time. They settled under the covers after picking out two books each for her to read.

"This one first," Sadie demanded.

"Then mine," Stevie chimed in.

"Okay, okay, let's do this." Lavender slowly read all four books and by the time she closed the last one, both kids were sound asleep. She scooped up Stevie as gently as possible and carried him to his own bedroom and tucked him in. She took one last look at Sadie, pulled the blanket up around her and made sure both rooms had their nightlights on. Stevie and Sadie were sweet and cute when they weren't running around terrorizing the house with their screams and messes, but she was glad they were down for the night so she could head back downstairs.

Lavender opened the fridge and saw there were seven bottles of beer on the bottom shelf. Plenty on hand for her to have one or two. *Maybe I should skip it tonight.* She was hesitant to partake in her questionable habit of drinking at the Gordon's house for two reasons. One, they were going to be back in an hour and a half, and two, she wanted to prove to herself that she wasn't addicted to beer and could choose to say no whenever she wanted to. She closed the refrigerator door without taking a bottle off the shelf. *I can do this.*

Lavender grabbed her laptop out of her bag on her way to the living room. She didn't feel like tackling any homework but had another idea. She found the AmeriCorps website and started reading. She read the *About* section, the history of the organization, she studied the programs currently in place and the opportunities for her age group willing to make a full-time commitment. Lavender reviewed every single FAQ. She couldn't remember a website that she had examined so thoroughly before. She looked for reviews and stories from other teenagers who had joined after high school. Her belly was fluttering, but with excitement. She hadn't felt that in a very long time. Maybe ever.

Lavender found some stories of AmeriCorps volunteers in California. There was Kayla who helped find housing for eighty-five adults who were living on the streets in Santa Barbara County, and Thu who was a first-generation immigrant from Vietnam who taught English as a second language to new citizens, and Carey, who helped teens in foster care transition out of the system and find independence safely. With each story, the buzz in her stomach amped up a notch. The organization even maintained a VISTA branch that began in 1965 that still focused on lifting entire communities out of the endless pit of poverty. *VISTA is what grandma did.*

Lavender finally felt a small piece of what Martin had. Clarity. Confidence. Direction. That was what she would do. She was sure of it. There were people who needed help and she could give it. That was her way out of the mess she'd created. Lavender was sure she could teach English or help teenagers who'd had a much tougher life than she had in Siena. She could tutor children and adults in literacy programs. She could run a food bank, or work with the elderly. She could make a difference. Her relationship with Louise had formed a soft spot in her heart for the vulnerable in the United States who were aging. The idea of sharing her newfound passion and adventure with Martin was a bonus. It was an opportunity to really do something big. Together. For the first time in her life, Lavender felt a pull on her soul that she'd never had before.

Lavender registered and created her account on the website. Before she lost her momentum, she dove headfirst into the eleven-page application form and the new life she'd found for herself. She listed her skills and experience and work history, which mostly consisted of babysitting and scooping ice cream. There was a whole section on Community Service, which was perfect. *Thank you, Ms.*

Clarke. She detailed her time spent at The Betsy Ross Home and the weekly visits she had completed. She conveyed her appreciation for a viable long-term care system that allowed the aging population grace and dignity while their lives were winding down. Lavender hadn't answered questions that clearly and quickly, ever.

Two sections gave her pause. The first was the motivational statement. *What was my motivation?* It had started out as finding something, anything, that would get her out of going to college, and out of Siena. Then it was the idea of meeting up with Martin to see if their relationship would feel as good in person as it did long distance. But now, after seeing the need and the possibilities to help those who were suffering, she could honestly say that she was motivated by the new call on her heart to make a difference, to build things, to create change. To use her intelligence and education and personality to help people who needed it. There was a big world outside of Siena, and she wanted to know every part of it. The eight-hundred-word minimum for the motivation statement was no problem for her to complete.

The second section that almost stopped her momentum was the last one, asking for references that weren't relatives or personal friends. She wouldn't have used relatives anyway since they all still thought she was going to BSU, and she didn't have any friends, so that was easy...she mentally ran through everyone else she knew. It was a short list. Could she trust Mrs. Gordon to not say anything to anyone? Probably not. She would use Martin. After all, he didn't live in her town so he wouldn't appear as a classmate. *Ms. Clarke!* Ms. Clarke would be a perfect reference. That was right up her *It's a Small World* alley. Lavender would love to use her grandma but there were two problems with that. They were related, and if they contacted her, she would probably say, Lavender who? *Oh, maybe Evelyn though...* Tattoo girl wasn't a girl at all. She was a grown woman with a job at Betsy Ross. That was perfect. She was sure Evelyn would be into it and willing to help her out. They weren't exactly friends but they had developed a mutual respect and rapport over the last few months. That was it. Her application was complete. She just needed to ask Evelyn and Ms. Clarke if they'd be a reference for her and add in their contact information. She assumed Martin was a no-brainer.

Mr. and Mrs. Gordon would be home any minute. She didn't have to stress about rinsing out beer bottles, getting them in her bag, or if she'd had enough time to metabolize all the beer to drive home safely. She hadn't missed the beer buzz or given it a second thought. It felt good, like maybe she didn't have a problem after all.

Lavender clicked on save and downloaded a copy of her application. She didn't want to risk losing all that she'd accomplished that night. She couldn't wait to tell Martin. Hopefully he would be excited and not think she was a stalker girl. Those two fifty-pound weights on her shoulders felt lighter and she could take a full, deep breath for the first time in months. Lavender still had to work out how to tell her parents that she wasn't going to college, and why, so it would have to be yet another secret. But there was the tiniest little crack in the wall of lies and shame surrounding her. That crack let in a glimmer of light big enough for hope. That was enough for now.

THIRTY-THREE

"79! SIENA, DID YOU HEAR ME? 79 days until graduation. You guys…" Hillary Charles was trying to be heard above the low rumble of distracted students in Ms. Clarke's Global/Lit class. Lavender might be the only one in the room who really did hear that number. *79. Holy shit. That's like, two and a half months.* "Also… Senior Superlative votes are due too-dayyyyyy…"

"Thank you Hillary." Ms. Clarke stood at the center of the room. "You're always so good at keeping everyone on track." Hillary reluctantly sat down, but her shoulders were pushed back and her head was high, turning to the left and right while she smiled just enough to make Lavender want to punch her.

"Class. It is true, we are winding down the school year. You should all be finishing the last round of discussion questions for *The Great Gatsby*. You should have, at least, thirty-two hours of community service logged and signed off on so far. And you should be almost done with the pen pal project. You only have one final email assignment, and that is to discuss the future of technology. What could be the greatest invention or discovery to date? What could technology give us that we desperately need? There's no right or wrong answer. Please use your Easter break wisely."

Even though the clock was ticking on Lavender's life and future, at least she was well ahead on her assignments for that class. She had more than completed the community service requirement and her and Martin emailed each other at least three times a week.

She'd scribbled some notes for the book club questions, but she'd finish that, no problem. Her real deadline was figuring out how to tell everyone in her life that she wasn't going to college without also telling them why she'd changed her mind, and then break the news that she was leaving for California with a boy none of them had ever met. She hadn't told anyone about Martin. How close they had become. The dates they'd had. How she felt about him. The plan to meet up after graduation. She didn't know why she'd kept it to herself. That was one secret that she didn't really need to keep but for some reason, she'd become secretive about everything. Because she'd locked down the truth about the party, the BSU application, her college plan, she automatically locked down everything in her life. Her parents didn't know how close she and Martin had become, or how much she'd grown to love Grandma Louise. She was keeping everything inside. Behind the walls. It was safer that way. But it was making it harder to transition to the new life that she was also planning covertly. *I need to talk to Jana. She could help me with my plan.* Lavender looked to her left and found Jana in her usual spot, doodling while Ms. Clarke droned on. Jana looked up just then and saw her staring at her. Jana held her gaze for just a moment before looking down again. *Does she miss me as much as I miss her? She probably hates me. I would.*

"I don't want to start anything the Friday before a break, so let's have some fun today." Along with the rest of the class, Lavender paused and looked up, waiting to hear what Ms. Clarke considered fun. "Who knows how the town of Siena got her name?" Silence. "Come on class. Most of you have lived here your whole life. You never thought about it?" *Actually, no, Ms. Clarke, never crossed my mind. Lol.*

Ms. Clarke projected her PowerPoint on the wall which started with a blank map of New York State. Each click of the remote triggered another town or city name to bounce, twirl or flash onto the map and land in its proper place. For the first round of slides, Ms. Clarke filled in those places rooted in the Native American legacy of the state.

"Did you know that even Manhattan was a Native American word? It means the *place where we get bows*. Who knew?" Ms. Clarke stood with her arms out waiting for someone to share the excitement she was bursting with. The next slides began to fill in a few of the neighboring cities and towns to Siena and Ms. Clarke asked the class what all those place names had in common. The room was still. "This is your biggest clue. Come on…" Ms. Clarke was desperate for someone to guess. "Verona. Florence. Turin. Rome. Siena…" The room began to hum as Lavender's classmates repeated the name of cities and towns that surrounded them, trying to place the connection. "Italy!!! They are all cities in Italy." Ms. Clarke sighed deeply at the ignorance and ambivalence of her students.

"For real?" Trevor asked.

Ms. Clarke turned around, ready to leap at the prospect of class participation. "Yes, Trevor, for real."

"Huh. Can't believe I never noticed that before," Trevor said.

Ms. Clarke finally had the class in her net, just like she wanted, and spent the rest of that period telling us about the Classical Naming Period and how it was common to name cities and towns in the new United States for old European towns. Even Beauville was European. France. By the end of class, the whole room was in her boat. Ms. Clarke was beaming. *This would be a good time to ask her.* After the bell rang, Lavender hung back to talk to Ms. Clarke. "Ms. Clarke?"

"Hi Lavender."

"I have a favor to ask."

"Oh? Sure, whatever I can do to help you. You know that." *Easy target...*

"I need a reference for something, and I wondered if I could use you."

"Sure. I'd be happy to do that for you. What's it for? A job?"

"Um, not exactly, but sort of. I'm applying for AmeriCorps."

"Whaaaat? You are?" Ms. Clarke looked skeptical, like she was on the verge of full-blown excitement but tempered with surprise. "Instead of college?"

"Yeah. I haven't told anyone yet, so...can it stay between us?"

"Definitely. That's amazing Lavender. AmeriCorps is part of the Peace Corps, you know."

"Yes, I know. All the work we've done this year on your *It's a Small World Project* has really inspired me." She knew she was laying it on thick, but she wanted to seal the deal and inspire Ms. Clarke to keep her promise on not telling anyone.

"That makes my heart so happy. You have no idea." Ms. Clarke wrote her full name, email and cell number on a sticky note and handed it to Lavender. "Let me know if I can help with anything else." Ms. Clarke wrapped her arms around Lavender and squeezed. "Sorry, I can't help myself."

"Thank you, Ms. Clarke. This means a lot." After escaping the embrace, Lavender moved to her next class. Her plan was moving forward. The second reference was nailed. She only needed one more before she could submit the application to her new life.

THIRTY-FOUR

LAVENDER POPPED THE TRUNK on the Malibu and pulled out the basket of goodies she had been collecting for her grandma. There was a box of the oatmeal raisin cookies that she loved, a soft brown bunny with pink ears, a chocolate rabbit, jelly beans and a tube of moisturizing hand and foot cream that smelled like spring. Outside Betsy Ross, the tulips and daffodils were bravely defying the cold and seemed determined to stand straight in the sunlight. The weather was cooperating with her plan.

"Hi Evelyn, Happy Easter."

"Hey. I thought maybe you weren't coming today."

"I know, I'm later than usual. But I did that on purpose. I waited until 11 when *Mary Tyler Moore* would be over. Is it cool if I take her out of here for a short road trip and lunch?"

"Sure. I just need you to sign something. No problem." Evelyn pulled out the drawer to her left and took out a piece of paper. "Just sign and date here and write Louise's name up here."

"Thanks. Hopefully she's up for it." Lavender did what Evelyn asked and returned the form and pen across the counter with a half-smile and shrug. Then she remembered what else she needed from Evelyn. "Um, can I ask you something else?"

"Sure, what's up?"

"I'm applying for this AmeriCorps program, you know, for after graduation, and I need references. They can't be family. Since I've been doing community service here, I wondered if I could use you?"

"Yeah, sure. No problem. What do you need?"

"Could you text me your last name, cell, and email? That should do it for now." Without another question, Evelyn handed Lavender her cell.

"Just put your number in here and I'll send you everything."

"You're awesome. I appreciate you."

Before Lavender reached the TV room, there was a text with all the information Tattoo girl had promised. *Sweet. That was it. Application will be done this weekend. California, here I come.*

With their favorite show over, the ladies in the TV room had moved on to debating the lunch menu.

"Smells like ham."

"No it doesn't. Besides, tomorrow's Easter, we'll have ham then."

"I thought I heard someone say pork chops."

"Smells like spaghetti to me."

"Hi Grandma," Lavender announced and then presented the basket to Louise who was in her favorite chair. Her grandma's face was blank at first. She was hoping that after all they'd shared for the last few months that her grandma would remember her name and who she was. They'd shared so many intimate things—the secrets, the stories, the songs, the foot rubs. They'd had moments together that connected their souls in ways that Lavender had never imagined they would. Lavender had told her grandma that she loved her and had truly meant it. She had hoped that all those moments could somehow penetrate the dementia and forgetfulness that Louise suffered with. Even though Lavender knew in her head that wasn't how it worked, in her heart, she wanted to believe she could love her grandma so much that her brain would heal, at least the part that knew

Lavender was her only granddaughter. She wanted love to be enough.

"I brought you presents for Easter."

"You did?"

"Yup."

"Wow, look at that," Rita said. "Nice basket."

"Are those jelly beans?" another woman said.

"I never liked Easter. All those bunnies and eggs," Sharon said.

"Shut up Sharon. Easter is sacred."

"The hell it is."

"Let's go. Lunch is ready."

Sharon, Rita and the other woman left for the dining room, leaving Lavender and her grandma in the TV room.

"Thank you. That was very nice." Her grandma picked up each item, held it up for examination and returned it to the basket. "I like all these things."

"Good." Lavender smiled at her. "Hey, I have another idea for Easter. Do you wanna get out of here for an hour or two and get some lunch with me?"

"You mean leave here?"

"Yeah, for lunch. Then I'll bring you back."

"Yes." Her grandma got up and carried the basket down the Potomac hallway to her room. Lavender followed close behind. "I just need to put my shoes on, my lipstick and my coat. Just a minute."

Lavender sat on the bed as her grandma fluttered around her little room, placing the Easter basket on her table by the window, sitting in a chair and tying her blue Keds on her size five feet, opening the top drawer of her nightstand and passing her finger over the whole row of little white lipstick sample tubes until she found just the right shade. A light pink. Finally, she grabbed her winter coat out of her closet and put it on.

"I'm ready to go," her grandma said with a smile.

"Let's do this."

They walked back to the center of the building and then headed for the front desk.

"Hey Lav." Evelyn stood up before they opened the double doors. "You have my number. Just in case." Lavender stopped and looked at her, then nodded.

"Have fun kids," Evelyn said as they moved out the door.

Lavender held her grandma's elbow as they headed for the white Chevy Malibu that used to belong to Louise. "Here's my car." She unlocked the passenger door and opened it for Louise. Once they were both inside, she started the car and turned up the heat. Lavender found the radio station that played jazz and kept the volume on low.

"Nice car," Grandma said.

Should Lavender tell her grandma that it used to belong to her before she *gave* it to Lavender when her parents sent her to live at Betsy Ross? Should she tell her that the dream catcher hanging from the rearview mirror was really hers and had been hanging there for fifteen years or more? Should Lavender tell her how she used to ride in the front seat as a little girl and wish her grandma would invite her to stay overnight at her house?

"Thanks. I love it." Lavender decided it was best to just let the woman be and not try to force her to remember things she didn't. She'd let the universe take care of that.

"Where are we going?" Grandma asked.

"I thought we'd go for a drive along the lake and then have lunch. How does that sound?"

"Okay."

She navigated the streets of Siena and turned north out of town towards the lake. She made sure to keep her speed under the legal limit and was extra careful all around. *Precious cargo.* Her dad used to say that whenever they would steal away for a ride, just the two of them. Lavender would get to sit in the front seat of his truck, her legs dangling without reaching the floor. She felt like a VIP riding high next to him. Like she was the most important person in the world. Whenever someone would pass him, or honk at his cautious driving, he'd say, *That's okay buddy. I got precious cargo.*

They drove in silence for almost thirty minutes with only the sound of low jazz horns blowing on the radio, watching the passing landscape that was fighting to be green again with spring grass and leaves budding on trees.

"This is what I miss the most," Louise finally said. "All of this. I used to pack up my babies and take them for rides. Especially when they were being fussy or difficult. I'd get them in the car, turn on the radio and just drive."

The Black Lantern was an old diner at the far end of the lake. Lavender pulled in and parked the car. "You hungry Gram?" "Famished."

They got out of the car and sat in a booth by the window. Lavender ordered a cheeseburger with fries and her grandma ordered a Reuben sandwich and chips. The diner had red paper placemats with scalloped edges and lightweight silverware. Their water was served in hard plastic tumblers and the waitress was all business. When their sandwiches were served they were all business too, eating everything on their plate. They didn't talk much.

"You want dessert?"

Her grandma snorted, "I couldn't eat another thing."

Lavender went to the register at the front counter to pay the check and returned to the booth to get her grandma in her coat.

"That was good, wasn't it? Let's get back before it gets dark, okay?" Lavender said.

"Alright."

Back in the car, Lavender headed down the opposite side of the lake. She changed the radio station to the oldies channel where they played all the songs from the sixties, seventies and eighties. They were reaching the town limits of Siena when her grandma began to get a little fidgety in her seat.

"You were supposed to turn back there."

"We're good Gram. I'm going the right way."

"No. My house is back there. You need to turn around."

"Really gram, it's okay. This is how we came from Betsy Ross, right?"

"I need to go home."

"We talked about this, remember? A ride, lunch, and then back to your new home. At Betsy Ross. With Sharon and Rita..." Lavender was nervous. Maybe it was a mistake to take her out.

"Can you please just turn here?"

Lavender took the next right. She thought that maybe if she went along with her grandma, she'd realize her home wasn't anywhere near there and give up the idea.

"Do you see it?" Louise was looking intently at every house on the street. "No. This isn't it. Take the next left." Again, Lavender complied and turned left. "This isn't it either."

"How about I head this way Grandma?" She would pretend to look for her house but really head towards Betsy Ross.

"No, I said. Go that way." Grandma pointed right that time. Lavender had an idea.

"I need gas. Let me fill up and then we'll keep looking, okay?" Lavender pulled the Malibu into the next gas station and rolled up to the pumps She got out of the car and pulled out her phone to text Evelyn.

> Hey. I need help.

What's up?

> Louise is insisting we drive around
> and look for her house. I've tried
> everything i can think of.

Oh boy. Take her for some ice
cream.

> Wtf????

Seriously. Try it. Promise, it works.

What the hell? Take her for ice cream? Lavender got back in the car, confused as ever, but willing to try anything at that point. "Let's get some dessert Grandma." She drove straight to Ren's Sweet Emporium on Maple. "What's your favorite? Chocolate? Vanilla?"

"I like a twist."

"Okay, twist it is. Be right back."

Lavender went inside and ordered two small twists on plain cones and brought them back to the car. They sat in the car and ate their ice cream. When they were over halfway done eating the cones, Lavender started up the car and got back on the road. Without a word, they drove back to the Betsy Ross Home.

"Here we are." Lavender got out and walked around to the other side. She held out her hand and her grandma grabbed it and let her tug her out of the front seat. Lavender was expecting a fight but didn't get one. She held her grandma's hand as they walked back through the front door.

"Hi Mrs. DuBose. Welcome home," Evelyn said while pushing the clipboard towards them. Lavender mouthed the words *thank you* while signing them back in.

"Are you tired Grandma? You want to take a nap before dinner?"

"Okay."

Lavender held her hand all the way down the Potomac hallway to her room and helped her out of her coat and sneakers and then covered her with the afghan after she lay down on the bed. She sat next to her and held her hand. "Thanks for coming with me today Grandma. I had fun with you."

"It was nice." Louise closed her eyes and loosened her grip on her hand.

Did she really enjoy it? Or did I just stress her out for my own selfish reasons? Lavender bent over and kissed her grandma on the forehead. "Love you. See you soon." She turned off the light on her way out and closed the door to her room.

The woman in the white hair and purple house dress was coming down the hallway. "Will you take me home?" she said while grabbing her breasts. Lavender couldn't respond. She was fighting the squeezing pressure in her throat that wanted her to cry. For her grandma, for that woman in purple, for all those people stuck in that purgatory between the homes they were desperate to go back to and their inevitable fate that was waiting for them. The hopelessness of mortality struck Lavender at her core in that moment. *This sucks. Is this what we all have to look forward to?*

"How's she doing?" Evelyn's voice jolted her out of her pity party.

"She's asleep. Your trick with the ice cream really worked."

"Yeah, I don't know what it is, but it always works. I think it changes the channel in their minds. Gets them out of that loop they get stuck in."

"Sucks for them being in here, doesn't it?"

"I guess you could look at it that way. I imagine that what we do here is helping them find their way, you know? They've done their duty on this earth and now it's our turn to walk beside them, wherever their journey takes them."

"You are a wise person, Miss Evelyn. Thank you for all you do for my grandma." Lavender opened the front doors and sucked in a lung full of the dusky air. Yes, she would walk beside Louise DuBose and help her find her way home.

THIRTY-FIVE

LAVENDER STARED AT THE CEILING wondering how she could avoid the family time that was expected on Easter Sunday. She ran through a list of possible scenarios to use. Sudden onset diarrhea so no one would want to be around her. Homework or studying for a test was a weak excuse because she had the next week off for Spring break. Newfound beliefs that prevented her from participating in a quasi-religious holiday would be a hard sell since they weren't going to church anyway. There was no way out of it.

Lavender decided to delay going downstairs for as long as possible and would prepare herself by getting her head right. She took out the diary that Martin gave her for Christmas. Moving her thoughts from her brain to the paper gave her mind some relief from the usual turmoil. She read her last entry before launching into the latest.

Easter Sunday
77 days until graduation. Tick. Tick. Tick.
Today is going to suck. The entire family is coming here for
dinner because Aunt Beck's kitchen is under construction,
so my mom volunteered our place. Which normally, I would
be all about not having to leave the house. However, having
dinner here is going to make it so awkward for me and Jackie.
I can hide in my room except for the actual meal at the table.
But... what would Jackie do? Would she expect to come to

my room and listen to music or watch movies? We haven't hung out in months. She gave up texting me. She gave up asking me what was wrong. It. Will. Be. Weird. The biggest bummer is that in spite of all that, I am so excited about my new plan to go to AmeriCorps after school. I wish I could tell my family. I wish I could tell Jackie. I wish they could be excited for me...oh well, you know what they say, if wishes were horses, beggars would ride. At least I have Martin. I'm going to tell him tonight. He will be excited.

Lavender took out her pic of Martin from her bedside stand and studied his face. She couldn't wait to see him in real life. *I wonder if his lips are soft.* She ached for his embrace even though she'd never known it. She was convinced that he would give the best hugs and that she would feel safe in his arms. She was sure of it. Thinking about her and Martin kissing and hugging and more, gave Lavender a warm buzz in her body, but unfortunately that line of thinking also triggered flashbacks to Travis. His lips were cold. His tongue was awful and unwanted. His fingers. The weight of him holding her down. Him inside her. *Noooooooo.* Lavender threw back her covers and stood up. She was tired of those memories haunting her and she hated that they took over her mind when she was thinking about Martin. He was good. He was her friend. She wanted him in her life. She wanted to feel him. *How will I ever get rid of that asshole Travis?*

She realized that staying in her room like that with too much time to think left space for the ticking countdown timer in her brain and the bad memories from that BSU party. She couldn't stay still. She must get up and get on with the day, no matter how awkward it was going to be. She would shower, dress in her Easter loungewear of a hoodie and joggers, and help her mom and dad get ready for company. Her strategy for the day would be to just keep moving. Keep trying to paddle so that wave wouldn't take her under.

"Hey Rosebud. Good morning. Happy Easter." Her dad was sitting at the counter drinking his coffee and reading the paper.

"Lavender. You're up." Her mom gave her a hug. "Happy last Easter before you go to college, lol." *So much for getting away from the timer.*

"Morning." Lavender sat next to her dad. "So what time is everybody coming? What's for dinner?"

"I told everyone to come at three, so you know this family, everyone will be here by two! We are having the usual suspects. I'm making the ham and rolls, and everyone else is bringing the sides and the dessert."

"Sounds great. Who's coming?" She was trying to find out if Jackie had found a worthy excuse to not show up.

"Mmmmm.... I think everyone is coming. I haven't heard otherwise."

"Nice," she said.

"Oh. Almost forgot. Your Easter basket." Her mom placed a *Home Goods* storage basket in front of her with green Easter grass holding an assortment of chocolate peanut butter eggs and Starbursts and gum, a coffee mug that said *Be Irreplaceable* in cursive, and a new pair of running tights. "You can use that basket in your dorm."

"Thanks Mom. This is great. I needed those tights."

"Here's another package." Her mom slid over in her direction a small rectangular box with a fitted lid, covered with a pattern of muted pink and purple flowers.

"What's this?"

"It was delivered yesterday to me. But when I opened it, this box was inside with a note."

"That said?"

"Something like, Hello Mrs. Finch. Please give this to Lavender on Sunday morning. Look forward to meeting you someday. Thanks, and Happy Easter. Martin." Her mom raised her eyebrows and did something weird with her lips.

Lavender took the box and lifted the lid. It was full of light purple M&Ms with the letter L printed in the center of each piece. There was a small, folded card. She opened the card just far enough to read the words but not so open that her mom could read it.

Happy Easter to my favorite person. May these delicious pieces of fake chocolate and all kinds of dye that is bad for you, fill your cute little tummy with pleasure. Haha. Seriously though, we are getting closer to seeing each other in person, and I can't wait. Love, Martin

Her mom and dad sat in silence, waiting for her to say something that would explain the present. "It's from Martin. The guy from my class assignment."

"I haven't heard about this guy. Where's he from?" her dad asked.

"He's her pen pal," her mom said.

"Is that still a thing?" her dad said.

"We had to email high school seniors around the world as part of an assignment. He lives in Cuba."

"Cuba?" Her dad said.

"His dad is stationed at the base there. He's a Chaplain."

"Huh." Her parents said in unison as they passed a looked to each other.

"I think he likes you," her mom said.

"Why?" Lavender thought she had done a good job of keeping her relationship with Martin a secret, and her feelings for him securely under cover.

"Well, I know you talk to him on the phone every week. He sent you Christmas presents, Valentine's Day presents and now Easter candy. Boys do not do that for a girl if they are not interested."

"He's nice. We have become really good friends. That's it."

"What are his plans after graduation? Is he going to college in the States?"

"He's not going to college."

That statement caused her mom to suspend the ham-glazing brush in mid-air and look at her dad again. "Really?" her mom asked.

"Yeah. He is spending at least a year in this program called AmeriCorps. It's like the Peace Corps only in the US."

"Huh." Her dad uttered the phrase again with a perplexed look on his face. It was all news to him.

"He's super smart. Loves photography. Wants to get some real-world experience first. I'm sure he'll go to college someday."

"If you don't go right after high school, you won't go. Trust me." With that wisdom drop her dad picked up the Sunday paper again.

"Interesting," her mom said. Lavender could tell she was trying to be non-judgmental and feign open-mindedness. "Hopefully we'll get to meet him someday. That is, if you guys are going to stay in touch after the assignment is over."

"I think we'll be friends. He's not like anyone else I know here in Siena." Her dad peaked over the top of the paper at her mom. Lavender stood up. *Keep moving. Keep paddling.* "What can I do? Want me to set the table?" She needed to jolt her parents back to the present situation where twenty people would be descending on their small house in just a few hours. "Let's put on some music while we work."

"Great idea Lav." Her dad got his Bluetooth speaker and turned on some eighties classic rock.

Lavender spent the next hour helping her dad put the leaves in the dining room table and set up the folding chairs and extra tables for the drinks and dessert stations, while her mom got the ham in the oven and the bread dough mixed for rising. It was the perfect solution for distracting them from looking too closely at Lavender's life. She knew they were curious and interested but she just wasn't ready to fully share Martin with them, or anyone yet. *Soon.*

Promptly at two o'clock, just as her mother had predicted, cars started rolling into the driveway until that was full and then they parked on both sides of the street. In a matter of fifteen minutes their quiet holiday vibe ended as their small house was overrun with her dad's family. Jackie arrived on her own twenty minutes after the initial rush.

"Lav, Jackie's here," her mom announced. Lavender pretended to be extremely interested in Aunt Rox's scalloped potatoes and the new method she had tried for layering the casserole. Anything to avoid the awkward. Jackie walked into the kitchen and gave Sara a hug and all the other adults in the room. She made her way to Lavender and stood in front of her.

"Hey," Jackie said.

"Hey, what's up?" Lavender said while avoiding direct eye contact. "Your hair looks great." *Keep moving.* She took the glass dish from Aunt Rox and looked for a place to set it down on the counter. "Everything smells so good."

That group hadn't been all together since New Year's Eve so there was nonstop conversation and catching up. Rather than escape to her room, Lavender sat at the kitchen counter and pretended to be interested in all of it until it was time to eat. After everyone found their seat at the extended table, her dad stood up to deliver a version of his usual pre-dinner toast.

"Let's take a moment and be grateful for the food before us, the family that surrounds us, and the good health and wealth that follows us. Cheers everyone." The adults clinked their wine glasses and responded with "Cheers." Jackie reached across the table to knock her water glass with Lavender's. "Cheers Cuz." Lavender nodded and knocked her glass. She had no right to miss her cousin so much. She was the one who closed off any form of communication and abandoned their relationship. It was all her fault. She had to figure out a way to fix it.

"So, Lavender. Are you counting down the days?" Aunt Beck asked. Lavender inhaled sharply and almost choked on the piece of ham she had just put in her mouth. "You know, until graduation? Are you having a party?" Not to be left out of anything, her aunts and uncles swerved into the conversation, like shark following chum.

"Party...am I invited?"

"What's the date? I want to get it on my calendar."

"You can use my two pop-up tents if you want."

"What should I bring? Potato salad?"

"My neighbor makes the cutest custom graduation cakes."

"You know, we haven't talked about that yet," her mom finally chimed in with. "I guess we'll have to look at the calendar and pick a weekend."

"I'm not sure I'm having one," Lavender said.

"No party?"

"Why not?"

"You'll get lots of cash that will come in handy your first semester at college."

"I don't know. We'll see." Lavender continued to focus on her plate of ham, scalloped potatoes, green bean salad, some sort of corn dish, and her buttered roll. For the fourth or fifth time that day her mom and dad exchanged a look. She could tell they knew something was off with her. How could they not? For the past seven months or so, she had been keeping secrets and lying to all of them.

Eventually they all moved on to discussing Aunt Beck's kitchen project. She breathed a sigh of relief and relaxed a little while she finished her food. *I wonder if Martin is having dinner right now. Next year at this time, we'll be in California together.* When the meal was over, she helped clear the table, put the leftovers away and load the dishwasher.

"We got this, Lav, if you and Jackie want to go hang out in your room," Aunt Beck said.

"Oh, that's okay. I want to help. Maybe we can play some pitch after we clean up. We haven't done that in a while." When she was younger, the family had legendary pitch tournaments. The card game was best played with teams of two who sat opposite each other. Each family brought a deck of cards, and they split up the group in multiple games and played to a score of eleven. The winning pair from each game then played another until they were down to the final match with the last two surviving teams. That game played to a score of twenty-one. Lavender was always the scorekeeper and there was an old notebook somewhere that held the column of numbers from years of games played, counting the points from High, Low, Jack, and Game.

"That's a great idea Lav. We haven't played cards in forever."

For the rest of the afternoon and evening, her aunts and uncles laughed, drank wine, played cards and never asked about graduation or college again. Lavender and Jackie stayed downstairs and played with them and avoided any alone time. *Keep moving.*

Lavender was exhausted. It took a lot of effort to hide behind that wall she had built by avoiding one-on-one conversations and honest answers to people's questions about her life and her future. At least that was the last family holiday for a while. By the time July 4th rolled around, everything would be out in the open. Lavender still didn't know how or when or what she would do to make that happen, but she needed to figure it out. She was at her desk with the laptop open to the AmeriCorps site. She logged into her account and clicked *Resume.* She added the contact info she had gathered for Evelyn and Ms. Clarke and added in Martin's details as well. She knew he wouldn't mind. Lavender read through the entire application again and was ready to hit submit. There was a knock on her door. Had to be her dad. "Come in."

"Hey Rosebud. Just wanted to say goodnight."

"Goodnight Dad." She looked up from her laptop.

"Long day, huh?"

"Yeah, but it was fun."

"You good Sweetie? Everything ok?"

Her dad was the most sincere, genuine, and hard-working person she knew. He had absolutely zero drama in his life. She felt the worst lying to him. She knew someday soon she would have to break his heart when he found out the truth about his only daughter. That made her sad. "I'm good Dad. Really."

"Ok. If you say so. Love you." Before he closed the door, she looked at him and half smiled so he'd believe her. She had to keep moving towards her new plan and find a way to make it happen. She refreshed her screen and stared at it for a minute or two. The submit button was highlighted and ready for her click. *Can I really do this? California? Martin? Leave Siena?* Of all the questions and thoughts and scenarios that traipsed around her brain on the daily, that one felt right. She felt a pull on her soul. Just like she did with Martin. *Yes. I can do this.* She clicked on submit and closed her laptop. *Done.*

Lavender moved to her bed and slid under the covers. It was almost ten and Martin was always on time. Her phone buzzed but when she picked up, it was a video call. *What the fuck? Video?* She ran her fingers through her hair and then under her eyes to get rid of the smeared mascara she knew was there. No time to do anything else.

"Hi," she said, trying not to sound surprised.

"Hey you."

"FaceTime? I didn't know we were doing that."

"I know, I'm sorry. I should have asked ahead of time. But I just really wanted to see your face tonight. It sounds weird, but I missed you."

"It's fine. But don't judge. I'm a hot mess."

"You look beautiful."

Lavender was distracted by her face on the phone screen and tried to find an angle that was flattering. The light in her room was dim so that helped. "Thank you for the box of M&Ms. Custom made!"

"Haha, you're welcome. I couldn't resist. How was your Easter?"

"It was good. We had dinner here. The whole family came over, so it was a lot. But it was fun. We played cards. How was yours?"

"Nice. We did church, an egg hunt after that, and then dinner. It was all good. But this is what I was looking forward to all day." Lavender sighed and smiled. Tears started to form in her eyes and then she remembered she was on camera and he could see everything. *How does this boy that I've never met in person know me so well? How did he know I needed this today?*

"Hey guess what?" She kept the conversation moving.

"What?"

"I made a decision."

"Sounds serious."

"Kind of. I applied to AmeriCorps too." She watched his face.

"You did?" He smiled and pumped his right fist in towards his waist as he mouthed a silent and long *yes*.

"Yup. I used you as a reference. I hope that's okay."

"Of course. That's the best news I've heard in a long time."

"Really? You don't think I'm like, a stalker girl? Following you?"

"No. It's great. We are going to change the world together. Me and you, Lavender Rose Finch. You...made my night."

They spent the next hour talking. About when AmeriCorps would notify them of their acceptance and assignment. They made lists of what they would need to pack and take with them. About California. They made lists of what they wanted to do and see while they were there. The Hollywood sign. The beach. Redwoods. Big Sur. Golden Gate Bridge. Surf. Lavender hadn't been that excited about anything all year, maybe ever. It felt good. It felt right.

"You ready for a song?" Martin asked. It was late. They had covered a lot of ground in the last hour.

"I am." Lavender considered for a moment whether she should say what was on her mind, or not, but decided to be brave. "Martin?"

"Yes?"

"You make me happy." She wasn't used to expressing feelings like that to anyone, much less a boy on FaceTime that she'd known for just a few months.

"Same," he said and nodded his head. "Goodnight Lavender. Sweet dreams." They turned their cameras off while they played their songs to each other. She went first with the Led Zeppelin song, "Going to California." Martin followed her theme and ushered them into sleep with "California Dreamin'."

THIRTY-SIX

51 DAYS... FIFTY...TICK...ONE...TICK...BOOM. Her life was about to implode, and Lavender had no escape plan. She was stuck. Frozen. Unable to figure a path out. A path out from behind her wall of lies, secrets and shame that she'd been hiding behind for two hundred days or more, depending on when she started counting. The day after the party at BSU when she knew that she would never, ever, set foot on that campus again? Or maybe it was less than two hundred days if she counted from when she lied about submitting her college application or was it that day Lavender let everyone believe she had been accepted and her mother placed that college sign in the front yard. *Go Bulldogs*. None of that really mattered because the countdown timer was only focused on one thing, and that was June 16th. 51 days away.

Lavender looked around the auditorium. She sat in the last row. Jana was on the left side closer to the front, sitting with new friends. Hillary was positioned in front of the microphoned podium on stage. Ms. Clarke and the other teachers stood along the right side where they gave an appearance of adult supervision, but Lavender imagined they were really talking about the weekend and where they were meeting for happy hour. There were probably two hundred and fifty seniors in the rows in front of her, all talking to those seated around them and shouting to more who sat a few rows away. Wadded up paper was tossed to knock somebody in the back of the head. Shrill notes were randomly let loose while the whistler pretended it wasn't them. Messages were passed. High-fives, fist bumps, the occasional hug. They were giddy with excitement. Excitement about the announcements today, about being seniors, about having only fifty-one days left in the school that they'd all inhabited for the past four years. She could see their lightness. Their anticipation. Their nervous energy. She knew what it looked like, but Lavender could not feel it. She was numb or maybe not even that because numb suggested a certain sensation. She felt nothing. The absence of any identifiable emotion. Lavender looked at the faces around her, most she had known since elementary or middle school, and yet they were like complete strangers. Like she was an extra on a movie set. She was on the outside looking in, no more than a casual observer of her senior year of high school. She was alone.

Hillary Charles ran down the list of all the important days that were left in the school year. There was the last day to buy tickets to the Ball. Then the actual Senior Ball. Class Night. Graduation. Tick. Tick. Tick. Once the announcements were complete, Hillary moved on to the purpose for the assembly. Senior Superlatives. The votes were tallied, and the names of the chosen were in sealed envelopes that the Class VP handed to Hillary, one category at a time. Hillary did her best Hollywood-award-show-host impersonation as she announced the category and what it meant. "We all want to find that perfect person, our soulmate, and have the kind of romance we only read about or watch on Netflix. The winners of this award that we're call-ing RELATIONSHIP GOALS, are…" A moment of silence while Hillary unsealed the oversized envelope… "Of course it is you two lovebirds. Sooooo jelly. Abby and Brandon, come on up." Abby and Brandon held each other around the waist as they walked on stage while the audience applauded, whistled, barked, and in some cases stood. Lavender and Jana used to roll their eyes and silently gag whenever they walked by them at lunch time, huddled in the corner with their mouths in a lip lock and their hands looking for a fast grope before the bell rang. Lavender almost gagged watching them walk up on stage. By Hillary's definition the couple had been soulmates since the eighth grade.

Lavender considered the possibility that Martin may be her soulmate. They'd had another date last weekend where they browsed a bookstore while drinking coffee at the same time on Sunday afternoon. They texted each other updates after the coffee was purchased, and then again when they entered their respective bookstores. They had planned to browse by section. New titles first. They were always on display at the front of the store. Then nonfiction, fiction, photography, and history. They spent hours looking at book covers, reading the backs of those that caught their eye as well as the opening sentence. If it made an impression after all that, they texted the other the title and author so they could try and find the same one on the shelves in their store. Lavender bought her mother a novel that was rated high by the book club crowd and Martin helped her find a book of photos that her grandma might like. Louise was stuck inside that Betsy Ross home for the rest of her life and Lavender wanted to bring her some beauty to behold. She would give both their books on Mother's Day. Later that night, on their Sunday phone call, which had been a video call since that first one on Easter, they shared their top five finds of the day. With Martin she felt something. He saw her. He knew her. He was curious and interested and relaxed about all of it. He was easy. She'd never had a soulmate before, but she imagined it felt something like him. Abby and Brandon had probably never been to a bookstore together or had discussed how a writer earned their attention with a powerful opening sentence or the reasons why a certain scene in a story moved them.

The awards continued and were announced in the same dramatic fashion and the winners were ushered up on stage by the applause of their fellow seniors. The male and female version of the MOST ATHLETIC, the MOST LIKELY TO GO VIRAL, followed by the two to have the MOST FOLLOWERS, then the comedians who lived to make everyone laugh and the two whose big mouth or suspect behavior might get them canceled someday. Didn't the animals of Noah's Ark go two-by-two? Lavender would ask Martin about that later.

Jana's dedication and devotion to her appearance and her wardrobe paid off as she was escorted onstage by her co-winner of the WHO WORE IT BEST category, Chad Daniels. That was the only award that Lavender clapped for. There were only two awards left and Lavender was watching the clock, wishing for time to speed up, just that once, so she could get out of the Senior Superlative scene that she had no interest in participating in. The HAIR category was next. Hillary opened the envelope, and for the first time, maybe ever, was speechless. It looked like her head might pop off her neck. Hillary stuttered and stammered and read the guy's name first. John Manetti had a thick mane of black wavy hair, that was almost to his collar, parted on the side. That made sense. Hillary looked at her Vice President. The pause and silence caught Lavender's attention. Hillary was upset about something. Then Hillary read the girl's name on the award and Lavender knew why.

"Hillary Charles." The class whistled and cheered. Hillary Charles read her own name as the winner for the I WANT YOUR HAIR superlative. To be fair, Hillary's hair was her best feature.

It was very Jessica Chastain or Emma Stone and it had been the same color since Lavender first met her in kindergarten. Back then, she wore pigtails or braids but for the last five or six years, it had been in the same longish bob. Lavender had to admit, Hillary's hair was consistently on point. Hillary's surprise was obvious when her face filled in with color, her speech slowed its cadence, and her tone lowered an octave or two as she introduced the very last award. She was definitely not expecting to win the HAIR award.

The final award, MOST LIKELY TO BE CEO, was for those that showed academic success but more importantly, was a leader among their peers. That was the award Hillary had been working for her entire academic career. Was it possible to win two superlative categories?

"Noah Stone and…" Again, Hillary paused and looked at her vice president like something was very wrong, her face pinched in a weird shape. "…and Lavender Finch?" Hillary said in a whisper, her tone rising at the end in a question mark.

What did she just say? Hillary said the names again, replacing the question mark with a period. "Noah Stone and Lavender Finch. Please come up on stage." Hillary closed the envelope and took a step back. The room full of strangers applauded. *Is this a prank?* Noah Stone was out of his seat, his arms raised in the air, his fists pumping, moving towards the stage. There didn't seem to be a punchline coming, so Lavender slowly stood and moved out of her seat and walked the long aisle to the front of the auditorium, her legs trembling, her arms hanging uncomfortably at her side, unsure of what they should be doing. Lavender didn't understand why her classmates would think she could be CEO of anything. Her life was a complete mess. True, her grades weren't far behind

Hillary's and were probably in the top ten percentile, but Hillary would be valedictorian. There was no doubt about that. Shouldn't the valedictorian be CEO?

Lavender climbed the steps with Noah at her side and they walked to the end of the line of winners. Hillary explained that the yearbook deadline was looming, and no one could leave the stage until the photographer that was standing by got their pics. Two-by-two, each group of winners were pushed over to the photo booth at stage right so they could select the appropriate props and pose in front of the Instagram-worthy screen. Lavender congratulated Noah and he said the same to her. She watched Jana wrap a pink boa around her neck and set a tiara on her head while Chad picked up a pair of dark shades. After their turn in the photo booth, Jana walked towards her and stopped right in front of Lavender. They looked at each other for a long moment. Jana's face softened, "I miss you Lav. Congratulations. You probably will be CEO somewhere someday. Good for you." The words Lavender wanted to say back were on the tip of her tongue. Words of apology and excuse and regret. She wanted to tell Jana how much she missed her too, how the school year had sucked without her, how her life was so empty now. But how could Lavender say all that? She was the one who walked away. She left Jana. Not the other way around. Lavender wanted to tell her about Martin, and her grandma, and how she wasn't going to BSU but had a great plan to help people on the opposite side of the country, so far away from Siena. Lavender wanted to tell her all of it. But instead, she smiled and said, "Congratulations Jana. You always knew you'd get that award, and you did. Good for you. You deserve it." Jana nodded and looked down before she said she'd see Lavender around and walked off stage.

The photographer convinced Lavender to put on a blazer, pose with her hand in one pocket, with her legs wide. A confident stance for a future boss. A strong, independent woman. As if she was in an airtight chamber, void of any sound or movement, Lavender was once again a silent observer through the glass, looking at a life that was supposed to be hers. Instead, she was just a girl, fighting to jump and catch the ball that was supposed to be her life, her people, her future, but was always just out of reach. Monkey in the middle.

THIRTY-SEVEN

"I CAN DRIVE MY CAR," Lavender said.

Her mom paused for just a second at her unexpected offer but then nodded and said, "Okay. Go for it," and opened the passenger door of the Malibu and got in.

For the past nine months, Lavender had been going to Betsy Ross by herself to visit Louise. She had purposely kept her developing relationship with her grandma to herself. Not that getting to know her grandma was a bad thing; it was just the opposite. Her connection with her grandma was more intimate and closer than it had ever been, and Lavender wanted to savor every last bit of it by herself. She didn't want to make any moves that would jinx it or change what had been happening between the two of them. She finally felt like she had a grandma and didn't want to lose her.

"Hmph. I haven't ridden in this car in a very long time," her mother said.

"I like it. It's the only thing of Grandma's that I have."

"Do you think you'll take it to campus? I'm not sure freshmen can have a car. We'll have to check on that."

Lavender stared straight ahead and turned on the radio. She hadn't thought about her car, but her mom was right about one thing, she couldn't take it where she was going. Or could she? She knew Martin would fly from Cuba, so she just assumed she would fly too, but maybe...he could fly to New York, and they could ride to California together. Road trip. Romantic? Or Foolish? *Would the Malibu even make the trip?*

Lavender parked in her usual spot and they both commented on how full the parking lot was that Sunday and how beautiful the flowers were that bloomed in front by the flagpole. Evelyn was in her usual spot as they both signed the visitor log. Lavender was caught off guard when Evelyn greeted her mother with the same friendliness that she greeted Lavender with. Her mom was a regular there too.

"Happy Mother's Day Grandma," Lavender said as she bent down to hug Louise, "How are you doing today?" Her grandma jumped slightly in her chair and looked up with wide eyes trying to place the voice, the touch, the face. "It's me. Lavender."

"Oh. Hi," her grandma said, trying to get a look at who was standing behind her.

"Hi Mom," Sara said.

"We came together today. Remember? I'm Sara's daughter," Lavender said.

"I know." Louise stood up.

Sara handed Louise a bouquet of flowers. "These are for you. Happy Mother's Day." Her mom hugged Louise and gave her a kiss on the cheek.

"They are beautiful." Louise looked at them both, her eyes unsure but smiling. "Let's take them to my room." Louise led the charge while Lavender and her mom followed behind as they walked down the Potomac hallway. She grabbed the vase by the window, leftover from the Valentine's Day flowers, filled it with water, placed the new bouquet inside and settled the vase on the small table. "There. That looks nice," her grandma said.

"It does. I brought you another present Grandma, and you too, Mom." Lavender pulled out the photography book that she and Martin had found on their date at the bookstore. She handed the oversized package in gold paper with a purple bow in the center to her grandma, and a smaller one with the same wrapping to her mom. Lavender watched her mom and grandma as they both loosened one piece of tape at a time and carefully unfolded the paper to slowly reveal what was inside. Watching both women unwrap their presents and register the identical look with raised eyebrows and a small smile, Lavender was struck by the sameness of their mannerisms. She tended to think of her mom in a vacuum, as a singular entity who had only existed to be her mom, but Sara had been Louise's daughter longer than she'd been Lavender's mom. Same with her grandma. Lavender appreciated her newfound relationship with her grandma so much, but in that moment realized that her daughter, Sara, had won her heart first, many years ago. That realization didn't trigger envy in Lavender. Instead, it made her feel like she was part of a long line of love. Imperfect and filled with disappointment, untruths, and sadness, but love, nonetheless. Did her mom know that her brother Michael had a different father named Miguel and that grandma was pregnant before she married? Did Lavender's mom know that grandma drank to nurse a wound, inflicted by the loss of her love Miguel, the loss of her baby boy Michael, and the betrayal of a man who broke every vow? None of that seemed to matter so many years later. In spite of it all, the love between the mother and daughter was still there. Lavender could see it.

For a moment, Lavender considered the possibility of telling those two women her own secrets and trusting that they would embrace her and tell her it all was going to be okay, that she was okay. If she told them about Travis and what happened to her at the party, about her lies that she applied and was accepted to BSU, and that she was instead joining AmeriCorps with Martin, could they handle it? Or would they be so surprised by her deceit it would change how they saw Lavender permanently? If they knew everything about her, would they still love her?

Her grandma sat at the table with the photography book. "These are wonderful pictures."

"I thought you might like them. They are supposed to be the most beautiful scenes from each country around the world."

"So lovely. I will look at every one of them later," her grandma said.

"Thanks Lav. I've heard great things about this book. Everyone is talking about it," her mom said.

"Cool. Glad you like it," Lavender said, "Martin helped me pick them out." She threw out that little tidbit and waited for the response.

"He did?" her mom said immediately, while whipping her head one hundred eighty degrees and sucking her face into a pinched and withdrawn look, that only a mom could pull off. Lavender laughed out loud. "How? Isn't he in Cuba?"

"Lol, yessss, but we went to the bookstore, together," Lavender said, making air quotes with her hands.

"Huh. You'll have to explain that one to me on the way home."

"Well tell your friend I said thank you. I love it," her grandma said, saving Lavender from having to explain any more. That little tease of information was enough. She had given her mom a little peek on the other side of her wall.

"Are you hungry Mom?" Sara asked. "I think the luncheon is about to start."

"What luncheon?"

"For Mother's Day. They're doing something special in the dining room."

"Oh? Let me put on some lipstick and then we can go."

Her grandma led the charge again, back down the hallway, through the center lounge with the TV, to the dining area. Evelyn waved at Lavender when they walked into the decorated room, set up with round tables of eight draped in white tablecloths, pastel-colored paper flowers in each center, along with a card that announced bold numbers on a metal stand. They found three seats together at table 09. They spent the rest of the afternoon at that table with two other sets of mothers and daughters. Evelyn was the emcee of the event and introduced all the residents at each table and had them stand for applause. She also coordinated the awards for the mothers in the room who had the most children, the one who drove the furthest distance to get there, the oldest mother and the youngest mother. Evelyn also played DJ and turned on some classic soft rock while she called each table by the number they'd been assigned. When table 09 was called, Lavender looped her arm through her grandma's and walked with her to the buffet line. Once they both filled their plates, Lavender carried her grandma's back to the table for her. The three of them commented on how the roast beef was good but the ham was dry, and the mac and cheese was yummy but the potatoes needed salt, and they talked about the spring weather and the rain that was coming, and they listened to the music playing in the background.

Her grandma didn't each eat much food. Her plate was still full. "Weren't you hungry Gram?" Lavender asked.

"Meh. Not really."

Lavender exchanged a look with her mother.

"You should try to eat a little more Mom, I'm not sure if they'll have a big dinner later."

"I'm fine. My appetite isn't what it used to be."

Another look.

"You feel okay?" Sara asked.

"A little tired, but I'm not sick. Just not hungry." Her grandma's voice was sharp, like she clearly wanted to stop that line of questioning and focus away from her eating and health. The volunteer staff cleared away the dishes. Lavender got up and walked over to where Evelyn was counting individual plates that already had slices of cake on them.

"Hey."

"Hey Lavender. What's up? How was dinner?"

"Everything was good, but I wanted to ask you about Louise. Has she been okay lately?"

"Mmmm. I did notice that she overslept a few days this week and missed *Mary,* which is highly unusual, as you know. Why?"

"She didn't eat much today and said she was tired. She just seems off."

"I'll leave a note for the nurse to check her out and let you or your mom know if she has any concerns."

"That'd be great. Thank you."

After the cake was served, Louise announced that she was done and stood to leave. Rather than try to convince her to stay for the games that were planned, Lavender and her mom followed her back to her room.

"Why don't you lie down and take a nap. I'll rub your feet," Lavender said. Her grandma got on the bed, slipped off her Keds, and lay back. Lavender grabbed the afghan and covered her up. She opened the top drawer of the bedstand and took out the lotion that she had given her in her Easter basket. "This one smells nice. Is this okay?" Her grandma nodded. Lavender found the speaker and turned on some soft instrumental music they might play at a spa during a massage. Lavender looked up and noticed her mom was in a chair at the table, watching them. She removed her grandma's socks and slowly rubbed her tiny and worn feet with the lotion and the lightest of pressure. No one said a word. After her grandma was asleep, Lavender and her mom turned out the light and shut the door and walked to the parking lot.

"She always loved you, you know?" her mom said.

Lavender nodded but kept her head straight. "I know."

"I know she wasn't always there when you were growing up…"

"It's okay."

"It's not okay, it was never okay, but…I'm glad you two…," her mother's voice trailed off.

"Me too Mom."

"You know, she wrote a poem when you were born and gave it to me at the hospital."

"She did?"

"Yup. I have it somewhere, maybe in your baby book. It's how you got your middle name. I'll find it when we get home."

The low music from the car radio played while they rode the rest of the way in silence. Lavender went straight to her room for homework and to think about her new idea of driving to California. She would mention it to Martin that night on their Sunday call. A few hours later, her mother knocked on the door and handed Lavender a small scrap of paper with worn edges, kissed her on the top of the head and said, "Goodnight. I love you."

Lavender stared at the faded blue ink in neat cursive writing and tried to imagine a younger Louise whose hands penned those words, about her. *Did she hold me? Did she buy me a newborn outfit? Did she kiss my head or whisper in my ear?* Maybe. Maybe not. Maybe that's why she wrote that poem.

Little Lavender Rose

Her small demanding presence fills
My heart with wonder and with song.
She is so tiny and warm and sweet!
So fair and rosy-limbed and strong.

Her eyes are blue delphiniums,
Her tiny mouth, a rosebud red.
Such blond hair. It almost curls
Around her lovely little head.

"Isn't she beautiful?" We cried,
in fond maternal ecstasy.
"Oh! I don't know," you replied,
"All babies look alike to me."

THIRTY-EIGHT

30 days until graduation. Tick. Tick. HOLY FUCKING SHIT.

To be honest, I was never one of those girls who started dreaming of the Junior Prom or the Senior Ball when I turned thirteen. I didn't have a fantasy dress that I'd been designing in my head. Jana did. She'll have her hair in a fancy updo tonight and will wear something classic. A long gown with a slit, some killer shoes, not too much cleavage. Jana's told me so many times what she dreamed this night would be like. I hope it is. I miss her.

I also never had any romantic delusions about losing my virginity to the 'one' on a night such as this. That's off the table now anyway thanks to...Stop! Not going to let my mind go there today. Too many good things to think about. I finally have a real plan for after graduation! I must figure out how to break the news to everyone, but at least Martin and I will meet each other (can't wait!), road trip my car to the opposite coast (California!) and work together to change the world for AmeriCorps. FU BSU. I don't need you...

"Lavender!" her mom said, outside her bedroom door.

"Yeah?"

"Can I come in?"

Lavender closed her diary and dropped her feet off her desk to the floor. "Sure."

"This was just delivered, for you."

"What is it?" She accepted the small square box from her mother.

"I don't know, silly," her mom said, "you have to open it."

Lavender loosened the clear tape at the top and slowly lifted the cardboard cover. Inside was a beautiful white rose surrounded by delicate green shoots of something, nestled on cream colored tissue paper. She gently lifted it out of the box.

"It's a corsage!" her mom said, "for your wrist…"

"What? Why?"

Her mom took the box and found a folded card at the bottom and read it out loud. "Dear Lavender. This is for you. Just in case you decide to go to your Senior Ball tonight. A beautiful flower for a beautiful girl. And if you decide to stay home instead, wear this corsage anyway knowing that there's a boy in Cuba who wishes he could be your date tonight. Love, Martin." Her mom didn't move a muscle for a solid sixty seconds. Neither did she. "Wow, Lav." Her mom's mouth was still open, a hand on her left hip. "You did not tell me this was so serious."

Lavender took the card from her mother's hands and read it again. She smelled the rose and wished Martin was there with her. She wished he could be her date too. *Maybe I could go to the Ball tonight. Martin would sort of be with me.*

"You know…I can call Aunt Beck and get one of Jackie's dresses. We can make this happen…" Not only did her mom read her mind, as only moms can do, but she also understood that Lavender couldn't text Jackie herself after all those months of ghosting their relationship.

"Really? Isn't it too late? I don't have a ticket…or a ride…or a plan…"

"I'm sure you can get a ticket online. Your dad can take you or you can Uber. I'd rather you didn't drive."

Lavender looked at her mom. She looked at the rose from Martin. She looked out her window.

"Ok. Let's do it. I'll go to the Ball." Lavender stood and put her hands on her mother's shoulders. They were the same height. "But Mom…this is low key…don't be extra today…no big deal… promise?"

"I can be cool. Low key. I'm on it." Her mom gave her a nod, touched her nose with her finger and then pointed at Lavender. "I got you girl."

Lavender rolled her eyes at her mother's attempt to be chill. Sara left the bedroom to secure a borrowed dress. She sat back down at her desk and opened her diary.

…OMG!!!! Martin sent me a white rose and now I'm going to my Senior Ball! My mother is calling Aunt Beck right now to see if we can borrow one of Jackie's dresses. This is either going to be fun or a complete disaster! Either way it will be a night to remember. Stay tuned.

Lavender made a mental list in her head. Ticket. Shower. Dress. Ride. She picked up her phone and started to text Jana. An old habit. Muscle memory at work. She stopped herself. Could she? Should she? She opened her laptop instead and went to the school website. Hillary's handiwork was front and center with a large clickable button, "Buy Senior Ball Tickets Here!" Lavender had to admit, it took a special kind of person to be class president, and Hillary was it. She was in her zone in that role. She followed the instructions to secure a single ticket and scanned the code to send the money through the app on her phone. Within seconds she had a digital ticket saved in the phone wallet. Ticket. Check. Next up, shower.

Lavender moved across the hall to her bathroom and hit the power button on her Bluetooth shower speaker to play some music. She sang along with Harry Styles while she washed her hot spots, shaved her legs and pits, and did an extra round of conditioner on her hair. She hadn't felt that light in a long time. Maybe the dark cloud of the last nine months was starting to move on. Lavender channeled Jana's voice while she considered the few pieces of makeup that she did own. *You need some color on your eyelids. For god's sake please put some blush on your cheeks. Your lips need to shine.* She searched through the bathroom closet for her hair dryer/brush combo that was as close as she ever got to straightening her hair. After twenty minutes of carefully drying and smoothing and glossing, Lavender looked in the mirror and didn't recognize herself. She hadn't seen that girl in a long time. There was a flicker of hope in her eyes and her face was open, ready to be seen, to come out from the shadows. *Am I crazy for doing this? Just keep moving...*

Her mom delivered on her promise a few hours later when she came back upstairs with a dress. "I got it. It's perfect." Her mom held out a hanger with a zippered garment bag. "Aunt Beck couldn't find one in Jackie's closet, so we called Aunt Rox and her neighbor had three daughters that are now in college, so...anyway...I think we nailed it." The FFTNN always came through in a crisis. Lavender found the zipper handle and slowly moved it around the bag. She pulled the dress out and held it up against her frame. She moved to the full-length mirror on the back of her bedroom door. The dress was navy blue with elastic for the neckline so it could be off the shoulder. It was a long and flowy maxi with pleated short sleeves that would hang low on her biceps, and a loose layer across the chest, above a tiered skirt that fell from a high waist, with a slit long enough to move it out of the prairie dress category. It wasn't the typical I-need-to-be-as-hot-and-sexy-as-possible dress that most of the senior girls at Siena High would be wearing. It was more retro. Old School. It was perfect.

"You did good Mom." Lavender whirled around. "I love it."

"It is perfect for you." Her mom's whispered voice had an edge to it. No doubt fueled by an emotional lump in her throat and some tears fighting to spill out of her eyes. "I can't wait to see it on you."

It was time. Lavender had waited just long enough to not be the first one there, but not so long, the night was almost over. She was fashionably late. She'd also spent the last hour drafting a pros and cons list in her diary, playing through possible scenarios and picking up her phone to text Jana or Jackie but then remembering that she was on her own. She slipped the white rose corsage on her wrist. Martin would be with her. That was all she needed.

As soon as her parents noticed Lavender walking down the stairs, they jumped up off the couch and muted the television. She couldn't help but smile watching them, watch her.

"Rosebud..." her dad said, with an unusual look on his face. "You look gorgeous." Her mom elbowed her dad.

"Ross. Shhh. I told you..."

"It's okay, mom."

"Just trying to be chill…," her mom said. "You do look amazing though Lav."

"Thanks. For everything. The dress, the shoes. It feels good."

"What's your plan? Can we help?" her dad asked.

Lavender considered her options, thinking through how lame it was to have her dad drop her off and pick her up, but it was probably lamer to drive herself, all dressed up like that.

"Can you give me a ride there? And then I'll Uber home?" Her parents looked at each other, trying to conceal their eagerness to be a part of her life again, especially that night. "But first, can you take a few pics of me?" She would send them to Martin.

"Of course. Here, give me your phone." Her mom took a bunch of pics while Lavender stood in front of the staircase and then handed her phone back. "Have the best time. Enjoy every moment." Her mom's voice had the same edge she'd had earlier that day, but Sara really was restraining her needy mom vibe. Lavender hugged her mom and walked out the back door with her dad at her side.

"Can we take my car?" Lavender asked and handed the keys to her dad.

"Of course. Haven't driven this since it belonged to your grandmother."

Lavender settled on the passenger side while her dad adjusted his seat and mirrors. She pulled the visor down and checked herself. "Hey Dad. Do you think this car could make a long road trip?"

He thought about it for a second. Checked her odometer to see the miles. "It should. You going somewhere?"

"Thinking about it. After graduation." This was the perfect opening to tell him everything. Should she tell him how she changed her mind about college and BSU? Should she tell him about Martin and how they got accepted to AmeriCorps together and were going to California? That she needed the Malibu ready for a cross-country road trip with a boy he'd never met in person?

"Hmmph. Yeah, it should. I could take it to the garage and get it checked out. Tuned up."

"That would be great Dad. Thanks." The problem with telling him the truth was that he would ask why. Why did she decide to abandon BSU when she had dreamed of going there almost her whole life? She couldn't bear to tell him about the party and what she let happen to her. She couldn't bear to tell him the shameful events that chained her up to all those secrets.

"Here we are." The trip to the High School was short so Lavender was relieved of having to say anything further. "Where do you want me to drop you?"

"Back here is fine." Her dad pulled up to the sidewalk, about fifty feet from the entrance where all the limos pulled up and dropped off the groups of friends going to the Ball together. "Thanks Dad." Lavender opened the car door and turned to step out. Senior Ball night wasn't the right time to blow up her life. The truth would have to wait. It had been almost nine months, what's a few more weeks?

"Rosebud?"

"Yeah?"

"You'll be the most beautiful girl there."

Lavender smiled at her dad and closed the door. *Keep moving.*

Round paper lanterns lit the hallways instead of the bright fluorescent school lights. The gym was unrecognizable with small round tables covered in white tablecloths, a stage with a DJ, a dance floor, the disco ball hanging in the center casting drops of light around the room. It was a makeshift night club. Her classmates were also unrecognizable. In their short dresses and suits, fancy hair and extra makeup, they looked like they were playing adults in a scene from a movie. Lavender searched the room, looking for a safe place to stand while the *ootz ootz* of the music beat overtook her ears and mind. She'd never been in an actual club, but it felt real.

"Lavender? Is that you?" Jana had walked up behind her.

"Hi." They hadn't spoken since that day on the stage at the Senior Superlative ceremony. "Believe it or not, it's me."

"You look amazing. That dress is fire on you."

"Lol, can you believe I have actual makeup on and a dress? I asked myself when I was getting ready, 'what would Jana do?'" They both laughed. For a split second it felt like old times. Like the distance between them, created by Lavender and her wall of lies, was filled in with their many years of friendship and history and how well they knew each other. It seemed like Jana felt it too, for a split second, but then remembered how her best friend had ditched her at the most important time of their lives and Jana backed up a little.

"I'm having an after-party tonight at my house. You wanna come?"

"Yeah? That's awesome." She couldn't believe Jana invited her over. "Ok. I'll plan on it."

"See you later." Jana walked away and Lavender watched her hook back up with her date and group of new friends. Maybe there was hope for the two of them after all. Maybe they could be friends again someday. Maybe.

Lavender walked to the drink bar and ordered a ginger lime mocktail from the bartender. She stood in the back of the room for the next hour and watched. Just like that day in the auditorium. Lavender was on the outside looking in. Like she was a stranger in her own school, in her own hometown. The buzz she had felt getting dressed and ready for the Ball was fading. But Lavender saw it on everyone else that night. They were dancing to every song the DJ played, their faces lit up with adrenaline and passion. Once again, Lavender knew what it looked like, but she could not feel it herself. She felt nothing surrounded by classmates who had become strangers. She was an extra on the movie set, on the outside looking in. She was alone. Her hand drifted to the soft petals on her wrist. Martin loved her. She knew that. But she couldn't help but wonder if he would still love her if he knew everything about her. Lavender would find out soon enough.

The Uber driver dropped her off at the corner of Jana's block. Lavender wasn't exactly sure why she was going to the party. It would be more of the same. Lavender would be surrounded by people yet overwhelmed with loneliness. But some long-lost part of her hungered for things to be different. To go back to the way they used to be. The way *she* used to be. Lavender had never been the most social person. Jana was the extrovert who plugged Lavender in to the social machine of Siena High.

Fashionably late again, Lavender climbed the front steps that she had climbed a million times before. It felt like she was returning to a place she used to live. The same *ootz ootz* was pumping out the front door. Kyle from Ms. Clarke's class was playing DJ with his phone and a Bluetooth speaker. As Lavender's eyes adjusted to the dim light in the living room, she searched for a friendly face, or a familiar corner to hide.

"Lavender Finch is here?" She whirled around to see two boys from her homeroom.

"She is here," Lavender said in a moment of witty strength, waiting for the next sarcastic comment.

"Cool. Will you hire us when you become CEO?" They high fived each other and moved away bumping shoulders and laughing. Lavender spotted Jana across the room and made her way over.

"You came." Her usually highly animated friend had a poker face. Lavender couldn't tell if Jana was happy to see her or what.

"Yup."

"Help yourself. There's beer in the kitchen, and some cocktails in a can...plain soda...whatever you're into."

"Got it. Thanks Jan." Lavender nodded at her. How could she expect anything more than a chilly greeting? She'd been radio silent and absent all freaking year. Lavender deserved any attitude Jana threw her way. She dodged dancing bodies while she made her way to the kitchen. The same kitchen where Lavender and Jana used to forage for late-night snacks and where they taught themselves to cook scrambled eggs and pasta and steak, because they heard some chef on Instagram say that every adult should know how to make those things. Lavender couldn't resist opening the long narrow pantry to see the heart they'd carved into the door jamb late one night. J + L forever, it said. The counter was lined with buckets that had bottles and cans nesting on ice. Jana's parents didn't seem to be anywhere in sight. Lavender grabbed a beer and popped the top with the opener hanging off the side of the bucket. *Ahhhh. That first sip. This should help.*

Lavender held her beer and surveyed the scene. Would Martin have a beer or a cocktail? Probably not. He didn't seem like the type. Like, he just didn't need it. Martin would hold her hand or maybe put his arm around her. He would definitely dance. A girl walked by that she didn't know and said, "Nice dress. And shoes. Rocking it."

Lavender grabbed another beer and took that one into the living room. She sat on the empty couch. She was proud of herself. It had been a long and lonely year and she had missed a lot of things. But not her Senior Ball. For better or for worse, at least she was there. She had been present. It wasn't so bad. Maybe the isolation was all meant to get her ready to move away from home. Lavender was excited about her plan, but also nervous to be so far from Siena and her family. Her grandmother. Her bedroom. Would she miss it? She wouldn't be able to come home to do laundry or for every holiday. California was a lot further away than BSU.

"Is this seat taken?" Lavender looked up to see a face she didn't recognize. He looked like he was in high school. He was wearing jeans and a black t-shirt. Where did he come from? Had he changed his clothes after the Ball?

"Nope. It's all yours."

"Cool. I'm Madden."

"Lavender." He had brown hair and long eyelashes. Not bad looking. But not Martin.

"Do you go to Siena?"

"Yup. You?"

"No. I came here with some friends who go to Siena."

"Ah. Nice." Lavender nodded, trying to be polite, but also signal that she wasn't interested in a conversation or anything else with him.

"How's the beer?"

He was persistent. Clearly not noticing the vibe she was giving off. "It's good actually."

"Do you have a boyfriend?"

That was none of his business. If she said yes, then she'd have to explain why he wasn't with her. "No, not really…"

"Cool."

Cool? Why was that cool?

"You wanna go get another drink?" Madden asked.

"I've still got some." Lavender was starting to feel uneasy on the couch, next to him.

"You wanna dance?"

"I'm good." Lavender wanted him to go away, but instead he jumped up on his feet.

"Let's dance." He grabbed her hand and pulled her up. Her head was swimming in dull noise. Lavender couldn't think straight. Was she at Jana's house? Or was she back at the BSU party? In the big house with the basement and the futon and Travis pulling her hand. Pulling her on top of him.

"No, I don't want to." Lavender shook her head.

"Come on. Have some fun." Madden started gyrating his hips in front of her. He was four inches from her face. He smelled like stinky cheese and dirty feet. He was too close. *He pulled her back down and kissed her, hard. He moved on top of her. She could feel him, bare against her stomach. He pulled her pants down. No. Lavender couldn't tell if she had made a sound. Did I say no out loud? She should scream. If she screamed, Jackie would hear her. No, no, no.*

"I said, No." She pushed on Madden's chest with both hands until he stumbled and fell onto the coffee table. "No. No. No." The dancing stopped and all eyes were on Lavender. The buzz of the room quieted except for the music.

"Geez. What is your problem?" Madden said, still on the floor looking up at her like she was a freak.

Lavender looked at the house full of people who were watching her like she was the stranger. She ran out the front door of Jana's house, ripped off her heels, and didn't stop running until she'd run the whole two miles home, in her bare feet with tears and snot staining her beautiful blue dress that her mom had found for her.

She plopped down on her backstep to catch her breath and figure out what just happened. *I should have just stayed home. What was I thinking?* She slipped off the wrist corsage, that had mostly survived the run home, and held the soft petals of the white rose to her cheek. *Martin.* She wished he was there to tell her that she wasn't a freak. She wished he was there to hold her and tell her everything was going to be okay. *If wishes were horses, beggars would ride.*

THIRTY-NINE

LAVENDER GRABBED A BOTTLE off the bottom shelf, popped off the top, and took her first sip. Well, it was more than a sip. More like a gulp or guzzle. *Ahhhhh.* The moment she'd been waiting for all week. The warmth trickled all the way down to the bottom of her belly. Her shoulders sank a few inches. Her mind relaxed. The Gordons must have restocked the fridge. The shelf was full of beer, but there were a few already missing, so they shouldn't notice a few more gone.

It seemed to take forever to get Stevie and Sadie down for the night. They both wanted an extra book read to them and then did several rounds of, "I need a drink," or "I have to go potty," or "I need the hall light on." Mrs. Gordon said they'd be back late so Lavender had a few hours before she'd have to drive home. Plenty of time to have a beer or two. Or maybe three. Definitely no more than three.

Lavender settled on the couch with her feet pulled up under her, her backpack next to her and a beer in her hand. Just one week ago, she was at the Senior Ball and then the party. It had been one whole week since she made a complete ass out of herself after that guy at Jana's triggered memories from Travis to play in her head again. When Lavender laid her head on her pillow at night, she saw him, felt him, smelled him. She dreamed of the giant wave chasing her on her surfboard again, threatening to crash down on top of her and her future.

Lavender took a swig of beer and ran through the night, one more time, trying to nail down exactly when things blew up and why. The night had started off solid. Yes, she went to the Ball alone, without a date or friends, but she had been okay with that. She loved her dress, and the white rose corsage Martin sent her. And even though she felt unseen and disconnected at the actual dance, she was glad to be there. Lavender was glad to be a witness to her Senior Ball. She knew it was important for the year to not be a total loss. She probably should have ended the night then and just gone home to bed. Everything would have been fine. But no… Lavender had to test fate and go to Jana's house. What was she thinking? Was she trying to pretend she and Jana were still best friends, in spite of the past year? What did she think was going to happen? Lavender finished her bottle and set it on the coffee table. She held her face in her hands.

"I'm thirsty," a voice said from behind her head. Lavender whipped around to see Sadie standing there holding her favorite elephant blanket.

"Sadie. You scared me." Did she see the beer bottle on the table? "Sorry."

"Ok. Let's get you a sip of water and then back to bed." Lavender took her to the kitchen for a drink and then carried her back upstairs. She tucked in the little girl and nestled the elephant blanket in her arms. "Go to sleep, okay? It's way past your bedtime."

"Your breath smells funny."

"Oh that's just the snack I had. I was eating cheese puffs."

Sadie stared at her like they were in a no-blink contest. Like she knew Lavender was lying. Would Sadie tell Mrs. Gordon that her babysitter's breath smelled like beer? Probably not. Hopefully not. Maybe Sadie wouldn't remember in the morning. If Mrs. Gordon said anything, Lavender could blame it on Sadie being half asleep when she came downstairs. The little girl closed her eyes and Lavender exhaled.

Lavender traded in her empty for a new bottle before she returned to the couch. She shouldn't risk it, but that unexpected interruption had hijacked her beer buzz vibe. Lavender had been looking forward to it all week and wasn't ready to give up on it yet. She pressed play on the playlist of songs that she and Martin had shared with each other over the past months. Everything from Ella Fitzgerald to Sting to classic eighties rock to Drake. It was another thing they had in common. They both liked music across all genres, as long as it made them feel something.

Lavender was getting her beer buzz vibe back, but Travis was still haunting her. How would she ever get rid of him and what he did? That guy at Jana's party was probably not like Travis. He probably just wanted to have fun. Jana had said so when she texted Lavender later that night, after she had pushed Madden over the coffee table and ran out of the house, like a lunatic.

> Hey. Wtf? Why'd you freak out?
> Lav? Tell me so i can do something
> to make it right.
> Did madden say something to piss
> you off? Let me know, k??
> I see ur ghosting me again. Not cool.

Lavender honestly didn't know if Madden was a creep or not. He clearly was clueless and didn't pick up her signals. He ignored her answer of no, but did that mean he was going to try what Travis did? Maybe. Maybe not. But the whole scene felt so familiar. The music. The beer. He sat so close she could feel his thigh touching hers. Why did he think that was okay? That she was okay with that? Just because he was a guy and she was sitting alone at a party, did he think that Lavender was fair game? Did he think she didn't mean it when she said no to dancing? It was all so confusing to try and sort out. Is that what kids her age did? Was she the weird one? Was what happened with Travis normal, and she was unreasonably freaked out? It had been way too long, but she answered Jana's text from a week ago anyway.

> Hey. Sorry about your party. I just
> didn't want to dance with him.

Lavender hit send and waited for the three little dots to pop up to let her know Jana was answering her. But they never did. Jana was ghosting her now. Who could blame her?

Lavender just had to get through a few more weeks of school...23 days until graduation...tick...figure out how to break the news to her parents that she wasn't going to college...tick... that she was leaving for the West Coast...tick...and starting a new life. Boom. After graduation, her and Martin would meet up and drive, far away from Siena, from BSU, from Travis and the bullshit at the party she just couldn't get out of her head. Lavender finished her third beer and checked her phone. No text from Jana or Mrs. Gordon.

She moved to the kitchen to rinse her bottles, gather all three caps, wipe down the counter and the sink with an extra spray of cleaner to make sure there was no stale beer smell, and moved all the evidence to her backpack. She figured she had at least an hour before the Gordons were home. Lavender lay on the couch and closed her eyes just as "Wake Me Up When September Ends" began from the playlist. Perfect timing.

FORTY

LAVENDER PULLED INTO HER USUAL last-row parking spot at the Betsy Ross home. She'd visited that lonely and dull one-story building at least thirty-five times over the past ten months and had more than met the forty hours of community service that Ms. Clarke required to pass her class. The pansies were blooming again around the flagpole. Lavender would miss that place. She had been so uneasy and unsure of what to expect when she started the assignment last September, but on that Saturday in June, going to Betsy Ross felt like going home.

Lavender walked through the double doors and signed her name to the guest log. Evelyn was on the phone as usual but winked and waved. She pointed at the phone and twirled her finger in circles. Lavender laughed and waved before heading to the TV room. The woman in the purple housedress passed her, "Will you take me home?" she said while clutching her oversized breasts. "Not today, but someday..." Lavender said back. Her grandma was in her chair with her eyes locked on the television.

"Hey Grandma. How are you today?" Even after all the visits, her greeting always started with "Hey Grandma," giving Louise an opportunity to remember and place that familiar face on a stranger in front of her.

"Hello. How are you today?"

"I'm alright."

"You wanna watch TV with me?"

"Yes, of course, *Mary's* coming on." Lavender pulled the ottoman next to her grandma's chair and silently watched the entire episode with Rita and Sharon and another new lady she'd never seen before. Once she heard the last line of the closing music... *you're going to make it after all...*Lavender opened her backpack and pulled out her laptop.

"Hey gram, remember how I started coming here as an assignment for school?"

"You did?" Her grandma looked at her with wide eyes. "I don't remember."

"Well yes. I mean, I wanted to visit you anyway, but I had to do forty hours of community service, so I thought I'd kill two birds with one stone, you know?"

"Okay, if you say so."

"My last part of the assignment was to write a summary and answer a few questions from my teacher. Is it okay if I read you what I wrote?"

"I guess. Sure. Sharon, turn off the TV. The girl has something to read us." Sharon obeyed and clicked the remote off and everyone in the room sat down with eyes locked on Lavender. She had an audience.

"Ok. Here goes." She opened her laptop and held it in front of her.

"Wait. You should stand," Rita said.

"Good idea. I can't hear you unless you stand," Sharon said.

Lavender smiled at the eager faces in front of her and stood. "Ok. Here goes," she said again and took a deep breath.

To fulfill my senior community service requirement, I chose the Betsy Ross Nursing Home. With its dull white exterior and scarce landscaping, it doesn't look like much on the outside. It also doesn't look like much on the inside, with its beige walls and floors and drapes. The hallways are cleverly named, Washington, Delaware, Pennsylvania, Potomac and Maryland and there's a strange funky smell always hanging in the air. I haven't quite figured out what it is yet.

"She's right, it does smell bad in here. I've been saying that..." Rita whispered.

But despite the questionable odor and the bland décor, what I've discovered over the past ten months, is that this place is full of life.

The people I've met here, I'll never forget. From Evelyn at the front door who really runs this place, and keeps tabs on everyone here, to Rita and Sharon and the lady in the purple housedress who always asks me if I'll take her home.

"That's Edna," Sharon said.

But my favorite person who lives at the Betsy Ross Home is a woman named Louise Rachel Dubose. Louise Rachel Dubose was born in 1956 and after she graduated high school, she moved to California to work in the VISTA volunteer program, which was the new domestic version of the Peace Corps. After helping migrant families with literacy and education, she returned to Siena and married. She had two children, Michael, who tragically passed away as a little boy, and a daughter named Sara, who is my mother.

When I was a little girl, my grandmother seemed mysterious and far away to me, even though we lived in the same town. We didn't know each other as well as a grandmother and granddaughter should. This assignment not only allowed me to get to know this woman, Louise Rachel Dubose, it also taught me things I will never forget.

Number one, I learned about Mary Tyler Moore. My grandma and her friends are so devoted to this woman and her television program, that I wasn't allowed to speak until the episode was over. If you showed up at ten-thirty in the morning on any given day, you'd find my grandmother and her friends enraptured by this iconic woman of the seventies who defied traditions of the time and blazed a new trail for women who were determined to be independent and free. Before this assignment, I had never watched an episode or heard of this woman, Mary Tyler Moore. I was hooked after the first one. But what really spoke to me, was the way these women of Betsy Ross, who are in the twilight of their lives, are still inspired and touched by the idea of living a life that is of your own making and choices. That our desire to have control over our bodies, our minds, our lives, never leaves us.

The second lesson I learned from spending time here is that you can create home wherever you are. Regardless of what the physical aspects of the space are, the idea of home transcends all that. My grandma has a room with a small bed, a table and two chairs, another chair next to her bed, a closet and a bedstand. There's a window where we sat together and listened to Christmas music and watched the snow fall. Her bedstand is the place she keeps everything that is precious to her—the photo album that has captured her life in pictures, the diary from her youth, her legendary lipstick. She has a homemade afghan on the end of her bed. I covered her with it when she was sick. I sat at the foot of that same bed and rubbed her tiny feet with lotion. Having a place for all your things, where you feel safe, warm, protected from the harsh elements of the outside world, is home. Home is also more than a place. It is being surrounded by people who care about you, where you can be yourself—allowed to have days where you're grumpy or want to stay in your room and also have those days when you are the one lifting everyone up with your generous vibe. It is sharing your life with others who accept you and the life you've already lived, exactly as you are, full of mistakes and regrets that are inevitable if you live long enough. If you can find a place and people that give you these things, you are home.

The most important lesson I've learned, is that it's never too late. It's never too late to get to know someone or to repair a broken relationship. As long as you are here on this earth, breathing new air every morning, you have another chance to turn it all around. After spending the last ten months or so with this woman, Louise Rachel Dubose, my grandmother, I know now that the ultimate act of love is to be brave enough to see others, exactly as they are, and to let them see you. I know what her hopes and dreams were as a young girl, I know about her first love and her first heartbreak. I've seen inside her life in a way that I never expected. I felt the tragedy she lived through and the unspeakable loss that she's endured. She let me in. And now I understand. That when you let others see you, when you're honest about the good stuff and the not so good, when you're brave enough to risk others seeing those parts of you that you are inclined to hide, that is what opens your heart and allows you to be seen and loved in return.

I'm so grateful, Ms. Clarke, for this assignment. Not only has it changed my life, it gave me my grandmother.

Lavender closed her laptop and exhaled. Sharon, Rita and the other woman began to clap.

"She should get an A plus for that."

"What a smart girl."

"Can you believe she never saw *Mary* before?"

Louise rose out of her rocking chair with the big blue cushions, raised up on her tiptoes and wrapped her arms around Lavender.

Lavender would stay forever in that embrace if she could. "I love you grandma."

"I love you too Lavender."

FORTY-ONE

THE GREAT THING ABOUT JUNE was that there was enough daylight to get a run in before school. Summer running allowed Lavender to travel light down the sidewalks through Siena in just shorts and a t-shirt. Without ice or puddles to dodge, she could focus on strength moves like the step-ups and step-downs on and off the curbs. She also worked on her speed by sprinting between light poles on long stretches of road.

Running was the only thing that could save her from the ticking time bomb that was scheduled to explode in less than 12 hours. In approximately eleven hours and thirty-three minutes, Lavender would be forced to come clean. There was no way she could lie at the microphone in front of all those people, including Principal Edwards and the Chancellor from BSU. When it was her turn on stage to announce her name and post-graduation plans, she couldn't say BSU like Jana would or the many other Siena students that would be freshmen in the fall. She wasn't one of them. Never had been. She would be surrounded by classmates who had made plans for student loans and tuition payments, who had been assigned a dorm and a roommate, who had selected a major and a schedule of classes. Tick. Tick. Dead.

It was hard to believe that her senior year of high school was over. Lavender didn't go into it with romantic or Hollywood ideals of what a senior year should look like, but she never imagined that her and Jana would be apart, or that her and Jackie wouldn't speak for so long. Lavender never thought of herself as a liar before the last ten months, or that she was capable of living a secret life. She hadn't counted on the loneliness.

Yet, in the midst of all the shitty surprises of her senior year, there was Martin. Who knew that a boy from Cuba, who she had never met in person, would be the one light in all her darkness? She engaged her glutes and quads to bounce up a high curb and smiled thinking of how cute and old-fashioned he was on their last Sunday night call. "Lavender, would you allow me the privilege of being your boyfriend?" he said. She didn't answer right away, not because she was unsure about him, but because she was wondering if it was wrong to accept his proposal without full disclosure of who she really was. Lavender made a quick promise to herself that she would come clean and tell him everything when they met in person. "I'll say yes, on one condition," she said back to him, "that I get to be your girlfriend." Martin's smile filled his whole face, "I've been telling everyone here for months that I have a girlfriend in the states. You, my dear Lavender, are old news in Cuba and the Adams household." Lavender felt bad she couldn't say the same thing to him. No one in her life knew how much they meant to each other.

With their relationship status settled, they began to make real plans about their summer and the trip to California. Martin was on board with flying to upstate New York and driving her Malibu to the West Coast. He took on the responsibility of mapping out their road trip and figuring out the hours they would need to drive each day and the places they would stop along the way. It didn't sound like he had the most efficient route in mind but had places like Graceland, the home of Elvis Presley's mansion, and Roswell, New Mexico with all the alien folklore and Tombstone, Arizona, then the Grand Canyon as the grand finale before they drove straight to Venice Beach to put their feet in the water. Lavender was in charge of getting the car ready, creating the playlist, snacks and the budget. It was going to be the time of their lives and they couldn't wait. He also told her that night on the phone that he wanted to set her expectations about the first time they met. "I'm not going to kiss you in the airport," he said, very seriously. "You're not?" she answered. "Nope. I want our first kiss to be special. And I wanted to tell you ahead of time, so you don't jump to conclusions or anything…I just wanna wait until we're alone." Lavender laughed and said, "That's okay, we've waited this long, what's a few more hours?"

Lavender ran as hard as she could down the last stretch of road before she reached Sycamore, stretching out her stride as far as her legs could reach. Pushing her body to its limits helped sort out the chaos and worry in her mind about Class Night and everyone finding out the truth. As usual, she had trouble imagining how it would all play out. She rounded the corner and saw her house up ahead. Mrs. Gordon was standing in the driveway talking to her mother. That was strange. Did she need a sitter? Why didn't she just text?

Lavender slowed to a stop and paced back and forth. Her mom and Mrs. Gordon quietly waited for her to catch her breath. "Hi Mrs. Gordon. I'm sorry if I missed a text. I'm not so good with my phone sometimes."

"Lavender. That's not why Mrs. Gordon is here," her mom said, in a weird tight voice. Sara's face looked like it was either angry or on the verge of tears.

"I need to ask you a question," Mrs. Gordon said. "Have you been drinking beer at my house?"

Lavender stopped moving and looked at Mrs. Gordon. "Why would you ask me that?"

"Answer the question."

"It's not true, is it Lav? You wouldn't drink while you were babysitting, right?" her mom said.

"No...well...I mean..." Lavender knew she should just confess but couldn't come up with the right words. The wave was closing in on her.

"Please don't lie. You know how I feel about you Lavender. How I felt. I loved you," Mrs. Gordon said.

"I don't know what you want me to say."

"Sadie told me that your breath smelled funny because you had an adult drink. Did you?" Mrs. Gordon asked.

Lavender was caught. Busted. In the worst possible way. Subconsciously she'd been hoping that she could just move away, and no one would ever know about her sketchy beer-drinking habit while babysitting. "Mrs. Gordon, I'm sorry...I didn't mean..."

"To be honest, I suspected it before. Not that you were drinking when I entrusted you with my babies, but I knew that beer had been missing from the fridge. I could just never put my finger on it. I never would have guessed it was you."

Of course not, because you never really knew me. "Mrs. Gordon. I would never do anything to put Stevie and Sadie in danger. I love your kids."

"But you did put them in danger, and you betrayed my trust." Mrs. Gordon looked at Lavender as if she was a complete stranger, or worse, someone who she despised or was disgusted by.

"I only did it after the kids were asleep. I swear to God." Lavender began to cry. Her mother was not offering any help. Lavender was on her own. "And I would only have one or two at the most…I'm so sorry…I'm so sorry…I did it to relax…I didn't do it every time…I was never drunk." She left out the part about New Year's Eve when she had driven home after too many beers in too little time. She also left out how the warmth of the beer in her belly helped her forget about Travis and BSU and all her lies. Mrs. Gordon wouldn't understand.

"I don't know what to say Janet. I'm sorry," her mom said. "We didn't raise her like this." *My own mother throwing me under the bus.*

"It's not your fault Sara. I won't tell anyone…except my husband, of course." Mrs. Gordon turned toward Lavender. "I'm just so disappointed. And heartbroken. I thought I knew you."

Well, you didn't. Maybe you shouldn't have been so quick to throw the love word around. "Mrs. Gordon, I am so sorry. It will never happen again."

"You're right, it won't. I'll be finding somebody new to take care of my kids." With that last gut punch, Mrs. Gordon got in her car and backed out of the driveway.

Lavender sunk to her knees on the grass, her hands over her face, waiting for her mother to say something. Anything. To punish her. Ground her. Take away the keys to her car. Anything. Instead, her mother turned around and walked away.

The first of many explosions had been detonated. Lavender had taken the first hit.

FORTY-TWO

LAVENDER SAT LOW IN HER SEAT in the last row of the student section. On Class Night, the seniors sat together while their parents, grandparents and other interested parties filled the rest of the auditorium. Which was just as well. Sitting next to her parents would be awkward since the incident with Mrs. Gordon in the driveway that morning. After Mrs. Gordon had left, Lavender went straight upstairs, cried some more in the shower and dressed for school. She left without another word...or breakfast. Lavender and her mother had never crossed paths again in the house. She imagined that her father knew by now. What must he think of his *Rosebud*?

Lavender felt like a soldier going into war. Unprepared. Not properly armed. Unsure who the enemy really was. What was that saying? Keep your friends close, but your enemies closer? She was her own worst enemy in that situation. She had only herself to blame. Lavender wasn't ready for it but knew it was time. Tick. Tick. Tick. Hillary Charles was onstage along with the school's principal and other important people. The university was close enough for the Chancellor to make the trip to welcome and shake hands with all the new freshmen who would be attending her campus.

"Hellooooo Siena High. This. Is. Our. Night. Woot. Woot. The last night in this place that has held our minds for the past four years. The place where we grew up, together. Tonight, we celebrate our future." Hillary's introduction was met with applause. Her classmates high-fived and fist-bumped and half-hugged each other. *Hillary Charles was born for such a time as this.*

Jana was four rows in front of her surrounded by people who were not Lavender. On either side of the stage were life-size cutouts of the superlative winners, including Lavender and her fellow CEO. She scanned the audience for her parents. Would they still come to the event now that they knew their daughter was a delinquent, beer-drinking babysitter? They did. Lavender saw them in the middle section. They were solid people.

Principal Edwards began announcing the scholarship winners and recipients of perfect attendance awards. Once he was done, it was time for the two hundred plus seniors to announce their post-graduation plans. *This was it.*

Hillary was back at the helm. She called the class of 2025 forward. They had practiced how to do that in Ms. Clarke's class and had been given a schematic of how they should file out of their seats, row by row, and follow each other in a civilized and orderly fashion. Lavender tracked the person next to her as she was instructed to do and followed the long line in front of her. Like a lamb to the slaughter.

One by one they filed on stage, pausing at the mic, to announce their name and their commitment after graduation. "Kayla Avaline. Nursing School. Brett Coletta, Marines." They stayed onstage after their announcement and walked to their pre-assigned location, creating a formation of seventeen-year-olds grouped by their choice of how to spend their future. Ten of her classmates received a standing ovation when they announced their enlistment in the Navy, Air Force, Marines and Army, some were wearing their uniform and already had their hair buzzed.

It was Jana's turn at the microphone. "Jana Brown, BSU. Go Bulldogs!" Her new friends cheered. She walked to the right side of the stage to shake the Chancellor's hand and stand with the other college-bound graduates. More followed with acceptances to BSU and also Harvard, Yale, Syracuse, Notre Dame, Duke, Georgetown, Princeton, SUNY schools like Buffalo, Binghamton and Oswego. Her classmates were impressive. Lavender was running out of excuses. She was running out of time. The long line in front of her was dwindling fast. Lavender counted twenty in front of her. Then it was ten. Five. Four. Three. Two. One. Boom.

"Lavender Finch." She managed to get her name out of her mouth. Should she stop there and just move off stage? Hillary stood at her side, waiting to take back the podium and mic since Lavender was the last student of the night. Hillary whispered, "Don't forget to say BSU." Lavender looked over at Jana. Their eyes met. Jana looked happy. "Psst. Lavender." Hillary nudged her with her elbow.

Lavender looked out at all the faces in front of her. She found her mother and father. Her dad smiled. Her mom's look was hard to read. She wanted to remember that moment. The moment before the bomb was dropped. "Sorry...My name is Lavender Finch and after graduation I will be joining AmeriCorps and working in California."

"Lavender, what did you say?' Hillary looked at Lavender like she misunderstood the assignment. Lavender moved away from the podium but didn't know where to stand. There wasn't a designated location for liars. No one to greet her. A few in the audience clapped. Most of them had no idea that her announcement was a surprise. Lavender avoided looking in her parents' direction but imagined they were stunned and confused. "What about BSU?" Hillary wouldn't stop.

Lavender didn't answer. She stood her ground in the center of the Siena High School stage. The eyeballs behind her burned bullet-sized holes in her back. She felt a slow and steady heat rise up from the bottoms of her feet, through her legs and stomach and chest all the way to her head. She just might spontaneously combust. The whispers from the strangers she'd known almost her whole life buzzed in her ears.

"What did she say? I couldn't hear."

"Why isn't she with the BSU crowd?"

"What the hell is AmeriCorps?"

"No idea."

"To be honest, she's been weird all year."

"Remember Jana's party?"

Principal Edwards was at the podium, dismissing the crowd and the students. His words were muffled and distorted. The lights were so warm. The fifty-pound weights were back on top of her shoulders. Lavender couldn't move. She closed her eyes. She was lying on her surfboard, paddling as fast as she could. The giant wave was chasing her. It was close. Too close. No matter how fast she paddled, she couldn't outrun it. Not anymore. As it crashed on top of her, Lavender fell off her board and sunk into darkness.

"Lavender. Wake up. Lav."

"Rosebud, are you okay? We're here."

Lavender opened her eyes to her mother and father kneeling beside her, her mother's hand on her forehead and then on each of her cheeks.

"Are you sick? Should we take you to Urgent Care?" her mom said.

"She just fainted, I think," her dad said.

Hillary stood peering over her father's shoulder. "Should I call 911?"

"How about some water?" her mother asked. Hillary was on it and returned in less than sixty seconds with a bottle of water.

"I'm fine. Really. I'm fine." Lavender sat up before a stretcher was called.

"Are you sure?" her mom asked.

"I just got lightheaded. I didn't eat lunch..."

Lavender took the water bottle from Hillary and took a few sips to prove that she was fine. That there was nothing to it. She wouldn't mention the wave. She stood up, her legs a little wobbly at first.

"Stay down."

"Take your time. No rush."

"I'm good. Really," Lavender said.

Her dad hugged her. Her mom grabbed her arm. Hillary and Principal Edwards stared.

"Let's get you out of here," her dad said. *Thank god for my dad.*

He led the three of them off the stage, out the first side door of the auditorium that they came too and then another door marked *emergency only* into the parking lot. The fresh air filled Lavender's lungs and brought color back to her cheeks.

"So much better. Not sure what happened back there. Guess I can't skip meals." Lavender was hoping to play down the fact that she had just passed out in front of seven hundred people.

"Lavender, we need to talk about what just happened."

"Now Sara? Can't it wait."

"She said she's fine Ross, and I'm more confused now than I was this morning. I feel like I don't know my own daughter." It was rare to see her mother so irritated. So angry.

"I'm sure she has a perfectly good explanation for all of it. Right?"

"First, drinking while babysitting, now springing this Peace Corps thing on us in front of the whole school?"

"Not the Peace Corps. AmeriCorps. I'm not leaving the country."

"But you're going to BSU, right?" her dad asked.

"You applied to college and were accepted. We've had a sign in our front yard since December Lavender," her mom said.

Her dad looked confused. Her mother looked pissed. Lavender sighed.

"Actually no. I never applied and therefore was never accepted." She looked over their heads, avoiding eye contact.

"You lied to us? To everyone?"

"Well, not technically. I think everyone just assumed that I did...I just didn't say anything..."

"Are you seriously going to argue the technicality of lying to us? Come on," her mom said.

"Can we finish this conversation at home and not in the parking lot?" her dad asked.

"You told Mrs. Gordon it was okay to drink because her kids were asleep, and you were *just relaxing* and now you're telling us it wasn't really lying because you didn't say the actual words *I applied and was accepted*?" Her mother began to cry. "What is wrong with you?"

Her dad put his arm around Sara and started walking to their car. "Come on. It's late. Let's go home. Get a good night sleep and figure this out tomorrow." He turned to Lavender and said, "Why don't you ride with us? I'll bring you back tomorrow to get your car." But by the time he finished his sentence Lavender was already gone.

Lavender drove faster than what was safe in a parking lot full of people, but she had to get as far away as she could from that place, from Jana and her new friends, from all the other kids who'd become people she didn't know, and from her parents' disappointment and anger and disbelief that their daughter was capable of all those things. Her hands shook as she held the steering wheel trying to decide if she should turn left or right or go straight. Where would she go? What would she do? Jackie was out of the question. Her boyfriend wasn't there. Lavender had no friends in that town. She turned on the radio and drove.

She turned right. Then left. Before she knew it, she was on a familiar street. *Grandma.* That's exactly who she needed. Was it too late for visitors? She crossed her fingers hoping that Evelyn worked Friday nights and would let her in. Betsy Ross was sleepy with just a few lights shining in the windows of the resident's rooms who were still night owls, and the entranceway was lit up. Lavender tried the front door but it was locked. She saw someone in a guard uniform at the front desk. It wasn't Evelyn. Lavender knocked on the glass. The person at the front desk looked up. She shouted through the glass.

"I need to see my grandmother."

The person pointed to the clock and shook her head.

"It's an emergency. Please..."

The guard pushed back her chair and walked out from behind her desk to the front door.

"How can I help you?"

"My grandmother lives here. I really need to see her."

"It's late."

"I know, I'm sorry, I wouldn't ask if it wasn't really important."

"What's your grandmother's name?"

"Louise. Louise Dubose. She's in the Potomac wing."

"Louise Dubose is your grandma?"

"Yes. You know her?"

"I'm sorry to be the one to tell you this, but your grandmother was rushed to the hospital about an hour ago."

Lavender lost all strength in her body. She dropped her car keys. "What? Why?"

"Not sure. She was found unresponsive in her room and they called 911."

"Oh my god." She wasn't sure what the next right question was. "Where did they take her?"

"The hospital."

"Ok. I'll go there."

"Do you know where you're going?"

"I'll look it up on my phone." She bent over to pick up her keys.

"Right. But there's two hospitals in Siena. Memorial and St. John's. Not sure which one they took her to." The guard must have sensed that that kind of crisis was new for Lavender. "Go to the Emergency entrance and ask if Louise Dubose was brought in. They should be able to tell you."

"Oh. Ok. Got it. Thank you. I appreciate your help."

Lavender ran to her car and pulled her phone out of her backpack. She had a text from Evelyn hours ago. *Damn it. Why don't I ever check my phone?*

Call me. 911.

Hey. Sorry i missed this. At br now.

Did they tell you?

Yeah. Is she going to be okay?

No idea. She's been a little off for
a few weeks. I could tell something
was wrong.

This sucks. I can't……

So sorry. Lmk what you find out.

With her fingers trembling Lavender switched to the Map app on her phone and searched for hospitals.

"Louise. Her name is Louise Dubose. Is she here?" Lavender came in hot to the front desk of the Emergency Room, desperate to find her grandmother. The man in front of the computer looked like he hadn't slept or showered in a week and was not affected by her breathless panic. After making brief eye contact, he typed on the keyboard and after what seemed like ten minutes, responded. "Affirmative."

"Can I see her?"

"How old are you?"

"Eighteen." Lavender lied, but she would be in ten days. June 24th.

"Are you family?"

"Yes. I'm her granddaughter."

"17C. Follow the orange signs." He buzzed open the locked entrance and held his left arm out to the side, as if to say, *you may enter here.* So dramatic. Lavender walked through the double doors and looked for orange. She hadn't been in an emergency room since she got a concussion playing field hockey in ninth-grade gym class. It was different in the middle of the night. The people working there seemed to be sleep-walking through their shift. No one was talking. For a place whose only mission was to keep people alive during emergencies, there wasn't an ounce of urgency in the halls or at the desks or anywhere she looked. Lavender seemed to be the only one in panicked pursuit of something. Someone. The spooky quietness was interrupted on a repeating cycle by an annoying beep. No one else seemed to hear it or be bothered by it. The sharp sound was like an alarm, or a warning of some sort, like of an impending invasion or explosion or some kind of attack.

After looping the entire floor, Lavender finally found an orange 17C above a white wall of curtains. She found the edge of the front curtain and pulled it back on its u-shaped track. *There she was.*

"Grandma," she whispered. Lavender looked down on the woman she loved, who looked so small and fragile lying on a bright white hospital bed. The chrome rails were up on either side, holding her hostage it seemed. The index finger on her right hand had a sensor over the end, with a cord that ran to a machine with a screen. There was a needle in the middle of her right arm attached to a bag of clear liquid. There was a slow drip moving the contents into her vein. The black screen with green numbers and lines that formed four different graphs, one in each corner, was flashing information. None of it made sense. Her grandma's hair was pushed back off her forehead unnaturally. No lipstick. She would have hated that.

"Let me get you a chair sweetie." Lavender jumped. A nurse had quietly entered the space and jolted her out of her trance. The nurse left and came right back with a cushioned folding chair. "Here you go."

"Thank you. What happened to her?"

"Are you family?"

"I'm her granddaughter, Lavender Finch."

"Well, the doctor will be around at some point, but it looks like she had a stroke."

Lavender swallowed hard, afraid to ask the next question. "Is she going to be okay?"

"I really shouldn't say more than that."

"Please..."

"With strokes it is hard to predict. We don't know the extent of the damage until she comes out of the coma. That's all I can say." The nurse smiled with her mouth only and walked out.

Lavender pulled the folding chair close and sat with her chin resting on the guardrail. She reached for her grandma's hand. It was warm. She didn't know much about strokes, but she knew enough to know that a coma was not a good thing. People woke up from comas and couldn't talk, or eat, or sometimes they never woke up at all. Lavender pulled out her phone and texted Evelyn.

> Found her. With her now in er.
>
> Stroke. Coma.

Lavender added a solid row of sad faces and sobbing emojis before she hit send. She and Martin didn't communicate by text unless they were on a date, but an emergency like this called for a break in their rules. That was when technology was useful. Lavender told him that her grandma had a stroke and that she was at the hospital. She also told him how scared she was that she'd never be able to hug her again or hear her voice. She figured Martin was asleep. It was almost midnight. But the three blinking dots appeared right away.

> I'm so sorry about your grandma. I'll
> have my dad say a prayer. I've heard
> people in a coma can still hear us. Talk
> to her. Tell her everything. I love you.

Martin was perfect. He just got it and got her. The last three words made Lavender take a sharp breath in. She knew they had fallen in love and were officially boyfriend and girlfriend, but to say it so casually and matter of fact in a moment like that was something. Lavender could only respond with a heart and would have to unpack the rest of her thoughts and feelings about that later. She put her phone away and rubbed her grandma's arm. She took a deep breath and even though she had a huge, tangled ball of fear lodged in the middle of her throat, she began to talk to her grandma.

"Hey grandma. It's me, Lavender. I'm so sorry this happened to you. You must've been so scared…I wish I was there." She imagined her grandmother all alone in her room, it must have hurt terribly before she passed out. Lavender couldn't hold back the tears and began to cry.

"I know I've told you how much you mean to me, and I meant every word. I wish we had had more years together like this last one. I think I really could've used your help and advice. I'm not so good at managing my life it seems. My parents are mad at me. Mrs. Gordon hates me. I've lost my best friends Jackie and Jana. If I could go back in time, I never would have gone to that party…

my life has been nothing but shit ever since that night." Lavender blew her nose with tissues from the small flat box on the rolling cart in the corner.

"I'm so ashamed to admit this to anyone, but I just know you would be the one person who would understand and not judge me. I met a boy at that party. His name was Travis. At first, I thought he was really cute and hot, and he was a college student, interested in me, of all people. We talked and danced. Played darts. We had a few beers. It was fun...until..." Lavender took a breath and blew her nose again. "Somehow, we ended up in this room by ourselves, on this blue futon...I can still smell it...it was like wet dog and boy's locker room...and he was on top of me...I told him to stop, I know I did, but he didn't. He didn't stop. I wasn't strong enough to push him off me. I couldn't stop him. I didn't stop him... Grandma, I didn't want it. I didn't want him on top of me, or inside me or..." Lavender hung her head and reached for more tissues. She waited for her sobs to slow down and then kept talking to her comatose grandma.

"After that night, I swore I would never step foot on BSU or any college campus again. I just couldn't. What if I saw him? I wouldn't know what to do. The only thing I knew for sure was that I never wanted to go to another college party again where some boy, stronger than me, could hold me down and do what he wanted with no regard for me or what I wanted. That's when the lying started. I didn't apply to BSU but let everyone think that I did. Then I let them believe I got accepted. I just couldn't tell anyone what had happened. I should have been sober. I should have been louder. I should have been stronger. But I wasn't. And I was ashamed of that. And so I hid it all from Jackie, from Jana, from Hillary Charles, even my mom and dad..."

"Oh my god…Lavender."

Lavender looked up in a daze of watery eyes and snot and brokenness. Her mom and dad had come up behind her. Lavender stood up so fast her chair fell over.

"How long have you been standing there? How much did you hear?" Lavender asked.

"We heard enough…come here." Her mother held her while Lavender sobbed out everything she'd lost over the past year. Her first time with a boy, her senior year, Jackie, Jana, all of it came out in wrenching, shoulder-heaving, sore-gut kind of sobs. After there was nothing left to grieve, her dad took her and wrapped his arms around her.

"I love you, Rosebud. I'm sorry I wasn't there to protect you."

Lavender handed both of her parents the box of tissues so they could wipe their own tears.

"Why didn't you come to us?" her mom asked.

"I know…I'm sorry. I couldn't. I was so embarrassed. I just wanted to forget the whole thing, but…"

"It's okay. Lavender. It wasn't your fault. What happened to you wasn't your fault." Her mother took Lavender's face in her hands and looked directly into her eyes. "Do you hear me? That wasn't your fault. He took something from you he had no right to take. We could go to the police."

"That's right. We should press charges…he can't get away with this," her dad said.

"It's been too long…I don't want to do that…I want to forget." Lavender began to cry again.

"Okay, okay. We'll do whatever you want, Rosebud. I'm sorry," her dad said. "Let's focus on grandma right now and we'll talk more about this later. Okay?' He grabbed her shoulders and said,

"Listen to me, Lavender Rose Finch. We love you, no matter what. Whether you go to college someday or stay in California in the AmeriCorps or think up something else to do, we love you. We are on your side. That's all you need to know."

The background noise of beeps and chirping machines hung in the air while she stood between her parents, their arms intertwined around each other, and watched Louise sleep.

FORTY-THREE

LAVENDER FED THREE SINGLE dollar bills into the machine and pressed E5. Her parents insisted that she go home and rest and get ready for graduation on Sunday. There was no sense in all three of them staying up all night, her mom said. But there was no way Lavender was leaving. She finally agreed to go to the waiting room and put two chairs together and try to rest her tired and red eyes. They would come find her if they heard any news, or if her grandma woke up. After she heard the thud, she pushed back the heavy flap and retrieved her bottle of water.

"Lavender?" People sneaking up behind her had become a theme in that hospital. She whipped around to see Hillary Charles in the same outfit she'd had on at Class Night. It seemed like the packed auditorium, the stage, her shocking announcement from the microphone happened a lifetime ago and yet, it was still the same night. Well technically the next day since it was after midnight.

"Hillary? What are you doing here?"

Hillary's usual, self-assured, class-president face was replaced with a somber and serious one. "My dad is sick. You?"

"My grandma had a stroke,"

"I'm sorry," Hillary said.

"Me too."

The two girls moved to chairs next to each other on the far wall of the crowded waiting room. There was a lady grasping her oversized mom-purse on her lap, in a staring contest with the clock on the wall. A man and a woman about her parents' age with their hands locked in a fierce grip. A woman holding a very unhappy baby. A man with a reusable shopping bag on the seat next to him, bursting with his belongings, it seemed like.

"So, what's going on with your dad?"

"He has cancer. Stomach. He's been getting treatments. Had some operations..." Hillary's voice trailed off.

"Oh my god. That must be so hard. How long has he had it?"

"We found out last September."

"Wow. I had no idea you were dealing with something like that." Lavender wasn't the only one who'd been suffering all year.

"Well, I'm pretty good at faking it."

"I know what you mean."

"Yeah, you dropped a bomb tonight. Or, I guess it was last night. What was that about? AmeriCorps?"

"Yeah. I never applied to BSU...I went to a party on campus last September and...." Could Lavender really say it out loud again? Would Hillary understand? She couldn't be sure of the outcome, but Lavender was exhausted from trying so hard to keep it in. Her parents knew, the wall was starting to crumble, and she felt like she could take a deep breath for the first time all year. It had to be right. Lavender took a deep breath and kept moving. "I was assaulted by this guy I met. It ruined college for me and I wasn't brave enough to tell anyone. So, I hid it and then lied about applying to BSU, because I didn't want anyone to know the truth about me."

Since the seal of shame had been ripped open by confessing everything to her grandma and accidentally to her parents, Lavender felt free. No more secrets. No more half-truths. No more staying silent and letting people assume things about her.

"Lavender...that's awful. I'm sorry that happened to you," Hillary said. "You could have told me."

"Yeah...I always feel like people just want to hear what they want to hear, you know? No surprises. When they ask how you're doing, they just want you to say, *I'm good*." Lavender shifted in her seat. "You could have told me about your dad."

"I didn't want people to feel sorry for me. I can't be weak and be class president. It's a lot of responsibility."

"You know you're very good at that kind of stuff, right?" Lavender nudged Hillary with her shoulder. "I mean who else would come up with a countdown timer for senior year and keep the whole mess of us on point?"

Hillary smiled. "I did that."

"Yeah you did. You're a boss."

"Yeah, but you got MOST LIKELY TO BE CEO!"

"I know. That was weird, wasn't it?" They both rolled in their seats, belly-laughing long enough for the waiting room people to look at them as if they were intruding on their sanctuary of anxious group silence.

"You know what I didn't get done?" Hillary asked.

"I can't imagine there's anything you didn't nail. What?"

"The class gift. We don't have a class gift. We raised all this money and I have no idea what to do with it."

"Hmmmm. That's right. I forgot about that."

"Everybody did."

"Hey, what about something to do with Ms. Clarke's *It's a Small World Project*? We could invest in technology, or set up a scholarship fund, or...hmmm..." Lavender thought about the women at Betsy Ross. "What if we purchased tablets and other technology for seniors in nursing homes? Their lives are so small and limited...

what if we could connect them to the rest of the world? Maybe they could have pen pals too, or join online communities, or..."

"Oh my god, that's brilliant. I love it. See? That is why you are a boss CEO," Hillary said, lifting her hand to high-five Lavender. They both belly-laughed again, with another round of stink-eye looks from the waiting room crowd.

Who knew that Hillary Charles had a sick father and worried about what people thought? Who knew that the smartest, strongest, and most confident person in the class of 2025 also had a sad secret? "In all seriousness, is your dad going to be okay?" Lavender asked.

"I don't know. We're hoping but...," Hillary sighed. "He had a bad day today. All year, I just wanted him to make it to my graduation..."

"He will. He has to. Graduation is tomorrow." Lavender put her arm around Hillary. "It's just one more day, Hill."

"Depending on what the doctor says, I may not even make it to the ceremony."

"Don't say that...you have to be there...you're the valedictorian."

"Listen, I have an idea...if I'm not there, will you give the commencement speech?"

"What? No, you have to do it. No one wants to hear from me."

"Lavender. Seriously. I've been stressing all night trying to figure out a solution and now I know. It's you. You have things to say. Things that people need to hear. I know it."

"Hillary..."

"Please? Future CEO...will you do it for me? I need to know the class will be in good hands."

A woman with the same deep auburn hair as Hillary came through the double doors and scanned the room until she laid eyes on the two of them. The woman waved her hand and lifted her head to the left, signaling Hillary to come. Hillary stood and looked down at Lavender.

"Go see your dad. I got you." Lavender nodded at her and sealed the promise with a look. Hillary looked relieved and whispered, "Thank you," before joining her mom on the other side.

Lavender pulled the chair Hillary had been sitting in around to the front of her and stretched out her legs, put her head back and closed her eyes. She had told her grandma everything. Her parents overheard and knew it all too. And now Hillary Charles was asking her to step in and speak at graduation. Lavender had survived the blast. The walls were down. The senior year from hell had taken a sudden turn and she finally saw light.

Lavender popped her head up and blinked a few times to clear the gunk from her eyes. The light was brighter in the waiting room and everyone was gone except for the lady and her purse. Lavender reached for her phone and saw that it was 6 a.m. She must have fallen asleep. Her legs were numb and heavy as she lowered them and put the chair back in line. She stood slowly giving the blood time to trickle down and bring her feet back to life. Lavender limped to the big doors. The man at the desk nodded and buzzed her through. The emergency room had a different energy and lightness to it with the new day. Everyone who was still there had made it through the night.

Lavender quietly peeked inside the curtain of 17C. Her mom and dad were in separate chairs next to each other, their heads leaning together, their eyes closed. Her grandmother was still out of it. She set her backpack down and searched for some lotion she carried with her. Her summer scent was always some kind of coconut and lime combination. Lavender pulled the white blanket back from the end of the bed and gently rubbed her grandma's feet with lotion. After she finished, she sent her mom and dad a text.

> Didn't want to wake you. Going
> home to get ready for graduation.
> I love you.

Before Lavender left the room, she looked for one more thing in her bag. She didn't wear lipstick, but she did have some tinted lip balm. She twisted the bottom until the light pink solid center came up and applied it to her grandma's lips. It would have to do.

FORTY-FOUR

"GOOD MORNING CLASS OF 2025." The sea of white-robed teen-agers in front of her erupted with cheers, woohoos and whistles. Lavender waited for them to finish before she spoke again.

"I know you were expecting to see our class president and valedictorian, Hillary Charles, up here this morning. So was I. She worked hard all year to get us…you and me…here. But she's dealing with some heavy things right now and needs our support. She asked for my help and so here I am. Before I go any further, I'd like us all to take a moment and send good vibes to Hillary and her family." Lavender placed her right hand over her heart and looked out. The Siena Civic Center auditorium was silent as every person in their seat followed her lead, placed their hand on their heart and closed their eyes. "To Hillary."

"Senior Year. It holds so much for us, doesn't it? It is full of opposing forces. Fun and responsibility. Fear of the unknown and excitement about what's coming. It is the end of school as we've known it, but not the end of our education. A season of our life is over while a new one begins. We celebrate, yet there is a certain sadness, a melancholy that comes when we realize life will never be like this again. It is change. Growth. Maturity. Friends."

Lavender looked at Jana in the second row. The strangers she'd been around all year were familiar faces again. In the crowd she saw the boy she had a crush on in third grade. The girl who lost a front tooth when a kickball hit her squarely in the mouth. Another boy who sat behind her in every homeroom since seventh grade because both of their last names began with the same two letters. Her locker neighbors. The driver of the red truck that always parked in the spot next to her. "We're no longer children, but not quite adults."

"For me, I thought senior year was going to be easier. I thought, if I could just get through Ms. Clarke's *It's a Small World* project, it would be smooth sailing, lol..." Lavender looked to her left and saw Ms. Clarke with the other Faculty and waved at her. "If you know, you know."

"But in all seriousness, Ms. Clarke, that project changed my life. Yes, technology gives us the tools to communicate, but it doesn't inspire hope or motivate compassion. Only love can do that. Through this project, I learned that love is the thing that connects us to each other and to the world. I think Ms. Clarke knew this all along and just waited for the rest of us to catch up. Love, not technology, is what makes it a small world after all.

"Before this year, I had given up on that four-letter word, love. I was convinced I was unlovable. In fact, I used to hate it when people said the words, *I love you*, to me. Which is hard to admit, I mean, who hates to hear that? But for me, it all seemed too easy, like a simple game of catch. It wasn't right. For me, it was always more like monkey in the middle. People said, I love you, but the ball was always just out of reach. I never quite believed them. It seemed effortless for them to blurt the words out on a regular basis. When I left for school in the morning, at night when I went to bed. On the phone. In a text. I knew loving me wasn't that easy. Or at least it shouldn't be.

"How could they love me when they didn't know me? Of course, my parents *know* me. I do have their genes after all. And I did come from my mother's body. But I believed that they still saw me as the baby who smiled at them every morning when I woke up, was never fussy and slept six hours straight through from the first night they brought me home. They knew me as the three-year old who picked dandelions from the cracks in the sidewalk to hand to my preschool teachers when my mom dropped me off. I was the kid who charmed strangers in the grocery store with my big blue eyes and polite banter. It was easy to impress adults. Just look them in the eye and talk to them, politely. Say please and thank you. Help them pick up the box of macaroni they dropped when they were putting it in their shopping cart.

"I had heard these stories repeated so many times I was convinced they all loved that version of me. The sweet, little, good girl. The perfect daughter. The best friend. The niece, the cousin, the classmate. Not the 17-year-old Lavender who had too much to drink at a college party and let horrible things happen to her." The auditorium full of people was stone quiet.

"I was assaulted at a college party last September. I will spare you all the details of that horrible night, but I can tell you that it was, by far, the worst thing that has ever happened to me. It was devastating and soul-crushing and I didn't deserve it. It wasn't my fault. And yet, after it happened, I didn't tell anyone. I didn't tell my cousin Jackie, who I was with that night. I didn't tell my best friend Jana. I didn't tell my parents. I was so ashamed of myself for letting it happen that I couldn't trust anything, or anyone anymore. So, I kept it a secret. Keeping it to myself seemed like the only way to control the shame that had settled over me, like a suffocating blanket that kept me afraid. Afraid that I was so imperfect and broken, so wrong, that if people saw the real me, if they knew what I had done, what I let happen, they would be horrified and turn away. Shame is no joke. It is a constant nagging feeling that something is off, something is wrong with you, but you just can't put your finger on it.

"And so, I avoided it. I avoided people. I stopped returning texts. I stopped hanging out. I closed myself off to keep the shame locked in. The only time I felt any relief is when I let the buzz of a few beers numb my brain, at least for a while. Shame ruined my childhood dream of attending BSU, or any college. Secrets and lies chased away my best friend, my family, people who had trusted me with their children. I hope you can all forgive me someday.

"I gave up on love, but...the good news is, it didn't give up on me. Thanks to Ms. Clarke and her project, I spent this year falling in love with a boy I've never met in person, and with a grandmother, who most of the time, isn't quite sure of who I am.

"It has taken me all year to learn that secrets not only keep shame locked inside, hidden from others, secrets also build walls that keep love out, locking us in a lonely place. Trusting people with our secrets is the one thing that lets us receive the love we need. Love that makes us feel seen and safe. Love that makes us believe that anything is possible, that we're okay no matter what. Love that changes us.

"To love me *is* to know me. My hopes, my dreams, my flaws, my secrets, my pain, my truth. From now on, I will catch every *I love you* thrown at me... and toss it right back."

Lavender stopped speaking and met the eyes of her classmates, Jana, her teachers, her aunts, uncles, Jackie, her parents. The walls she had so carefully constructed were gone. She was one of them. She knew them and they knew her. Lavender placed her right hand over her heart and nodded. The audience did the same. "To love."

Loving Lavender Finch hadn't been easy, but it finally felt right.

FORTY-FIVE

LAVENDER WAITED at the bottom of the escalator in the center of the Syracuse airport. The plane from Miami had landed ten minutes ago according to the big screen tracking the arrivals and departures. She wanted to ask everyone who passed by if they were coming from Florida. Her stomach was spinning in circles. For the millionth time that morning she had to pee. Her mouth was dry. Lavender was finally going to meet her boyfriend, Martin Luther Adams. She studied each face, looking for the one she'd only seen in a picture and on her phone screen.

Lavender had so much to say to him. They hadn't talked or written much in the last few weeks since Class Night, her grandmother's stroke, and then graduation. He'd been busy too with his own end-of-senior-year stuff, saying goodbye to friends and family and preparing for their road trip. Lavender's grandmother was out of the hospital and back at Betsy Ross, recuperating. Time would tell how much permanent damage there would be from the stroke. *Hopefully not much.* Lavender and Hillary had exhausted the class gift fund purchasing the tablets, smart phones, and Bluetooth speakers and presented them to Louise and all the residents at Betsy Ross They solicited the internet provider to show up and install boosters throughout the building so the wi-fi was fast and reliable in every hallway and room. Ms. Clarke recruited the Global/Lit class to host an *It's a Small World* event onsite at Betsy Ross teaching the residents how to play music and navigate video calls with friends and family or online webinars. Jana showed them all the magic of YouTube and how you can find videos on cooking, or gardening, or painting, or live web cams from all over the world. Ms. Clarke had even compiled a list of potential pen-pals for those residents who wanted to email with others in senior living homes.

There was a graduation party waiting at Lavender's house. The entire FFTNN was expected to be there, including Jackie. She and Jackie had stayed up until dawn one night and talked about what had happened at the party and everything since then. Jackie cried and apologized for not protecting her younger cousin from a creep like Travis, and then half-jokingly promised to hunt him down and ruin his life. Jana and her new boyfriend would be at the party. Hillary and her mom. Everyone was excited to meet the boy from Cuba who was taking their precious Lavender so far away. The plan was to leave the next morning for the West Coast.

Lavender had completed her task of creating the perfect playlist, including all the songs they'd said goodnight to, movie soundtracks, the eighties rock her parents had played around the house and other road trip classics. Her dad had kept his promise of getting the Malibu ready. Not only did he take it to the shop for an oil change and inspection, he also bought four new tires and had the car detailed. He filled it with gas and gave her a card with enough money on it to fill her tank all the way to Venice Beach.

The stream of people heading down the escalator had thinned out. Lavender's heart jumped into her throat as she considered, just for a moment, the possibility that he wouldn't show up. Maybe he changed his mind. Maybe he realized that it was crazy to meet up with your senior class pen-pal and get in a car to drive cross country together. *Oh my god, I'm turning into my mother. Stop the what-if game Lavender!* She took a deep breath and checked her phone. No messages. She turned around and looked behind her. It wasn't a huge airport so there were limited options to get to baggage claim. As she looked back to the top of the center escalator, she saw a shadow of someone approaching. *There he is.* She knew by the way his smile filled his face and lit up his eyes. Lavender smiled back. He was carrying a bouquet of white roses. How did he manage to fly all the way from Cuba and still be the perfect boyfriend who brought flowers? Martin waved at her with his other hand while he descended to the bottom. He set down his backpack and the flowers and scooped her up in a tight hug. She wrapped her arms around him and buried her face in his neck. He smelled like sun and earth and home. They stayed that way long enough for the distance of the last ten months to fade away. All the conversations, the letters, the texts, the gifts, the virtual dates, the friendship, the wishing, the hoping, the longing, all of it melted between them.

Martin stepped back, brushed her hair back from her face. "Let me get a good look at you, Lavender Rose Finch."

Seeing him face to face, looking into the eyes of this person who had found her very soul, brought tears to her eyes. He picked her chin up and put his lips on hers. They were soft and gentle and tasted sweet. She put her hand on his cheek. "I thought you weren't going to kiss me at the airport?"

"I wasn't. But when I saw you, I knew I couldn't wait another second."

He picked up the roses and placed them in her arm. Without a word Lavender and Martin locked hands, their fingers intertwined, like they had found their perfect match. Like they'd known each other forever, and their hands had finally found the one they were supposed to hold.

ACKNOWLEDGEMENTS

THANK YOU, READER, for taking a chance that picking up this book would be worthy of your time. I write for you. It is so easy in the business of writing to get caught up in gaining the attention and approval of the publishers, the award givers, the various parties who've given themselves gatekeeper status, but I write what moves me for one reason, and that is the hope that it moves you, too. Thank you for sharing this human experience with me and reading the words I've put down on paper. It means everything.

Thank you to my small little focus group and early readers—Lonnie, Denise, Pat, Craig—for believing in this story and loving Lavender as much as I do. Your honesty and feedback have been so important throughout this process.

Thank you to the team of professionals who made this happen: Linda Lowen, Debbie Horan, Gwyn Flowers/GKS Creative and Melanie Zimmerman.

Thank you to my husband, Craig Anderson, for taking my dreams as seriously as I do; and to my own tribe that runs deep, your love and support challenges me to do better, all the time. And to the leaders of our tribe, my parents, Carl and Jeanne Bargabos: It is impossible to find words to convey how much you've impacted me. In the words of my therapist, "I cannot be me, without you."

The hand of God is on my life, and he is the author and finisher of my faith.

www.ingramcontent.com/pod-product-compliance
Lightning Source LLC
Chambersburg PA
CBHW020651120726
47906CB00001B/223